𝕮𝖍𝖚𝖗𝖈𝖍 𝖔𝖋 𝕯𝖔𝖓

Church of Don

Rum makes everything better!

Don Thomas

Church of Don

Copyright© 2023 Don Thomas

All rights reserved.

This is a work of fiction. Names, characters, businesses, places, events, locales, and incidents are either the product of the author's imagination or used in a fictitious manner. Any resemblance to actual persons, living or dead, or actual events is purely coincidental.

No part of this publication may be reproduced, distributed, or transmitted in any form or by any means, including photocopying, recording, or other electronic or mechanical methods, without the prior written permission of the author, except in the case of brief quotations embodied in reviews and certain other non-commercial uses permitted by copyright law.

Dedication

This book is dedicated to all the people that think they see some aspect of themselves in the characters. Anything is possible.

So if you do self-identify as one of the offensively unpleasant characters, please try to be better. And if you self-identify as one of the characters that have aced the purity test, please try to dirty up a bit. The most interesting people are the ones that are generally good but with just the right amount of naughty.

Disclaimer

This book's character, "Don," is not the author "Don Thomas." However, they share a first name and probably a few cocktail recipes.

No aluminum folding chairs were injured in creating this book's cover photography. A stunt chair and visual effects produced the iconic aluminum folding chair likeness.

Acknowledgments

The cover photo of the model is by Oleh Panasenka (Ukraine), licensed through 123rf.com.

The Author's photo is by Guild West Agency (San Jose, CA).

Contents

Chapter 1 - Don't piss off Jane 1

Chapter 2 - An old aluminum beach chair 18

Chapter 3 - What are you going to do with a church 29

Chapter 4 - Sign on the dotted line 33

Chapter 5 - Jerry thought Olivia had caught him 35

Chapter 6 - I love the humble beginnings pitch 42

Chapter 7 - The aluminum chair recognizes 45

Chapter 8 - I want to christen this place properly 55

Chapter 9 - The church of dipshit will be gone 57

Chapter 10 - As sure as Bob's your uncle 59

Chapter 11 - I honestly think that we are a little weird 65

Chapter 12 - That old broad and her posse 68

Chapter 13 - An oasis from reality 71

Chapter 14 - Call him A-Wall since he's evolved 77

Chapter 15 - What's up your skirt 82

Chapter 16 - Gary from high school 87

Chapter 17 - A sure thing with easy Lana 90

Chapter 18 - That's just human nature, man 96

Chapter 19 - The seeds of uncertainty and doubt 100

Chapter 20 - You want me full of lust, don't you 104

Chapter 21 - All day long and into the night 109

Chapter 22 - The bartender is a cultural leader 119

Chapter 23 - Beaver in the pond 121

Chapter 24 - I have your back; may I have your heart 125

Chapter 25 - What's this, trouble in paradise 130

Chapter 26 - He and that chair belong together 136

Chapter 27 - Make it look like it was an accident 140

Chapter 28 - Something classy for my sassy chassis 147

Chapter 29 - Jane obliged 151

Chapter 30 - Call me hot bronze goddess 155

Chapter 31 - The nickel and dime crowd 159

Chapter 32 - We can be nudie buddies 162

Chapter 33 - I will be honorable and gentle with Red 167

Chapter 34 - Ally is my girlfriend, John is my buddy 171

Chapter 35 - His humble beginnings pitch 177

Chapter 36 - Jeanette should have one for the road 181

Chapter 37 - Jane won't put up with our shenanigans 188

Chapter 38 - Okay, yes, please, taser him for me 191

Chapter 39 - I will do forever with Don 196

Chapter 40 - The aluminum chair recognizes John 202

Chapter 41 - We need to get rid of the competition 213

Chapter 42 - It's going to be a busy night 218

Chapter 43 - Don't worry, Paul, I've got this 222

Chapter 44 - It's showtime baby 225

Chapter 45 - Smyth practiced his plan 231

Chapter 46 - I bet Jane says it first 233

Chapter 47 - Smyth angrily tugged at the zipper 236

Chapter 48 - Let me go; I have to save Don 239

Chapter 49 - Lady Luck cut me some slack, man 257

Chapter 50 - Rum makes everything better 265

Chapter 1 - Don't piss off Jane
February 26th 6:17 a.m. ~ Brite Rock, Massachusetts

When Jerry Palmer woke this morning, he had no idea that this day would start him down a path where he would find danger, intrigue, the love of his life, new friendships, and an odd yet welcoming community that he had no idea existed. And this wasn't even his story. That belongs to the two people he would visit on this day.

1:24 p.m.

Jerry Palmer carefully parked his new black BMW between a FedEx truck and an old rusty hot rod in front of the old two-story brick and wood building. Stepping from his car, he paused to survey the tight quarters before deciding it was safe to park there.

It wasn't the neighborhood; there wasn't a bad part of Brite Rock. It's a typical small Massachusetts coastal town with well-kept homes and a picturesque town center on nearly a mile of pristine beach protected by offshore sandbars. The town is home to almost twelve thousand year-round residents and a few small commercial fishing boats that dock at the beach's jetty at the south end. Brite Rock's population grows by over forty percent in the summer as people from hot inland areas come to enjoy the beach and cool ocean breeze.

After working in Brite Rock as the town's lawyer for seven years, Jerry finally bought a house and moved to town six weeks ago. He had broken up with his girlfriend and was tired of the commute to Brite Rock from Quincy, a southern suburb of Boston. Summer traffic from the Boston area to Cape Cod made his commute unbearable. Living in Brite Rock just made sense to him.

Jerry opened the back door of his car and took out an old folder stuffed with papers. They had that "been in storage" musty smell. He had never encountered a situation like this in his seven years as legal counsel for the town. Many documents in this unique arrangement between a trust and the Town of Brite Rock were dated 1920. Jerry knew he was in for an interesting experience in resolving this situation.

Pausing to look up at the old building, Jerry studied the Don's Tiki Cocktails & Lounge sign. The iconic bar sign, which has been there since 1948, definitely did not fit the Chamber of Commerce's recently chosen New England ocean and beach architectural theme for the town.

Ironically, the bar sign is protected by a grandfather clause in Brite Rock's historic preservation ordinance that was put in place by the Chamber of Commerce in the early 1970s. Much to their dismay, the Chamber's hired consultant considered Don's bar sign of architectural importance. Jerry found it humorous that the very sign the Chamber of Commerce wants to get rid of, it must protect.

Jerry liked the sign; it has character. Even the minor rust spots caused by the salty sea air added authenticity since the bar sits directly across the street from the beach.

He adjusted his tie and reached for the front door. The oak door was heavy and solidly built but opened with little effort. He thought *old-time craftsmanship* as he stepped into the dimly lit bar. A voice greeted him before his eyes could adjust from the bright daylight.

"Welcome to Don's Tiki Cocktails & Lounge. Sit where you like."

Jerry recognized the voice as belonging to Jane Gilman, bartender and outspoken bar co-owner.

"Hi Jane, is Don here? I need to see him on town business." Jerry rested the large folder on the bar.

"Is this about the sign again? I thought that was settled with those snooty old farts."

Jerry smiled. "Now Jane, I work for the town and have to represent said snooty old farts in legal matters. You made your views clear on the sign topic at the town meeting, and I agreed. Neither the Chamber of Commerce nor the Beautification Committee can do a thing about your sign except grumble. I'm here today about a personal matter between the town and Don. Is he around?"

Jane glanced at the large folder curiously, then at Jerry. "He's in the back receiving a delivery. It's a big one, and he has to count and sign for it. Maybe five minutes? Can I get you something while you wait?"

"No, thank you. I'm fine. I'll just wait."

"Are you sure? We do serve lawyers here!" Jane smiled and picked up a glass to emphasize the offer.

Jerry laughed. "I do appreciate your kind offer, Jane. But, unfortunately, I have to decline while I'm on the clock. Next time."

"I can make it nonalcoholic. When was the last time you had a virgin, Mister Palmer?"

Jerry's eyes grew wide. "Well...thanks for that offer too, Jane. Next time perhaps."

Jane giggled mischievously. "Okay, make yourself at home, and I'll let Don know you're here."

She glanced down at the floor. "Sorry about your shoes!"

Jerry looked at his expensive Ferragamo loafers. They looked fine. "What about my shoes?"

A quick smile flashed across Jane's face. "Oh, nothing. I'll go get Don."

Jane was a bit of an anomaly to Jerry. He wasn't sure if it was her feisty personality or her figure that commanded attention at the recent Chamber of Commerce meeting. He overheard one of the councilwomen telling another that she had taken high school gym class with Jane and could attest that Jane's figure was all-natural.

Jerry didn't give Jane's figure much thought either way. He was more intrigued by her big piercing eyes. At five feet seven inches tall, he and Jane are the same height. Eye-level. She had the habit of looking directly into your eyes when speaking with you. It was much more than a casual gaze. She held eye contact for an extended period. He wondered if she was looking for social cues or emotions. Perhaps it's curiosity about the person that she's speaking with? Maybe she's judging trustworthiness? Could it be flirting? Whatever the reason, you knew you had Jane's undivided attention, and she had yours.

Jerry picked up the folder and looked around the bar. This was the first Tiki bar that he had ever been in. As he walked around, he noticed the scent of the fresh lemons and limes that Jane was juicing. There was also the slightest hint of Jane's perfume. Something tropical. It was pleasant.

Jerry turned his attention to the unique décor. The long oak bar was vintage, at least one hundred years old. Behind the bar, a large number of bottles, most of them rum, were prominently displayed. On one of the travel websites, he had read that rum continued to be a hot trend in cocktails, but this was the first time he had experienced it in such a conspicuous way. Also displayed were what looked to be over one hundred different Tiki mugs on the shelf that ran the length of the back bar. These appeared to be for show as part of the décor. Jerry smiled, thinking the bar probably hadn't changed in decades; it was just the tiki trend coming back around, making the place relevant again.

Thatch roofs supported by bamboo poles sheltered several booths. They were lit by large red, green, yellow, and blue hanging glass balls once used as floats for commercial Japanese fishing nets. They occasionally still wash up on pacific island beaches, Hawaii, and the west coast from Alaska to southern California.

An eight-foot-tall Tiki totem stood in the middle of the bar entrance, with several smaller versions displayed around the bar. In addition, various Polynesian-themed items, including pufferfish lamps, added to the feel of the tropical island experience.

Autographed photos of old local politicians, movie stars, sports figures, and other notables covered the left side of the bar wall. Posters for the films Donovan's Reef, Hells Half Acre, and Pagan Island hung between leaflets for past events.

Old advertising handbills for surf guitar and tiki bands were stapled to the wall by the old jukebox; time had yellowed many of them. Newer ones were respectfully added so as not to damage the old ones.

The stage was relatively small and framed with bamboo and tropical woven matting. Jerry knew the bar had live bands and D.J.s several times per month. He had seen the flyers around town for the shows. Last weekend, the Hangin' Eleven and local favorites Kalani & The Ōkole Shakers performed.

Several framed menus from once-popular Tiki-influenced New England establishments were displayed on the wall by the stage. Bob Lee's Islander in the Chinatown part of Boston, The Polynesian Village at the Somerset Hotel, Kon-Tiki Ports at the Sheraton Boston, and Johnny Yee's on Cape Cod. All are long gone. A framed record album, *An Evening at Johnny Yee's*, was hanging by the menus.

Maps of the Pacific Islands, Oceania, and the Pasifika region were hung on either side of the jukebox. A sign next to the maps states *The tropical islands in this area inspired much of the tiki theme. While tiki is an aesthetic construct, the islands, the people, languages, and cultures are real and threatened by climate change. Like Brite Rock and many other coastal communities, they may be lost to the ocean in as little as 50 years. Be a voice for these people. Save them. Save Brite Rock. Save the planet.* It was signed; *Thanks, Brad* (Brite Rock Planning Department - Ocean & Environment).

Jerry thought for a moment. He was standing about five hundred feet from the ocean's edge. He suddenly felt a common concern with people a world away that he had never considered. He smiled to himself. The most important thing he learned today is hanging on the wall of an old bar.

A click and whir of the jukebox coming to life got Jerry's attention. The jukebox looked like something from the 1950s. It was heavily chromed, advertised 200 selections, and featured high fidelity. Jerry didn't recognize any of the bands listed or their song titles. A tropical-sounding song played softly. *Jungalero by Les Baxter*... music definitely for the Tiki enthusiast, he thought. It was relaxing, but not in the creepy elevator music kind of way.

The old oak floor creaked as Jerry turned to look at a vintage pin-up picture of a topless hula dancer painted on what appeared to be black velvet. Next to it was an old, smaller photo, maybe 5 x 7 inches, in a beautiful old wood frame. The tarnished silver tag said the photo taken in 1919 was Duke *The Big Kahuna* Kahanamoku. The koa wood surfboard in the picture is said to be 16 feet long and weighs 114 pounds. Jerry knew nothing about surfing, but even he was impressed by the massive surfboard.

Jerry turned his attention to a sign posted behind the bar. He laughed as he read it.

Bar Rules

1. Don't piss off Jane.
2. Leave your politics at home (it's like your underwear – best kept to yourself).
3. Bring your kindness, humor, knowledge, and respect to share with others.
4. No smoking in this bar – it's gross and stinky and evidently an actual Massachusetts law.
5. We are near the ocean – salty language may occasionally occur.
6. Don't piss off Jane (it's worth mentioning twice).
7. You CAN have too much of a good thing, so don't drive drunk. Uber yourself home!
8. Be Good! The Brite Rock Police Department is 1/4 mile away – 'nuff said.
9. Unattended children will be given an espresso and free marching band cymbals.
10. KAPU! – (ancient Hawaiian laws) it's forbidden to take bar tiki mugs without paying for them. Dis real! No steal!
11. Like preschool – you pee your pants, you go home.
12. Dick wants to fight. We throw Dick out. Don't be a Dick!
    Mahalo

A large flat screen framed in bamboo on the wall behind the bar showed short vintage tropical scenes, surfing, and the occasional 1950s topless sunbather video. There was something quaint about the old scratchy film of the partially nude women. Jerry was fascinated by the thought that they were all natural. Augmentation at that time meant stuffing tissues in their bra. And the...

"You looking for me, man?"

Jerry turned to find the bar co-owner, Don, standing behind him. He felt a little embarrassed about being caught admiring the voluptuous women in the old video.

"Yes, I am!" Jerry fumbled with the large folder as he reached to shake Don's hand.

Jerry thought of Don as one of the local characters of the community. He stands six feet tall, has an average build, somewhat long hair, and has a slight hippy quality. Don typically sports a well-worn Hawaiian print aloha shirt with a speaking style that often ends with the word *man*.

"Jane said that you're not here about our sign this time. Is the town ready to agree that it's legal and historical, man?"

Jerry smiled. "No, I'm not here about your sign. I think the town has given up that battle for now. But I do have something else that we need to discuss." Jerry did a quick scan of the bar. He counted seven patrons, the bartender Jane and a guy that was washing glasses. Jerry leaned in and asked, "is there someplace more private where we can talk?" Don looked around the bar slowly. "What's wrong with here, man?"

Jerry glanced down at the large folder. "Well, Don, it's just that this is... personal. And there is also something down the street that I need you to see."

Don looked at the thick folder that Jerry was holding and nodded. "Down the street. Okay, follow me."

Don and Jerry headed toward the door. Don turned and yelled back to Jane, "you're in charge, girlfriend. Keep an eye on Best so he doesn't organize the fruit in the garnish tray again. That's nasty!" Jerry looked back at James Freeman as Don walked out the door.

Jerry exited the bar to find Don putting on his leather jacket and getting into the old rusty convertible hot rod parked out front. Don gestured for Jerry to get into the car. He hesitated. "You know it's around forty degrees out. Why don't we sit in my car? It has a roof and will be warmer."

Don slipped on his sunglasses. "We don't get many nice sunny days like this in New England in February. Now, climb aboard Jenny, and let's enjoy some nature. You know, carpe diem, man!"

Jerry fumbled as he tried to open the rusty car door. "Jenny? Who is Jenny?"

"This is Jenny, man!" Don gently runs his fingers across the top of the steering wheel. She reminds me of Jane. She's fast... powerful yet gentle... can be hard to handle... has a mind of her own... and gives one hell of a ride!"

Jerry suddenly felt uncomfortable. "Are we still talking about your car?"

Don looked over the top of his sunglasses at Jerry. "Yeah, why do you ask?"

"Well, it um... the comparison."

Don leaned over and unlatched the car door for Jerry. He awkwardly climbed in and nervously looked around. "What is this...Jenny? Is this thing dangerous? It's like someone could get hurt just looking at it."

Don smiled and gently patted the tarnished metal dashboard. "She's a 32 Ford rod, man. And before you ask, she's supposed to look this way. This isn't rust, man; it's patina! It's a badge of honor. She's a survivor, man! If it ain't steel, it ain't real. Nothing fiberglass or pre-1963 on Jenny. She is an original wicked pissah street rocket!"

Jerry wasn't sure how to feel about being seen sitting in this rusty relic. He wanted to change the subject.

"Why did you call that man in the bar Best?"

"James has had the nickname Best since he was a kid. He's got some kind of thing, man. He tells everybody that everything he has is the best. He owns the best car. He vacations at the best resort and dates the best-looking women. He drives the staff crazy with his insisting on the best rum, the best juices, and even the best garnish for his drink! We have to watch him so he doesn't sort through the garnish tray for the best-looking lime wedge. Can't do that, man. The Board of Health and Jane have rules!"

"If he's disruptive, why don't you throw him out of the bar?"

Don shook his head. "That's not our style, man. We accept him as one of our bar family and adjust his behavior when he gets on people's nerves. Best is cool with that."

"Are nicknames common in the bar?"

"Sure, man, in my circle anyway! There's Carl; he's the *free tow bandito*. His 52 Chevy is always crapping out, and he has to have it towed back to his house. He usually stiffs *Cyclops*; that's Jimmy from Delmonte's Towing. Jimmy has a glass eye, so he's Cyclops. Cyclops' girlfriend is *Bent Betty*. Her real name is Marisa. She had some spinal thing as a kid, but the docs straightened her out. Kathy Schulz has a slow eye tick, so she's *Winky*.

Then there's Mike *Spider* Gordon. He was six or seven years old when he freaked out at summer camp when he thought a spider bit his penis when he used a portable crapper. He asked the camp counselor if someone should suck the poison out. The counselor said no way and told Mike that he would die. He didn't. Jim Cook is called Pudsy for asking Carla Stevens for a goodnight tug after senior prom. Carla declined to give him a handy and told the entire class about it. Then there's Geezer, who, at around ten years old, would yell at the neighborhood kids to get off his front lawn. So they tagged him with the moniker Geezer, which is ironic as he is now in his 70s and an actual geezer. Ah, I can't forget Jane's nickname; it's Witch. She is a descendant of someone that was offed for being a witch in Salem in the 1600s…or it could be that she can be a bit spooky at times. The list goes on, man."

All of this was both foreign and interesting to Jerry. None of his friends had nicknames or would be caught dead sitting in this rust bucket in the middle of town in the middle of the day. "So, what do they call you, if you don't mind me asking?"

Don sized up Jerry to be sure he wasn't making fun of him. "Ticky," that's what they call me, man."

"They call you what?"

"Ticky, man. My mom was born and raised in Brockton and had a regional New England accent. For example, she would say the name Sarah as say-ra, and tiki was ticky. So, I learned it as Ticky when I was a little kid, and my dad started to call me that. I kind of like the nickname. My family gave it to me. I carry it with pride, man. What about you? What did they tag you with?"

Jerry shook his head. "Nothing, we didn't have nicknames. As a kid, I was Jerry when all was well and Gerald when I was in trouble. So, Ticky..."

Don interrupted Jerry. "Whoa, slow down there, chief. You see, you have to be *in* to call me Ticky. Not just anyone can call me Ticky, man."

"In what, a club of some kind?

"Just *in*, man. You know, cool. No expensive designer suits. No top-shelf BMW parked out front. No Italian big buck loafers with $60 socks. That's not the down-to-earth tiki scene, man. That's the kind of stuff that can get you called a rich douchebag, but that's not a nickname; it's just a description. When you are cool, you will get a nickname. That's when you can call me Ticky, man." Don nodded to confirm his statement.

Jerry looked at his Ferragamo loafers while processing what Don had just said. He then turned his attention to the big folder on his lap, opened it, and took out the top piece of paper. Jerry wasn't sure how to approach this.

"So, Don, I need to draw your attention to a property in town. You see, according to town records, this property..."

"Hello, boys!"

Don looked over his shoulder and greeted Darlene as she walked around the back of his car, holding a paper bag and an empty Kahlúa bottle. She handed the paper bag to Don. He sniffed it and smiled. "And how is the hottest cook in town today? Jerry, do you know Darlene Rogers? Darlene owns and operates the Mariner's Shanty Restaurant next door."

Jerry smiled and greeted Darlene. He had been to the restaurant for lunch many times over the past several years but never had a formal introduction.

"What do we have here?" Don opened the bag as Darlene told him she thought they could use a slice of her fresh warm rum cake.

"You know we can always go for your rum cake, sweetheart. Rum makes everything better!" Don hands Jerry a take-out container and fork.

"What's the Kahlúa bottle for?"

"It's empty, and I need some for my Kahlúa cheesecake recipe. May I have a bottle?" Darlene's smiled flirtatiously.

Don nodded as he took a bite of the rum cake. "Sure, Jane's inside; she'll fix you up. And this is seriously tasty rum cake, as usual!"

Darlene thanked Don and headed to the bar's front door. Jerry watched as she walked away. He thought she was maybe in her mid-40s, medium build, just the right amount of curves, dark shoulder-length hair, a pretty smile, and a cute wiggle to her walk. Jerry wondered how this average-looking guy had some form of magnetism with the ladies. From outward appearances, it's not his looks or fashion sense.

"I've got to say, Don, this free dessert thing is a pretty good deal."

Don glanced at Jerry while licking the crumbs off his fork. "It's not free, man. It's a relationship."

Jerry was confused. "I don't understand. Do you mean that you and Darlene are...." Jerry realized that as town counsel, his personal question was inappropriate. Don laughed. "No, man. Nothing like that. Jane is my one and only. Maybe the whole story will help.

You see, man, my great-grandparents and grandparents were rolling in cash way back when. It was money made from their shoe tool manufacturing business in Brockton in the 1800s. Brockton had around 40 shoe manufacturers and was known as Shoe City. My family had a big summer home here in Brite Rock, on the north end of the beach. I understand they put on some pretty wild parties back in the day.

When Prohibition happened in 1920, my great-granddad built this building. His summer office for the shoe tool biz was in the front, and the speakeasy was hidden in the back. That same year Darlene's great-grandparents were given rent-free space in the same building and opened the restaurant. Darlene's great-grandmother, Emma, was the cook at my great-grandparent's summer home. Anyway, great-granddad could cater his parties at the speakeasy through a special door between the restaurant and bar without arousing undue suspicion, man."

Jerry didn't know that the bar had started as a prohibition speakeasy. "Where did they get the alcohol? Was someone making it locally?"

Don shrugged. "Locally made booze was probably below the speakeasy's upscale clientele. It had to be the good stuff. Rum runners would meet up with local fishing boats 12 miles off Brite Rock in international waters. Scotch whiskey and gin were shipped to the Caribbean from Europe. That scotch, gin, and rum came up the coast from the Bahamas on an old Gloucester three-masted schooner called the Lady Deborah.

The story is that the Lady was a fast sailer and outran the Coast Guard all along the east coast. Then, the rum runners offloaded the booze onto local fishing boats to smuggle ashore. The fishing boats would dock a few blocks from here at the jetty.

"Don, you called the rum runner boat a fast sailer. Is that where the odd spelling for Sailers Church came from? A fast rum-running sailing ship?"

Don laughed. "I believe it is, man. It was probably an inside joke to name the church that. My great-granddad's picture of the Lady Deborah hangs in my office at the bar next to the speakeasy photo."

Don sighed. "When the depression hit in 1929, my great-grandparents and grandfather, who was around 30 years old, lost nearly everything except one small factory in Brockton, this building, and the summer house here. Darlene's grandparent's restaurant would have been toast if it weren't for the deal my family had made to bring food from their restaurant into the speakeasy so that people could eat and drink.

That made it more than a watering hole or another restaurant about to fold. Instead, it was a way for the two families to make a living during hard times.

When Prohibition ended in 1933, the speakeasy became a legitimate bar, and they kept the arrangement going. They supported each other through 13 years of Prohibition and the depression. The bar and restaurant are still together today."

Jerry found this fascinating and was hanging on every word. "So during Prohibition, the local police had to know what was happening."

Don laughed. "Yeah, from my understanding, the mayor and police chief were regulars at the speakeasy. They are in one of the old photos on the wall in my office. My granddad once told me the booze was hidden in the church basement. He was a bit of a prankster, so I don't know if that is true, man. Who would suspect a church? He said the preacher and town cops, who were also speakeasy customers, helped move the booze to the bar as needed late at night.

You know, Prohibition was an exceptionally unpopular law, man. You could drink all you wanted to legally. You just couldn't make, sell or transport it. The booze at the speakeasy was free to members, but their monthly membership dues varied by what they drank. So, technically, no booze was ever sold at the speakeasy."

Jerry smiled. "I have to say that was pretty creative risk management, and I can see where that law would be unpopular. So, how does your bar and the Shanty restaurant relationship work today?"

"I do alcohol only. Darlene does food only. She pays for the Common Victualler License for both the Shanty and my bar so food can be made and sold in both businesses. She runs the bar food menu and keeps the profits. There's a small kitchen in the back of the bar for making bar menu items when the restaurant is too busy. It also allows food from her restaurant to be consumed in the bar.

I pay for the liquor license that also covers the Shanty. That way, our patrons can enjoy one of her tasty meals and our professionally crafted beverages served in the Shanty without her needing to pay for a liquor license or supporting a bar. We don't compete, and it drives customers to both our doors. We take care of each other. It's a pretty tight bond, man."

Jerry was still sorting out the story in his head. "So, the Mariners Shanty still doesn't pay rent to this day?"

"Darlene pays a modest rent for the Shanty that covers her part of the building upkeep and insurance. Jane and I don't profit from the rent. The restaurant biz is tough, man. For every dollar the Shanty takes in, seventy-three cents goes back out as cost. The Shanty has almost eleven percent net profit. That's high for a food-only joint. My bar averages nineteen percent net profit, and that's very respectable too. It's a symbiotic relationship, man. We both make a good living."

Jerry was impressed with this long-standing arrangement. "That's a great partnership with the restaurant. So, how did the bar go from a speakeasy to a tropical-themed bar? It's not very New England, is it?"

Don looked over the top of his sunglasses at Jerry. "You ask a lot of questions, man."

"Oh, I'm sorry. I'm not from here originally, and I'm just trying to understand…"

Don laughed. "I'm just dicking with you a little, man. So, the tiki bar…It was one of those right place at the right time moments. When World War II started, my granddad joined the Navy. He was in his late 40s and wanted to do his part. Because he made the sandwiches that were served at the bar, the Navy thought that qualified him as a cook and assigned him to work in the ship's galley in the Pacific.

When the war ended, he found himself in Hawaii. He was in no rush to get home, so he started hanging around and helping at the new Polynesian-themed bar that a couple of his sailor buddies had opened in Waikiki. It was decorated like it was on a south pacific island. Granddad liked the exotic tropical cocktails and the escapist vibe of the place and thought other sailors from the war would like it too.

My granddad returned home to his wife and son, my dad, to help run the bar when great-granddad died. They started planning the conversion of the bar and collecting exotic tiki drink recipes. And then box after box of Polynesian-style decorations arrived. My granddad and dad told me stories about the excitement in town when the new bar sign went up. They were both named Don, so they called it Don's Tiki Cocktails & Lounge. They say it was the first tiki bar in Massachusetts. The old newspaper clippings from 1948 talked about lines past Rudy's Clam Shack to get in, man. Times were good! A few years later, my dad met my mom, got married, and I showed up.

Jane and I took the bar over from my dad when he retired. He died when I was 32, and my mom a few years after. So, we carry on the Tiki tradition. It's what we do. It's our lifestyle, man."

"So, you and your dad grew up around the bar business?"

"Yeah, that bar holds nearly all of my most important memories. Jane, too, has a long history with the place. So you could say that Darlene, Jane, and I grew up in the bar and restaurant."

Jerry started to dig through the thick folder again. "That part about the family summer home and other local property holdings makes sense now."

"What other holdings are you talking about, man."

"Well, Don, there is a property that you own, and the town needs to know your intent."

Don had no idea what Jerry was talking about. "Are you sure you have the right guy, man? I don't own any other land in town, just the bar. The family summer home was lost in the two hurricanes in 1954 and never rebuilt."

Jerry closed the folder. "Maybe we should just go look at it and talk there. It's about six blocks away, on Main Street. We can take my car."

"What's wrong with Jenny, man? Buckle up and hold on. I'll drive; you navigate." The car body shook as the vintage Ford 327 motor with straight exhaust pipes roared to life.

Jerry's eyes were wide as he yelled above the noise. "How is it possible that this thing is street legal?"

Don smiled. "Jenny's registered as a parade vehicle. I just haven't found a parade worthy to be in yet, man." They made a U-turn, headed down Brite's Jetty Road, and took a left onto Main Street.

Chapter 2 - An old aluminum beach chair
February 26th 2:34 p.m. ~ Continued

Jerry hung on for dear life as Don pulled Jenny to the curb and stopped. Jerry shivered. "I don't think this is optimum weather for a ride with the roof down, Don!"

Don sat, staring in silence. Then, finally, he lowered his sunglasses and peered over the top of them at the building they had just pulled up to. He knew the small building with its white clapboard siding, wrought iron fence, and simple steeple. After all, Sailers Church is one of the town landmarks in family folklore.

Don smiled. "Who put you up to this, man? Jane? It took her two days to figure out that I had swapped all her new panties for ones a size smaller. So this has to be her payback."

"Put me up to what? I don't understand."

"The joke, man. Me owning a church? Someone got me good, so who gets the credit? It has to be Jane. Using you was the perfect set-up, man." Don laughed. "You know, I was actually starting to believe you."

"Don, I'm a lawyer. We aren't funny. This isn't a joke. I am here in a legal capacity representing the Town of Brite Rock."

"Okay...so if this isn't a joke, can you tell me what the hell this is all about?"

Jerry shifted his weight to his left to retrieve the folder on which he was partially sitting. He feared the contents would be blown away on the short but windy ride to the church.

"Well, Don, a legal document crafted and signed by your great-grandfather in October 1920 is a lease between your family and the town of Brite Rock. For one dollar a year, the lease enabled the town to have a church built by your great-grandfather on your family's land to provide comfort for those who earned a living working the sea. The town, in turn, would sublease the church property for one dollar a year to whomever they saw fit, as long as it was the predominant religious entity of the local commercial fishing community."

Don stared at the little building. "So, you are telling me my family still owns that church?

"In a sense, yes. It's in a family trust with the original agreement from the 1920s. As it stands today, you are the sole successor trustee."

Don continued to study the building. "Tell me more about this, man."

Jerry efficiently shuffled through the papers in the folder and pulled out a document. "Let's see…the property consists of the Sailers Church building, the rectory house directly behind the church, and the land that both sit on bordered by Main Street, Bay Colony Road, and Chapel Lane. The house has four bedrooms, five bathrooms, a library, a dining room, a living room, a house kitchen, a large rectory kitchen, and a meeting room. That's odd; there is a description amendment on the church building. The half-basement noted in the building plans appears to be full-sized, half hidden by a stone wall discovered about 20 years ago. The last Pastor also deconsecrated the church, so it was rendered non-religious and is now for secular use. So it's technically not a church, I guess."

Don pushed his sunglasses back up and sighed. This was starting to feel like a burden to him. "So how does this affect me, man? Why now?"

"Well, the lease states that after 50 years, if the church does not have an active congregation for a period exceeding ninety days, the property reverts to the family trust.

Someone in Pastor Smyth's congregation hit the lotto and handed his church the entire $386 million ticket. He bought a piece of land on South Main Street just about two miles from here and gave notice that he was done with this lease.

Smyth finished building his massive new church and moved everything out of here this past weekend. Nobody else appears to want to use this building as a church. It's very small. The maximum occupancy is only 62 people."

Don sat and listened as Jerry talked. He looked past Jerry at Ed Mattie, the local handyman, as he worked at painting over the name of the church on the sign by the street. He then glanced over his sunglasses at the small wooden structure again. The only thing remarkable about the building was that it sat on a triangle-shaped piece of prime real estate in the center of town, a short distance from the bar.

"So, have you been inside the church before, Don?"

Don looked at Jerry for a moment and wondered. Had he been in the building before? Not that he could remember. "No, man, I can't say I have. Maybe as a little kid…I don't know."

Jerry pulled the papers together. "Well then, let's go check this place out. The heat should still be on in the building."

Don stepped out of the car and headed for the walkway to the church. Hearing Jerry mumbling about the damn car door, Don walked back, reached inside, and popped the door open. He smiled… "not a car guy, are you, man?" Don turned and walked back toward the church, with Jerry following behind.

Ed looked up from painting over the Sailers Church of Brite Rock sign. "Sorry, Don, if you are here to get a little religion, they are closed."

"No, Ed, you know me and organized religion. If I want to chat with sky daddy, I go directly to the source. No need to involve some middleman's interpretation. Anyway, I guess I now own this place". Ed set his brush down and shook Don's hand. "Congratulations on your new acquisition. Will you keep it as a church?"

"It's not like that, man. I didn't buy it. I inherited it somehow. I don't know what to do with it. Like I said, I'm not a church kind of guy."

Ed picked his paintbrush up and asked Don what he wanted painted on the sign.

Don looked up at the building and scratched his head. "I don't know, man. What's wrong with the name people have called this place for decades?"

Ed shook his head. "Can't do that. Some suit over at the big new church told me they now own the Sailers Church name. Something about a trademark. They paid me a hundred bucks to paint over this sign to cover up the name, so here I am."

"Can they do that, man? Walk away with the name?" Don looked at a mystified Jerry.

Jerry shrugged his shoulders. "I doubt they have the right to claim the name for a trademark. Sailers Church has been leased to the town for around a century. I assume your family trust or the town holds the rights to the common law trademark just by using the name over the years. I'll look into it and let you know my opinion."

Ed picked up the paintbrush again. "So, do you want me to cover up the name or paint something different on the sign?"

Don was approaching being overwhelmed. The sign was the least of his concerns at the moment. "Paint anything you want, man. Except under new management. Don't paint that."

A bewildered Don walked up to the church door with Jerry. Ed looked at the Sailers Church of Brite Rock sign for a moment. He had already painted over the words Brite Rock, so he went to work on covering the word Sailers. Then, laughing, Ed opened a can of white paint and picked up a clean lettering brush to crudely add Don's name to the sign.

He took a step back to admire his work. "*Church of Don* looks good to me! I'll come back and finish the sign when he knows what he wants painted on it."

The church's front door burst open as Jerry reached to open it. A handsome man in his late 30s appeared in the doorway. "Step aside, boys, workmen coming through." He raised his hand to motion his workers to hurry. His Tom Ford suit, Rolex watch, and Tiffany gold signet ring were meant to be signs of personal wealth and power.

"I am late for a meeting, boys, and just needed to pick up the last things for my new church." Three men exited the doorway, one carrying a box and the other two struggling with the large cross that had hung on the church's back wall. It was a simple old eight-foot-tall cross made of white maple with a plaster figure of Jesus attached. "Stop by on Sunday for the dedication of my new place, the Brite Rock Cathedral by the Sea. It will be packed, so come early."

Don watched them walking away and turned to Jerry. "Who is the shiny guy in the suit, and isn't that big cross part of this building?"

Jerry sighed. "That's Pastor George Smyth. He was the Pastor here before building his Cathedral on South Main Street near the town line. I thought his face looked a bit shiny too. Maybe he moisturizes too much, or it was the reflection off of his jewelry."

Don pondered Smyth's skin care regimen. "He looks like someone a movie casting company would send over to play the part of the handsome shiny Pastor with a sketchy past. He almost looked life-like."

Jerry grunted in agreement and started thumbing through the thick stack of files again to see if he had a contents inventory list for the property. That may identify the owner of the cross. "Well, it may belong to the Pastor, you, or perhaps even the town. I'm pretty sure it was in the building when Smyth leased it. I'll have to get back to you on that one."

Don watched Smyth and his workers load the cross into the back of a Mercedes-Benz commercial van with the Brite Rock Cathedral by the Sea name on the side of it. Don grew more agitated at the thought. "I'm not religious, but I hope they didn't just steal my big Jesus, man! They just can't take another guy's big Jesus. Isn't there a no-rip-off policy in the Ten Commandments? You know, do unto others, don't take shit that doesn't belong to you, don't do your neighbor's wife, that kind of stuff?"

Jerry smiled as he opened the door to the church. "That's a rough interpretation of the Ten Commandments, but I get what you're saying. I'll look into it and let you know. I'll order its return if it belongs to you or the town."

Don entered the open church door mumbling to himself. "Rat bastard, big Jesus stealers!"

The building was a bit smaller than Don expected. The fire department sign near the door stated *Occupancy of 62 People*. The hardwood floor was slightly worn but in good condition. The pews were made of local thick white oak, simple in design but well crafted. The white paint on the walls was a bit dingy from age. The pulpit was a simple, unadorned podium on a raised stage, two steps up on either side. On the back wall was a clear outline of where the cross had hung for many years. It had the same kind of outline that you see when a painting is removed after it has hung on a wall for a few decades.

Jerry found the property description. "The property consists of the church building, fixtures, land…no specific mention of the cross, but we may be able to have that classified as a fixture. The main floor of this building is the nave and the stage. There is also an attic, a back room, a unisex bathroom, a closet, and stairs to the basement. I already mentioned the house on the lot that was the Pastor's home and rectory."

Don was getting nervous again. "A house and this building. This is a pretty big deal, man. Is this like a game show thing where I get these gifts and have to sell them to pay a ton of tax?"

Jerry laughed. "I don't think so. This property has been in the family trust for a long time. So you get the benefit of exclusive use without an inheritance tax."

Don scratched his head. "Tell me again why this is happening now."

Jerry closed the folder. "Since this isn't being used as a church now, the town hopes you will take ownership and use the property for commercial or private use. The town would rather have the property tax revenue they won't get if it is leased as a church again."

"This is a trip, man. I just need to figure out what the hell to do with it." Don had a perplexed expression as Jerry showed him around the building. It was authentic to when it was built, except for a complete rewiring of the electrical system in 1989 to bring it up to code.

Jerry showed Don the hidden door to a secret room in the basement. It was empty except for a few old wooden barrel cradles. Don smiled. Those were probably used to store barrels of beer.

As they were leaving the basement, Don spotted an old 1960s vintage aluminum folding beach chair in the corner. It had seen better days. One of the blue seat straps was torn and was hanging down, and one of the back legs was severely bent. Someone had tried to straighten the damaged leg and taped part of a broom handle to make it useable.

"Sorry, Don, that chair should have been tossed out by Smyth's people. I'll make sure it gets dumped."

Don paused for a moment admiring the well-used chair. "No, man, let it stay. It's a survivor. It probably had some cool experiences in its day. I like it!"

Jerry laughed. "Okay, the old chair stays. Now, I have another meeting to attend at my office, so I have to go. Here are the keys to both buildings. We have a few papers for you to sign tomorrow to end the lease arrangement. Can you be at the Town Hall Administration Office at 11:00 a.m.?"

"Yeah, I can be there, man. Oh, what about your car?"

Jerry picked up the large folder he had been carrying for the past couple of hours. "I'll walk over and get it after work. Now, look over this building and the house. I can answer any questions you may have at tomorrow's signing. Please remember to lock up when you leave."

Jerry shook Don's hand and exited out the front door. Don went out the church's back door and stood in the driveway admiring the colonial revival-style rectory house. It was a big two-story building in excellent condition. With keys in hand, he entered the house through the front door.

The first-floor living room spanned the width of the front of the house and featured a beautiful oak entryway, a sizable fireplace with an oak mantle, and built-in colonial-style windowed cabinets on both sides. The large living room windows faced Main Street. The hallway from the living room passed a den, bedroom, and full bathroom on the way to the chef's kitchen.

The sizeable primary bedroom was on the front's second floor and had an en suite bathroom with dual sinks, a jacuzzi soaker tub, an impressively large shower, and two large walk-in closets. It was significantly better accommodations than where he and Jane were currently living. Their apartment above the bar always felt too small to Don, but the million-dollar view of the beach out the front windows was entertaining. Jane enjoyed people-watching from them. "Jane is going to love this place."

Don locked up the house and went back to lock up the church. Lost in thought, he was startled to find someone sitting in the front row pew as he entered through the back door. The woman, who he estimated was in her mid-40s, was crying. Don had seen her around town. She had also been in the bar several times, always with a group of women.

Don sat down at the front of the stage. He was at eye level with her.

"Are you the Don on the sign?"

"Sign? Do you mean the bar sign?"

She wiped the tear from her cheek and shook her head. "No, the sign out front, the one that says Church of Don."

After a long pause, Don finally had an aha moment when he realized that Ed had painted his name on the Sailers Church sign. He would deal with that later. "Yep, that's me! Are you looking for Pastor Smyth, the guy who used to run this place?

She shook her head again. "No, I don't know him. I was wandering around town and thought someone here may be able to help me."

"Well, I'll give it a try. How may I help you?"

The woman wiped away another tear. "Well, my mom passed away this morning, and I don't know where she is."

Don was confused. "I'm not sure what you mean by where she is. Is she missing? What's your name?"

"Oh, that did sound a bit stupid. I'm sorry, my name is Karen...Karen Eastman. My mother passed away this morning at the hospital. I feel like she's gone, but I also feel that she's still here. Like she is trying to tell me something. I can't explain it. I guess I just need to know about her soul. Where is she now?"

This wasn't the first time Don had been asked something a little odd. Bartenders get all sorts of strange questions and hear all kinds of personal problems. Usually, they are things that people can't talk about with family or friends. Often it's someone looking for advice or needing someone to talk to.

Don studied Karen for a moment and figured some bartender advice might help. "You were very tight with your mom. You had a good relationship." Of course, he didn't know this as a fact but assumed her emotional state and her questions about her mother to be a reasonable guess.

Karen smiled. "She was more than my mom; we were best friends. We really were!"

Don leaned in toward Karen. "You had that feeling. If you thought about your mom, the phone would ring, and it would be her. You would both start to say the same thing at the same time. You always got her the perfect gift. You knew her. You were connected."

Don's comments surprised Karen. He was right on all accounts. "Yes, that is...was us. How do you know all that?"

"It's just how some people are. You have this connection, Karen, that you think is broken. It isn't. It's only changed. Do you still get that feeling like she is thinking about you?"

"Yes, I feel like she is okay, but I don't know if that is something I am making up in my head. Do you think I am? Am I making it up?"

Don took Karen's hand. "This is about feeling; it's not a head thing. Focus on the feeling that has always been there. It's a real positive vibe, yes?"

Karen smiled softly. "Yes! It makes me happy."

Don spoke compassionately to Karen. "I believe the relationship is still there; it's just in a different form now. Yes, you will miss her being physically here, but keep including her in your thoughts and putting out that positive vibe that your mom loves about you. It's okay to talk to her too. Tell her about your day. Tell her that you love and miss her. She is still your mom, and that will never change."

Karen took a deep, cleansing breath. "I suppose you are right. I need to stop overthinking this and go with the feeling. It's there, and I shouldn't question or deny it. I feel her. Thank you for helping me."

Karen stood and hugged Don. "May I make a contribution to the church?"

"The what? Oh, yeah – no. That's not necessary. I'm glad you're feeling better, and sorry I didn't meet your mom. She sounds like a cool lady." Don walked Karen to the door. She paused for a moment.

"My sister should talk to you. She had the same kind of relationship with mom as I did… I do. She is also struggling with this; I'm not as good at explaining it as you did. It would be helpful for her to talk with you. What time on Sunday?"

Don was puzzled. "Sunday, what about Sunday?"

"Yes, what time does the service start on Sunday? I want to bring my sister to meet you."

Don fumbled for words. "Well, you see, this isn't a.. well, it is, but it isn't a… you see, I'm not…" Don's attempt to explain that it wasn't a church anymore didn't matter to Karen. She felt that he could help her sister.

"How about eleven in the morning? Is that a good time?" Karen smiled and nodded in agreement, hugging and thanking Don again before she left.

Don mumbled to himself. "Eleven in the morning on a Sunday after closing the bar at two the night before. Jane is not going to be in love with this."

Don locked the front door to the church and walked down the path to the gate. He paused by the Sailers Church of Brite Rock sign that Ed had been painting over. "Oh, come on. That's not cool, man!"

Chapter 3 - What are you going to do with a church
February 26th 4:14 p.m. ~ Continued

Jane glanced up to see who was entering the bar. "Where the hell have you been? What did the town lawyer want with you?"

Don had a perplexed look on his face. He shrugged his shoulders as he walked up to Jane and touched his forehead to hers. They held each other for a moment. It was their way of connecting.

Don sighed. "It took a while for lawyer Jerry to give me the keys to my new church and our new house. Well, they will be once I sign for them tomorrow."

Before a stunned Jane could speak, a booming voice filled the room. "MOTHERFUCKER, MOM-MOM-MOM-HIP." The room fell silent. That same voice, now meek, was heard again – "sorry!" In unison and with a drawn-out cadence that had developed over time, the bar patrons replied, "it's okay, Brad!"

Brad, age 36, is the Civil Engineer for the town. He graduated from M.I.T.'s Civil and Environmental Engineering school. He is the perfect person for the job, having both town infrastructure and the environmental challenges of an ocean-facing beach, an inlet, and a jetty to manage.

Brad views himself as a townie; someone brought up in town with no plans to move away. He stops by the bar every Thursday night after work for a Mai Tai or two, a plate of Darlene's fried Ipswich clams, and a bowl of clam chowder. Brad always counts the French fries on his plate but never the fried clams. Counting is a mild obsessive-compulsive disorder associated with his neurological condition, a moderate form of Tourette's syndrome.

Brad has a few occasional motor tics, mostly a random fast twitch of his nose or facial grimaces. He also vocalizes a soft grunting sound or repeats a few words. Occasionally Brad may vocalize socially inappropriate and derogatory remarks when he is stressed. He also yells out "motherfucker" at random moments. Don's Tiki Cocktails & Lounge is one of the few places where he feels accepted and comfortable. It's a social sanctuary for him.

Jane intensely stared at Don, trying to read his face and body language. He has pulled some elaborate pranks on her in the past. However, she saw none of that in his eyes this time.

"Somehow, I inherited that little church on Main Street and the big house next to it. I will meet with Lawyer Jerry tomorrow morning to sign the papers. It's in a trust, but I sort of…we sort of own it all."

Jane laughed. "You inherited a church? Are you fucking kidding me? What are you going to do with a church? Should I buy a naughty Nun outfit from the costume shop?"

Don scratched his head. "I don't know, man. Oh, not about the naughty Nun costume, do buy that. I'm just trying to figure out if this is a burden or a good thing. The house is nice…big! And you will love the massive bedroom and bathroom. The shower sprays water at you from every direction except up. And the kitchen is restaurant quality. But the church building, what am I going to do with a church? This is weird, man."

Jane could see that Don was having difficulty sorting through all of this. He isn't religious, but he does feel that there is something after we die. Don reasoned that there is too much mystery and unknown in the universe for death to simply be lights out. It was a topic that Roger Avery, a recovering atheist alcoholic, occasionally brought up. Even though A.A. is non-denominational, Roger believes the spiritual awakening aspect of it to be a stealth religious organization. That bothers him. So, every Friday, Roger meets Don for lunch at the Mariners Shanty to talk about his week and get a pep talk to carry him through the weekend. It's bartender advice for the recovering alcoholic.

While missing the bar's social aspect, Roger tried a few Mai Tai mocktails one evening. Drinking all that fruit juice didn't end well. It was a rude surprise. He stood, grabbed his ass, and loudly declared,

"Oh shit, here comes the fruit juice," as he bolted for the men's room. That was the last time Roger set foot in the bar. That was five months ago. He said the cocktails were too enticing for him to be around. What he misses most are the engaging conversations and socializing.

Don remembered that he hadn't told Jane about his Sunday commitment. "Um…I've got to meet this woman, Karen, and her sister at the church Sunday morning. She showed up while I was looking the place over and asked about her recently deceased mother. Trying to make sense of it all, I guess."

Jane was confused. "What about her dead mother? What did she want?"

"I guess she just wanted someone to talk to and picked that church out of convenience. I don't know what she wanted from me, but I guess I said the right things because she seemed better after we talked. Her sister is a mess and a half, and she wants me to talk to her too. I don't know; maybe I can say something to help."

"Why didn't you ask them to stop by the bar instead of the church?" Jane gave Don side-eye and folded her arms. He recognized her disapproval stance. That was her reaction when she first saw the hot rod he bought from Spider.

"I don't know, man. The whole thing caught me off guard. She was just one aspect of a very trippy experience. I told her I would be there Sunday morning at eleven, so I guess I have to. Do you want to come along?"

Jane thought for a moment. "You know, I do! Not to watch you play barink (slang for bartender shrink) to a couple of skirts, but to check out the house. Sound like a plan?"

Don nodded his head in agreement. "A few kind words with the ladies and a tour of the facilities with you, and we are back for the one o'clock opening. That will work."

Laughter at the far end of the bar caught Don's attention. "I see the little old D.A.R. ladies are here for their Thursday afternoon tipple. It's good to see some of the old customers still come around after all these years." Don smiled and waved to the ladies.

Jane reached up and lovingly stroked Don's face. "I think they come back because the place holds many fond memories, and A.J. still tends to them. It's sweet of you to let him serve his old clientele."

"Of course! A.J. is family. He's been behind the bar here since the 1960s. Hell, I learned how to make most of the classics from him. Besides, those D.A.R. ladies drink pretty old-school. Let's see, Lily always has a Brandy Alexander and Doris has a French 75, while the more adventurous Millie has a Pain Killer, and designated driver Ginny has a Safe Sex on the Beach Mocktail. Have you noticed that Ginny is much nicer since she gave up the bourbon? Anyway, A.J. can make those in his sleep. And I think they also come here because A.J. is still a good-looking guy, and they are all widows. That plus, he charges them 1970s prices. Uncle Sam and I keep the old ladies in cocktails. I wonder if that young lady sitting with them is a new D.A.R. member. She looks familiar."

Jane glanced at the young lady. "That's Becca, Millie's niece. Her mom, Michelle, runs Rudy's Clam Shack when he goes on vacation."

Don made the connection. "Oh yeah, that's why she looks familiar. Do you think she can join the D.A.R.? It's good for older people to have younger friends and associates. It helps to keep us younger as we age!"

"MOTHERFUCKER!....sorry!" Again, in unison and with a drawn-out cadence, the bar patrons reply, "it's okay, Brad!"

Lily turned to Brad. "It really is alright, dear. My deceased husband would quite often yell that out too. Of course, he didn't have a condition like you. He was just a dick!"

Brad and the other little old ladies chuckled.

Chapter 4 - Sign on the dotted line
February 27th 10:48 a.m.

Don wandered around the Brite Rock Town Hall, looking for Jerry's office. He paused to read a plaque on the wall. *This three-story granite and brick town hall was built in 1844. It replaced the meeting house that was built in 1756. The town's first meeting house was built in 1643 by Alden Williams. All three buildings occupied this site. Colonial and Native American artifacts found during construction can be viewed in the second-floor museum room.*

After briefly visiting the museum room, Don found Jerry's office on the third floor. The door was open. "Wow, nice digs, man. Is this where I do the paper signing thing?"

Jerry smiled. "Yes, it is. And thanks for coming in today, Don."

Jerry had spread out the 16 documents to be signed on the large table in his office. The documents represented the original agreements and updates to keep current with the changing laws over the past 100+ years.

"First off, on behalf of the town, I would like to thank you and your family for providing comfort by way of the old church. It has served our community well for over a century. The town looks forward to returning it to you and your family's trust with our sincere gratitude."

"Just doing our part for the citizens of Brite Rock, man. Hang on a second; I've got to make a phone call." Don tapped a number on his vintage cell phone's contact list. "Roger, hey man, I can't make our weekly lunch today. I'm signing some papers at a lawyer's office. If this can wait until Sunday, I can meet you at the little white church in the center of town at 11:00 am. No, we're not going to church; we're going to meet at a church building. Big difference, man. As it turns out, I now own a church building. I'll tell you more about it on Sunday. Okay, man, see you then. Aloha!"

Don took his old five-dollar supermarket reading glasses out of his shirt pocket and put them on. "Okay, where do I start?" The oldest document was the first. It was dated January 18, 1920.

Jerry sat back in his chair, scrolling through his appointment calendar on his iPad as Don read every word of every document. It wasn't clear to Jerry if Don understood the legal jargon or just didn't ask any questions. It was almost 5:00 p.m. when Don signed the last of the documents.

"There, all signed! That was interesting reading, particularly the old stuff. They had a way with words back then. Superior lexicon, man!"

Jerry nodded in agreement as he pulled the documents together and paged his assistant to come and help with notarizing and copying all of them. "It will take a few minutes to get a set of these signed documents ready for you to take."

Don looked up at the clock on the wall. "Sorry, man, it's Friday night and happy hour. The bar starts to get slammed right about now. I need to jet out the door. Can you mail them to me or drop them off at the bar?"

Jerry thought for a moment. "Yes, I'll swing by and drop them off on my way home today. I'll see you in about an hour."

Don smiled broadly. "You know, for a lawyer, you're not half bad. I mean that, man!" With that, Don turned and walked out the door.

Chapter 5 - Jerry thought Olivia had caught him
February 27th 5:17 p.m. ~ Continued

Jane pulled two empty glasses off the bar and quickly wiped it down. The place was crowded. Two new young faces took a seat in front of her. Jane thought tourists, New York, maybe. "Welcome; what will you have?"

The couple looked around, trying to come up with something to order. "What is the specialty drink of the house?"

"If you are talking alcohol, I need to see some I.D. first." The couple quickly presented their New York driver's licenses. Jane thought to herself, *New York - nailed it*!

Jane handed Amber and Kyle their licenses and went into tourist mode, which often happens in the summertime in Brite Rock. She smiles and gives the couple a drink menu. "We are a traditional Tiki bar with over 300 rums, 73 exotic island cocktails, and prohibition-era libations. The house cocktail is the Mai Tai. It's two premium rums, orange curaçao, lime juice, house-made orgeat, and a touch of Demerara sugar syrup. We juice the citrus for your cocktail daily for maximum freshness and flavor. We also offer beer, wine, and other modern cocktails. In addition, we offer over twenty tropical and conventional nonalcoholic drinks."

The couple pondered the drink menu for a few minutes. "There's just too many to choose from. My wife wants a white wine, and I want something tropical with a bit of a kick but smooth. So I'm thinking maybe the Pussers Painkiller # 3."

"Okay, that's a Painkiller # 3 and a white wine. Chardonnay, Sauvignon Blanc or Pinot Grigio?" Jane picked up a wineglass and started pouring the moment the customer said Chardonnay.

"Kyle, your Painkiller takes a few minutes to make. Our cocktails are precisely handcrafted. Thanks in advance for your patience." Jane lets first-timers and people she doesn't know that it takes time to make a craft cocktail. On a night as busy as this, patience can wear thin on both sides of the bar.

Jane looks down the length of the bar. Kelly, the cute 32-year-old redhead, is holding her own tending bar in the middle. A.J. on the far end is fading fast. Then, just as Jane starts to get worked up, she sees Don coming in the back door.

"It's about time you got your happy ass back here! A.J. down there is used up. You take my station; I'll take mid-bar and have Red replace A.J. at the end. Shakemaster Sam can hit the tables for empties and fill in where needed." She flashed a smile, gave Don a quick kiss, then turned and walked away. She hadn't taken more than two steps when she heard the crack of a bar towel being snapped and felt the stinging sensation on her ass. She had gotten the playful reaction that she was looking for.

Don scanned the bar while filling cocktail orders. At his first opportunity, he adjusted the volume control on the jukebox sound system, turning it up just enough to provide background music that wouldn't compete with customer conversations. The 32-speaker system was designed and installed by one of his customers, Olivia. Usually, Don gives polite vague non-answers when anyone that has been drinking makes him an offer. Unfortunately, the best of intentions look very different in the harsh light of the following day.

But Olivia was at the door when the bar opened that following day, a warm Sunday morning last September. She had brought some electronic equipment on a portable luggage cart.

Olivia's white cutoff jeans and white Jake Shimabukuro t-shirt contrasted her dark skin and natural hair. A tattoo ring of dolphins surrounds her right ankle. A vintage large puka shell bracelet moved freely on her left wrist.

Don had noticed her as a new, somewhat regular in the bar over the past few months. She was usually alone and sat at a small table near the jukebox. It was common to see her iPhone up to a speaker to see if the app could identify the song. If it couldn't, she would often get up to ask Don what song was playing and who it was by. Then, writing it down on a drink napkin, she stuffed the notes in her back pocket.

This was the first opportunity Don had to talk to her for any length of time. As it turned out, she was trying to make her way into the tiki and hot rod scene. He was surprised at how much she knew about the tiki culture, history, fashion, music, food, and drink. Don didn't know any black women in the tiki scene this deeply. Black customers, yes! Black tikiphiles, only two came to mind.

"I'm impressed with your knowledge of tiki, but why are you here with your cart of…things, man?"

Olivia handed Don a business card – Senior Product Manager at Architectural Audio Corporation in Boston.

"The problem with your jukebox is that the sound is concentrated in a couple of pockets. So when I walk 10 feet from the juke or the two satellite speakers on a busy night, I can't hear it anymore, and that kind of sucks because there are some cool songs that I would like to hear without being stuck in the corner."

Don shook his head in agreement. "Yeah, the juke is hard to hear on most busy nights. Are you saying that you can fix that?"

Olivia's eyes sparkled with enthusiasm. "I sure can! I'd sound out the room, design a balanced, active sound distribution mesh, and install it. So, the jukebox will provide the signal to a bunch of speakers distributed all around the bar. Several microphones spread around will input bar ambient noise into an audio processor in the back room that will analyze the background sound and music to set the optimum sound volume per speaker dynamically. As a result, customers can hear the music in the background without needing to speak over it. What do you think?" Olivia fidgeted while she waited for a response.

Don scratched his head and looked deep in thought. "I sort of lost you back at the problem with the jukebox is… I must admit that the juke sound is lame, but I dig the machine. So what are you trying to sell me here? What's the cost, and where did you learn all this, man?" Don was skeptical about the offer.

"At M.I.T.! I have an E.E. degree and did my postgrad work in the acoustics and vibration lab. The audio hardware won't cost you anything. I have several real-world test sites going on currently. It's how I validate my commercial designs. The only thing you need to do is sign a few waivers. I will pull the required permits if any are necessary. Oh, and you also need to provide me with an internet connection so I can remote in for updates. That's it! Oh, and I agree, the juke is a cool retro player. There is no need to replace it with a streaming service, but I would consider it as a backup. I can also integrate control for both into a smartphone or iPad. My team can lay out and fab the hardware interface to add internet and phone control to the juke. We did that for a rich guy on Martha's Vineyard last year, and it works great!"

Don was impressed but still a bit skeptical. "Why do you want to do this? What's in it for you?"

Olivia laughed. "Do you mean besides my freedom to walk or sit anywhere in the bar and still hear the music? I want you and Jane to help me learn more about tiki. And I need help with finding a car. Not a hot rod like Jenny, more of a classic ride. A cruiser!"

Don nodded. "Okay, that's all cool. But what if I don't like the sound system after you're done?"

Olivia smiled. "That's easy; I put it back exactly as it was. You have everything to gain and nothing to lose. So, what do you say? Can I do this?"

Don thought for a moment and agreed to the offer. Free is good! Olivia installed the sound system six months ago, and it has worked flawlessly. She now sits at the first barstool closest to the bar's front door and the pass-through door into Darlene's restaurant. It's the best seat in the house for people-watching.

Don smiled. "Are you ready for another Jet Pilot, Olivia?"

"Yes, please! And what is the song currently playing? My app can't find it." Olivia was poised to make a note on her phone.

Don started making Olivia's cocktail and paused momentarily to listen. "Oh yeah, this one's a classic called Sun Stroke by the Bambi Molesters. The group is out of Croatia, I think. The gal on the bass guitar is cool. They got into the 60s surf music revival in the late 90s. I tell you, man, this scene has been underground for a while and is not just local. Surf guitar groups from America, Belgium, Germany, the Netherlands, France, and Japan are on the juke. It's global, man!"

Olivia was making notes on her phone as Jerry walked up to the end of the bar. There was an open spot, standing room, next to her. He handed Don a large envelope. "Here are the copies of all the documents you signed and an extra set of keys we held until the property was transferred to you. You are now the proud owner of a church and rectory!" Olivia burst out laughing.

Don's smile changed to a feigned indignant expression. "Why does everyone laugh when they hear about this, man? What is so weird about me owning a church building?" Don paused for a moment. "Okay, yeah, I can see where that might be amusing! So Jerry, thanks for the papers, and what will you have, man? The first one's on the house for helping me out today."

Jerry glanced around the bar. "Oh, I don't know. I'm not too big on sweet frilly drinks."

"There is nothing frilly about these, man. These are classic cocktails."

"Okay, what do most people have?" Jerry looked at Olivia's drink. "What are you having?"

"It's a Jet Pilot. Here, try it. I'll get you a straw."

Before Jerry could decline her offer, Olivia slid the drink towards him and stretched across the bar to get a new straw from below. Jerry noticed that Olivia was rather attractive. He also admired her lean, stretched-out body. The tropical print t-shirt and vintage Jordache jeans hugged her perfectly. For a moment, Jerry thought Olivia caught him checking her out, but if she did, she didn't let on. Olivia slid the new straw into her drink, and Jerry took a sip.

"Wow, that's good! Yes, I'll have one of those Jet Airplane drinks, please."

Don smiled and nodded, acknowledging Jerry's Jet Pilot drink order. Olivia grabbed the seat next to her for Jerry when it became available. They talked for a while and ordered another round. Jerry went to the Shanty to get them a seafood sampler plate to share and two forks. There is intimacy in dining from one plate.

They talked about their careers, and then Olivia schooled Jerry on the salient points of the Tiki scene. He was curious and asked detailed questions. Don was impressed with her knowledge and passion and with his curiosity. He watched Olivia and Jerry continue talking, smiling, laughing, and making sustained eye contact. Jerry touched her hand. Olivia touched his arm. Don didn't know either of these people well but thought a love connection might have just been made. Olivia and Jerry left together just after 11:00 p.m.

The crowd had thinned to a handful of regulars by midnight. Don tended to the customers while Jane restocked the bottles and Tiki mugs that were sold that day. Red collected glasses and washed them in preparation for tomorrow. Sam cleaned the juicing equipment in the back room, a job no one liked.

In the Mariners Shanty, Darlene placed the closed sign on the door at 11:00 p.m. and lowered the blinds in the front windows and door. Her crew pushed several tables together and set sixteen place settings. Don called the last round at 12:40 a.m. The last bar patron was ushered out at 1:05 a.m.

Brite Rock was too small to have a good 24-hour restaurant or late-night bar where food service people could go after work for that 1:00 a.m. meal and drink. So Don and Darlene improvised by putting on the weekly Friday night dinner. Darlene announced its Cajun night with boudin balls, crab and shrimp Étouffée, fried chicken, dirty rice, corn maque choux, and greens. Dessert is bread pudding topped with a warm sweet bourbon-based sauce. Jane always gets a couple of bread pudding orders to go for breakfast.

Darlene's line cook, Tommy, knocked on her door asking for work in October 2005. He was a young line cook at a New Orleans restaurant and was displaced by Hurricane Katrina. He came up north to stay with family and never went back. When it comes to authentic Cajun, Tommy is one of the best in New England.

Everyone assembled at the table, and Don and Jane took the drink orders for Red, Sam, Darlene, Tommy, J.C., Darlene's dishwasher David, Darlene's waitress Stephanie, Kevin and Lindsay from the Black Cat Diner, and Claire and Sarah from McCabe's Irish Pub. Officer Jim Dillard would join in after his shift ended. A.J. and Geezer may show up if they are out and about. This was a Friday night tradition. It's their lifestyle. It's their family.

Chapter 6 - I love the humble beginnings pitch
March 10th 9:51 a.m.

Pastor George Smyth settled into the high-back leather chair in his new spacious office at the Brite Rock Cathedral by the Sea. He watched as the workman installed the Sailers Church cross on his office wall. He viewed the cross as a spoil of war for the taking. Something to point to when he talked about starting his ministry. The cross was a prop that was necessary to help him sell his story.

None of this would be possible without Paul Caruso. Just over three years ago, Caruso met Smyth in a Narragansett, Rhode Island bar. He was impressed with Smyth's good looks, voice, and natural ability to be likable. These traits serve Smyth well in gaining people's trust and persuading them to spend more money than they should. He was selling yachts for a living, a job that typically receives a lot of *no's* and the occasional rare *yes*. Smyth's sales record and consumer complaints were rapidly rising. It was time for him to change careers, something he did every few years to avoid legal entanglements.

Caruso convinced Smyth that there was big money to be made in the church business. The goal was to form a ministry and build it into a highly profitable mega-church. Sailers Church of Brite Rock was available to lease, so they created a partnership and business. It didn't matter that Smyth knew or cared little about religion. The lease was cheap, and the little church was the perfect training ground for Smyth to learn and hone his skills. He watched hours of online church services to craft a persona and build a portfolio of plagiarized material to present on Sundays.

The arrangement was simple. Smyth would lead the flock as the religious figurehead, and Caruso would manage the business and income. They would suck as much money out of the operation as possible and divide it equally.

Thinking of protecting their investment, Smyth filed a trademark application to acquire the rights to the Sailers Church of Brite Rock name. The name had been on the church building since the 1920s but was never trademarked. People just didn't think to do that.

Six months after he started preaching, an opportunity arose when an elderly parishioner came forward to ask for advice and guidance regarding her good fortune in the lottery. It didn't take Smyth long to persuade the lucky winner to donate the winning $386 million lotto ticket to the church. Later he laughed when he told Caruso how easy it was to separate the old lady from her winnings.

"You are charming, George, but let's get back on task. Are you ready to give your sermon today? This isn't that shitty little church. It's the big time now, and a lot of money is riding on this. Are you ready to lead the flock to their fleecing?"

Caruso's question brought Smyth's wandering mind back into focus. Smyth had a case of opening-day jitters. He went over the details of his welcoming sermon for the third time. It would be televised on a local broadcast station in Massachusetts and streamed online. Smyth was okay with buying the time slot to broadcast his service. He and Caruso considered such marketing efforts an investment, not an expense.

Caruso hired a public relations firm, a social media specialist, and a broadcast television producer. These were necessary to grow the Brite Rock Cathedral by the Sea into their desired money-making brand.

With just over 2,850 plush theater-style seats, the venue was built on a foundation of conspicuous consumption to establish status. Smyth believed that such status would inspire confidence in his followers.

He told Caruso, "you have to touch the people's hearts to touch their wallets. This place will touch their hearts." While Caruso agreed that an extravagant display was a necessary attention-getter, he also reminded Smyth that the luxury of the Cathedral needed to be grounded in the ordinary person.

"Stop thinking like a yacht salesman and start thinking like a preacher. Your persona needs to be humble and approachable. That's why I recommended you take the cross from the old church and put it in your office. We need to link you to the old church to show where you came from. That way, we can head off any public conversation about the old lady giving us her winning lotto ticket. So let's start by establishing a different dialogue, one of your humble beginnings."

Smyth wasn't sure about the value in that. "Do you think anyone cares where I came from, Paul? If that were so damn important, why not just buy that shitty little church building and stick it on the front lawn? Hell, we've got over 25 acres here."

Caruso grinned. "That's not a bad idea! We can contrast your rise to fame right here. That little church building is small enough to fit next to the Cathedral. We can market the hell out of that. It's a tug on the heartstrings and a good money-making prop. Is it for sale?"

Smyth laughed. "Of course, it's for sale. We have to find the owner and figure out the number. It can't be more than $100,000 for that shack. We leased it from the town for one dollar per year. I guess they own it."

Smyth paused for a moment. "You know, when I was there getting the cross yesterday, the town lawyer, you know him, the Harvard guy with a stick up his ass. He was there with the guy that runs the weird old bar across from the beach. So let's have Jim Reed take the lead on this and see what it will take to get that little church building. If the bar owner is looking to buy the place, we need to top his bid. I want the building. I don't care about the land."

"What's your cap on the offer, George?"

Smyth's eyes narrowed as he contemplated the offer. "Let's start at $100,000 and see where it goes. That's a reasonable amount of cash to get the deal done. So let's go with that and have Deacon Reed start calling around on Monday. I'm honestly starting to love the humble beginnings pitch."

Chapter 7 - The aluminum chair recognizes
March 14th 10:02 a.m.

Jane removed the towel from her wet hair and stood in front of the mirror, studying her body. Being in her 40s, she thought that she still had it together. Jane guessed it was a toss of the genetic dice and a daily five-lap run on the beach that maintained her taut body. She also was on her feet for several hours a day working at the bar. Her activity tracker usually exceeded 30,000 steps per day.

It was common for men, and the occasional woman, to hit on Jane. She knew it was purely physical, all about looks, and had nothing to do with who she was. She disliked that feeling yet knew she could do nothing about it.

Jane felt that good looks had a downside as her family and friends sat in judgment when she started dating Don. They voiced their opinions that he was below her and that she could do much better with her looks. They didn't understand that she found Don to be everything she wanted and needed. The fact that he wasn't handsome and had a hippy vibe was endearing to her. There was just something about him that Jane genuinely wanted in her life. As far as she is concerned, they rock each other's worlds entirely and in all ways. That's more than most of her friends can say, particularly those who have cheated, divorced, or had numerous marriages.

The bedroom door opened. Don smiled. "Are you going like that, or are you going to put some clothes on?"

Jane struck a seductive pose. "Can we be a few minutes late?"

Don feigned a shocked expression. "Stop trying to have your way with me, woman! We will be late if you don't get your ass in gear, so cover that beautiful nakedness and let's hit the road. You'll get some sticky later if you play your cards right."

Don turned and started to leave the bedroom. He hadn't taken a step when the wet towel flew past his head and hit the door, knocking it closed. He turned to see Jane slowly moving toward him. "I am taking 10 minutes of your time …right now! I will get you to your church, but you must forgive me, for I am about to sin."

The squealing sound broke the Sunday morning tranquility. Jane smoked the tires on Jenny as she came to a halt in front of the church. Don grinned ear to ear. He enjoyed it when Jane cut loose.

As they climbed out of Jenny, Jane spotted Roger, the woman named Karen, her sister, Wally, Brad, a young guy that is a regular at the bar, and three other people whom she didn't recognize. Jane was bewildered as she stood staring at the nine people waiting for Don.

He took Jane by the arm. "Come along, my flock is waiting for me, and you must confess to being a naughty girl."

Jane didn't move. "What are all these people doing here, Don? I thought it was just going to be the two women and Roger. What are you going to tell them?"

Don took off his sunglasses and glanced up at the waiting group. "Well, I guess I'll pretend they are at the bar and have just come to hang out and talk. A half-hour of chat and all should be right with the world, I hope. And you'll be here too, so if I tank, you can work your magic. What do you think about that plan?"

Jane still didn't move. She had reservations about Don's plan, and he could see that doubt in her eyes. He gently brushed her hair to the side of her face. "Okay, you are right, as usual. Oh, not about talking to them, but that you've been a very naughty girl. How do you feel about a spanking as penance?" Don smiled and took Jane's hand. As they walked up to meet their guests, Jane was aware that he had again used humor to alleviate her uncertainty. She was okay with that.

Don greeted the waiting guests with a big "*aloha*" and made small talk as he fumbled with the door key. As they entered the building, it struck Don for the first time how small the church was. There were five rows of pews, six average-sized people per side for a total of sixty seats. A person playing the piano and the preacher make sixty-two, the maximum number of people in the building per the Brite Rock Fire Department.

"Everyone grab a bench and make yourself comfortable, man." Don sat on the edge of the stage but quickly realized he was too low. He couldn't see anyone in the second row back. There was a pulpit that he could stand and lean on, but he thought that would look a bit too churchy.

"OK, here's the problem, man. If I stand, it's like I'm preaching, and that's not my thing. If you stand, I can see all of you, but that feels weird too. Wait a minute...."

Don remembered seeing the old aluminum folding beach chair in the basement and quickly retrieved it. It had seen better days. Don wondered if the bent leg with a piece of broken broom handle taped to it and the torn webbing on the seat would hold up. It was better than nothing, but not by much. Don set the chair up on the stage. It creaked and squeaked as he gently settled into it. He smiled broadly.

Nobody seemed to notice or care that the person they came to hear was dressed in plaid shorts, sandals, and an aloha shirt with sunglasses hanging from the shirt pocket. Sitting in the slightly lopsided old folding beach chair only added to the odd sight.

"So, citizens of Brite Rock, what do you want to talk about? Sports? The price of clams? Why you are here this morning? Anything?"

Karen raised her hand to speak. Don suddenly realized that he was the impromptu moderator of the group discussion. He didn't want this to be about him, so he assigned the power the same way the British Monarchy had – to the throne. "The aluminum chair recognizes Karen. Unfortunately, for those that don't know Karen, her mom passed away the other day. That's a serious bummer, man! So, what's on your mind this way too early on a Sunday morning?"

Karen collected her thoughts for a moment. "Well, Pastor Don and I..."

Jane burst out laughing. Don interrupted Karen. "Stop the bus. Let's be clear here; I'm not a pastor, priest, shaman, or any of those dudes.

I own a bar, man. We're just here to talk and hang out. You know, chill and chat."

Wally balanced his iPad in one hand and raised his other as if he were in school and wanted to ask a question.

Don pointed to him. "Hang on a moment, Karen. I like the raised hand, man. Nice touch, and thanks to Karen for establishing that communication gesture. Now, what's on your mind, Wally?"

"Is it OK to record this for my video blog, and are there rules for talking?"

"Sure, man, video whatever away. This is a public forum. Rules, do we need those?"

Everyone looked at each other, and there was a consensus that having rules was a good idea. Don scratched his head for a moment. "Rules…ok, let's see…we already have the raised hand thing." Don rattled off a few more rules as they hit him. Most everyone chuckled and nodded in agreement as they heard the rules.

The Rules

1. If you wish to speak, raise your hand, and wait for the aluminum chair to recognize you.
2. This is just a building, not a church. There is no flock. You're just people, man.
3. Check your political views at the door. A diet of politics is bad for your mental health.
4. Be cool. Everyone has the right to speak and be heard.
5. You can disagree, but don't be a dick about it. As Dave Mason said, *it's just you and me, and we just disagree.*
6. The occasional obscenity is cool, don't freak out if you hear one; it's just words.
7. No hate allowed. Everybody respects everybody. If you can't, you know where the door is.
8. Jane is right! She usually is, and it's easier if you just accept that.
9. You get booted if you're being a serious jackass.
10. No gratuitous nudity.
11. Although rum makes everything better, no cocktails are allowed here. We may revisit that rule in the near future, probably this afternoon.
12. I don't know…oh, no fighting or weapons. Keep that shit outside of this building and our bar. You can't take back a violent act. Apologies, thoughts, and prayers don't cut it.

"That's about it. Talk it out. Hug it out. Hang around. Commune. You know, be a community." Don looked around at the smiling faces. "Sound groovy?" The answer was an emphatic yes with a loud Blow Me from Brad, followed by his familiar sorry.

Don smiled. "It's OK, man; you are covered under Rule #6, the occasional obscenity rule."

Sitting on the stage's right side, Jane raised her hand. "The aluminum chair recognizes Jane. Will I regret the aluminum chair recognizing you?"

Jane grinned. "Absolutely! So, babe, is that outfit you are wearing this morning covered by the obscenity rule too?"

Don looked down and studied his attire. "I see what you mean. The chair clashes with my outfit."

Jane folded her arms. "That's not what I mean, and you know it. We will address your wardrobe choices at home."

Don nodded. "There is room for improvement. There always is."

Brad raised his hand, and the aluminum chair recognized him. "For those that don't know me, I have Tourette's Syndrome, a disorder that causes me to make sounds or say things that can be socially awkward. I also have a couple of tics that look like a nose twitch, grimace, or real fast smile. The luck of the draw, I am one of the few that yells random things out. I don't mean to; it just happens. Although, being in church, I have to confess that I recently yelled out nice tits on purpose when Red served me. That one wasn't Tourette's…my bad." Jane chuckled as she recalled Brad doing that yesterday.

"It's cool, man. Thanks for letting the new folks know your thing. We all have a thing or two that makes us who we are. Okay, where were we? Ah, Karen, please proceed."

Karen took a deep breath and began. "Well, my sister Kathy and I lost our mom the other day. I wandered into this church, and…Don was able to…I don't know… to help explain things in terms I could understand. Can you talk about that to my sister?"

Don scratched his head. "Well, ladies, I can give you my take on life. It's simple. As they said in the movie Jurassic Park, life will find a way. It is amazing to me that any of us are here at all. Being born and making it this far is challenging, man, yet here we sit."

I think each of us is a big unique chemistry set that runs on electrical impulses. I believe that we relate to that same energy in others. We can feel it when someone is near us. We've all had that experience where we think of someone, and the phone rings, and it's them. There are all sorts of examples of how we connect to each other. My mom called it women's intuition. Jane calls it *just knowing,* and I've been busted a few times by that. The lady on West Street says she can read your aura, our body's energy field. If she can do that, that's pretty cool. So, what happens to that electrical energy and unseen connections when we die?

Albert Einstein was a pretty smart guy. He said that Energy could not be created or destroyed; it could only change from one form to another. I think our energy changes form when we die, but we still have a link to it. That's why we can still feel that connection with someone when they pass away. Kathy, do you still feel that connection to your mom?"

Kathy shook her head yes. "I do, it's like she is someplace, but I can't pick up the phone to call her. I do feel her, and I get what you're saying. Do you think that energy, that thing we connect to in life and after, is our soul?"

Don gently shrugged his shoulders. "It's something, but I honestly don't know what or where it is. I am in no way qualified to speak about the whole soul, heaven, and afterlife thing. I only know that, for me, it has been comforting to have that connection that binds us to each other. And I feel that it stays with us, even after we hit our expiration date."

Kathy smiled. "Thank you! It's truly comforting to talk about our mom passing and not get the same old awkward sorry for your loss sympathy. It's good to know others have this experience. Unfortunately, mom isn't physically here, but I feel that we're still connected. I really feel that." Karen mouthed the words thank you to Don.

An older gray-haired man raised his hand. "The aluminum chair recognizes.... what's your name, man?"

"Carleton, my name is Carleton. Where does this energy reside, if not in heaven? Do you know where heaven is?"

Don smiled. "I can show you where heaven is, man. Jane, stand up!"

Jane laughed. "Good one, reverend!"

Don composed himself. "Sorry, Carleton, that was the perfect setup. Anyway, we are getting into the religion zone here, and that's not within my sphere, man. I think the energy within us is this vibe, this frequency that harmonizes or clashes with other people's vibe. It's that subtle instant like or dislike when we meet someone new. It's the attraction or rejection. It's what we bond to. How that magic happens when we die and still feel the other person is beyond me, man. It's a total mystery, as it should be. I think our vibe parties on after we do. That's just my take on it, anyway."

Carleton stared at Don with a blank expression on his face. "Wow, that sounds more plausible than angels flying around up in the clouds. I need to think about that more. I do have another unrelated question. It's for Jane."

"Sure, man, ask away."

Carleton hesitated for a moment. "Well, Jane, are they real or augmented?"

Don was taken aback by the question. "What the ... Boundaries, man!"

Jane stood, put her arms in the air, and struck a pose. "It's all real! It could be DNA, or it could be shit luck. Whatever the reason, I started to sprout in eighth grade, and by the time I turned 17, I had the figure you see today. I am proudly rocking this 40-something badass body."

Jane took a bow in acknowledgment of the applause. "Thank you, and enough about my rack. Let's move on and talk about Carleton's testicles. How are the family jewels doing, Carl?"

Carleton was surprised and embarrassed by Jane's question. "Well, I...um. I see your point, Jane, and I'm sorry I asked such a stupid personal question. It's none of my business. Please forgive me."

"Sure, Carl. Let's chalk that up to your momentary lapse of judgment. So, Ticky, take two more questions, and I want to see the house before we go to work. The bar opens at 1:00 p.m., people!"

Roger raised his hand. "The aluminum chair recognizes Roger. What's on your mind today? Are you good?"

Roger nodded. "It's been another dry week. I still have little to no desire for alcohol during the week. It's the weekends that can be a problem. I feel like I am missing out, but if I have one drink, that leads to two, and then the self-control is not so controlled. I know better; I need to work on self-discipline some more."

"Do you need to talk one on one later, man?"

"No, Don, I'm in a good place this week. I've got a date Friday night with a gal from Scituate. Life is good!"

"Excellent, man! Let me know if you need to chat during the week. Now, who has something to put out there?"

"I've got a question!" The voice belonged to Paper Cut Paul, a 30-year-old tattooed Cape Cod Cruisers car club member. He has a scar on his forehead from a nasty cut he got loading cardboard boxes into a moving van, a career that lasted one week.

Brad reminded Paper Cut Paul to raise his hand. He did.

"The aluminum chair recognizes Paper. What's on your mind, man?"

"I've got a 1963 Buick 12-inch 45-fin aluminum brake drums set with cast-iron liners. They are factory originals in the box. The backing plates are totally unmolested. These are perfect for the purist who is building a pre-1964 hot rod. I want to sell them to buy a hood for my 40 Ford coupe. What do you think I can get for them?"

Don thought for a moment. "Okay, Paper, this is complicated, but if you trade the brake drums to Douche Bag Danny Swinton, you can get around $450 in credit for Douche to do some tuck and roll upholstery work. Take the upholstery credit and trade it to Fritzie for a new lawnmower from his shop. His wife has been bugging him about getting the seats in her T-Bird reupholstered. Negotiate hard, and you can get a good mower. Now, trade the new lawnmower with Been Dead Billy so he can mow that strip of grass beside his body shop before the town fines him again. Bill's dad raced '40 Ford coupes at Norwood Arena Speedway in the late 50s and early 60s. Billy has a half-dozen vintage Ford fenders and hoods in the attic at his shop."

Paper Cut Paul thought for a moment. "Shit, that just may work! Genius answer, Tiki God!"

Don stood and wished everyone to have a groovy day. Roger spoke up and said the meeting today was fun, and he would rather meet next Sunday again at the little church building than have lunch at the Mariners Shanty on Friday with Don. The others quickly voiced similar opinions about doing it again. Don looked at Jane, who hesitantly agreed to meet next Sunday.

Don closed and locked the church's front door after everyone exited the building. He followed Jane around the side of the church toward the house. While Don and Jane admired how well-maintained the lawn and shrubbery were, neither noticed the black SUV parked across the street or the camera lens protruding from the partially lowered driver-side window.

Chapter 8 - I want to christen this place properly
March 14th 11:56 a.m. ~ Continued

Don pulled a key from his pocket and unlocked the rectory house's front door. Believing it was necessary to show respect to the house, Jane wanted to go through the front door the first time she entered. Don never questions Jane's choices on these things. He had experienced too many *coincidences* to think otherwise.

That morning as they stepped out of Jenny, Don spotted and picked up a coin lying face down on the sidewalk. He asked Jane to guess the year the coin was minted. She didn't hesitate; she said it was 1986. She was right. She is always right.

The house smelled a bit musty. Nothing a good airing out wouldn't cure. Jane took note of the sunlight entering the large windows that were south-facing, perfect for indoor plants. The rooms were large, with tall ceilings and wide doors. The primary bedroom was on the second floor and faced Main Street. The east-facing window on the left side of the bedroom looked across the Town Common and up Main Street to the beach. She liked that view, the connection to the water. The west-facing window on the right side of the room offered a view of the back of Sailers Church and down Main Street.

The primary bath had a large jacuzzi soaker tub, a spacious walk-in shower with a smooth stone floor and walls, dual ceiling rain shower heads, dual wall-mounted shower heads, and indirect lighting. For a rectory house, it was not the austere monastic manner of living that she had imagined.

Walking down the front stairs to the first floor, Jane noticed one of the steps made a distinctive creaking sound. She smiled, knowing that Don would absentmindedly squeak that step every time he used those stairs, no matter how quiet he tried to be.

The kitchen was much more than Jane expected. The 6-burner range with dual ovens was enormous. The side-by-side refrigerator with a separate side-by-side freezer reminded her of Darlene's restaurant.

It was way more than two people needed. Jane imagined Don cooking the Thanksgiving dinner or making his family's old-world Christmas pudding. It felt like home. New memories would be made here.

"So, what do you think, babe? Should we move over here?"

"Yes, this house is bigger and better than our apartment. It's in great condition, and most of the fixtures in the house are new. Pastor Smyth must have spent some of his lotto money on this place. What's not to like about it?"

Don agreed. "I will miss the convenience of being close to work, the one-minute walk for morning coffee at the Shanty, and the beach view out our bedroom window. But I won't miss banging my elbows in that tiny shower or being above the bar on our day off."

Jane hugged Don and gently kissed him. She playfully held his lower lip between her teeth and stared into his eyes before closing hers and gently kissing him again.

Jane grinned. "We need to come back here with a very nice bottle of rum, some candles, pillows, and a soft blanket. I want to christen this place properly, starting on the bedroom floor and finishing in that beautiful shower."

Don knew what he would be doing Tuesday afternoon, their next day off.

Chapter 9 - The church of dipshit will be gone
March 24th 10:08 a.m.

Pastor Smyth's weekly Wednesday staff meeting had just started. He casually looked at the photos on the big flat screen on his office wall. Paul Caruso paid someone to take the pictures outside Don's church building last Sunday. Smyth was amused at the crudely painted Church of Don sign and the eleven people standing in front of the church building. "This reminds me of that animated Christmas video that my niece watches every December. You know, the one with the screwed-up toys that nobody wants!" Smyth and Caruso chuckled. Smith shook his head, "where does he find these losers?"

Reed looked at it with a bit more concern. "May I take over the screen for a moment?"

Still chuckling, Smyth shook his head in approval as Reed took the keyboard and went off to the internet. He brought up Wally's iPad video blog posting of the group meeting with Don at the church. Smyth and Caruso were in tears from laughing hard at the video.

Smyth tried to compose himself. "This is fucking hilarious, and that Jane, shit, she's got a smoking hot body! I don't get what she sees in that hippie bartender. Do you think those tits are real?" Smyth looked at Caruso, who shrugged his shoulders. "I tell you, Paul, they look real to me. Oh, did you see the blond that was here on Sunday? She sat in the third row back on the aisle and had a huge rack, obviously fakes. It looked like someone glued two melons to a flat board. Why do women try to pass those off? I'd rather enjoy small and real over big and plastic."

Still looking concerned, Reed waited for Smyth and Caruso to settle down. "You can mock them as much as you want, but let me show you a few things I found sobering. While we had just over 1,200 visits to view our web-based sermon on Sunday, the bartender had just over 9,000 visits. We spent well over $30,000 in online promotion and web placement while they did nothing and kicked our ass.

Smyth looked at Reed as if he had lost his mind. "Come on, Jim. You put a video of a monkey throwing his shit on the internet, and it will draw more viewers than the fucking hippie bartender. The difference here is that he is entertaining the losers while we are saving souls. Of course, he is doing this for free while we generate a little revenue along the way, but you have to feed the beast to be in business, and we are in the soul-saving business. Trust me; the church of dipshit will be gone when those idiots get tired of wasting their time listening to his bullshit philosophy, and the bills start piling up for maintaining that building and insurance. It's all a joke!"

Smyth is annoyed at having to deal with this. "Reed, where are we on getting that church building? This will all be over once we move that building to our lot."

Reed sighed. "We are stalled. Maybe visiting him and pointing out his financial burden on owning that building will get things moving. He may not have done the math yet, and as you say, the bills will start to pile up. We can take that financial burden off of his hands."

Caruso laughed. "He's right, George; you smooth-talked the old lady out of her lotto ticket. You should be able to talk the moronic bartender out of a building he doesn't want."

Chapter 10 - As sure as Bob's your uncle
March 31st 2:11 p.m.

George Smyth and Jim Reed had never been to Don's Tiki Cocktails & Lounge. Being from the church, they wanted to maintain their wholesome public image. Privately, Smyth enjoyed expensive single malt scotch and high-end California Cabernet Sauvignon wine that often cost over $100 per bottle.

The bar was nothing like either of them expected. The authentic vintage tropical decor and the classic turn-of-the-century design of the bar itself were unique. It felt old but in a good way. The place was clean and did not have that funky old bar smell.

Tropical music played softly in the background, and the lighting was subdued yet inviting. Amber light from a few odd-looking illuminated puffer fish lit several locations around the room, as did large, illuminated red, blue, green, and yellow glass spheres. It was a very comfortable environment, unique and with a subtle personality.

Smyth and Reed approached the bar and asked the bartender, Kelly, if they may speak with Don. She picked up the phone and called the apartment above the bar.

"Don is on his way; can I get you something while you wait?" Smyth smiled politely. "No, thank you, we are here on church business."

"Here on church business are you now? No beer for you then, vicar. Maybe a nice cuppa and biscuits?"

Smyth turned to see what appeared to be a woman, in her 30s, with short dark hair sitting at the bar. She wore blue jeans, a white T-shirt, a vintage green army jacket, and perfectly round glasses. She looked familiar yet didn't.

"Yes, I am here on church business. And your name is?"

Alexandra extended a hand and said in her acquired British accent, "I'm John Lennon. Who might you be vicar?"

Smyth was puzzled. "Is this some sort of a joke?"

Lennon exhaled loudly. "Look, when I said that we're more popular than Jesus, I was just trying to make the point that Christian churches in the UK were experiencing ever-falling attendance levels while we were becoming more popular. I wasn't comparing the Beatles to Jesus Christ, so please don't bring that up again."

"Pastor Smyth, what can I do for you?" Don walked past Smyth and Reed and settled into a booth in the corner. Both Smyth and Reed were perplexed by the conversation that had just occurred. They followed Don to the booth and sat with him.

Reed could not contain his questions. "Is that woman putting us on? Does she honestly think she's John Lennon?

Don studied both Smyth and Reed for a moment. "Well, man, I take it you don't know Alexandra DeCarlo. She's a local and has lived here all her life. Alex has a personality thing of some kind. She believes that she is John Lennon when she's off her meds. You know, from the Beatles! It's harmless, man. She's just a little different. That's all."

"She honestly believes that she's John Lennon? She's crazy! Have you called the authorities?" Reed turned back again to look at Alexandra, totally fascinated by this.

"Call the authorities? No, man, Alexandra and John are both cool people and welcome here anytime. Sure, John can be opinionated sometimes when he's had a couple of beers, but he's cool. He knows his shit about music too, man."

"What about her? What's she like when she's not John Lennon?" Reed was eager for Don's response.

That was a good question. Don thought for a moment. "I don't know, man. I don't think she's ever been in the bar as Alexandra. As far as I know, Alexandra doesn't drink." Don pondered for another moment. It was the first time he realized he's only seen her as Alexandra on the street, in the restaurant, and a few other places around town.

Smyth wanted to ridicule all of this as another one of the losers but decided better of it. There was plenty of time for that after he got what he came for.

"Don, we have a proposition for you. As you know, I started my career here as pastor of Sailers Church. While pastoring at that church, I brought together a community that needed comfort and a connection to our Lord. I provided that leadership and community moral compass they so strongly desired."

Don nonchalantly shrugged his shoulders. "I guess you did, man. I'm not too big on the whole religion thing, so I'll take your word for it."

Smyth wasn't sure how to take that but continued. "As you are likely aware, I have just opened the new Brite Rock Cathedral by the Sea at the edge of town. But as splendid as this new large church is, our roots and message are no different from the first time I addressed the parishioners at Sailers Church. That building, that holy little building, is part of who and what I am. It's part of our congregation. It's part of our community." Smyth paused a moment for dramatic effect.

"As I understand it, Sailers Church has come into your possession. Am I correct? Do you now own that little church in the center of town?"

"Yes, Jane and I do, and the big house behind it. Why do you ask?"

Smyth smiled. "I do believe this is your lucky day. I want to offer you a sum of money to buy the church building. I have no want or need of the land it sits on or the house next to it. I only want the church building."

Don sat back, looking at Smyth. And then at Reed. And then back at Smyth. He was growing uncomfortable with the conversation but wasn't sure why. He didn't want or know what to do with the church building. It was more of a problem for him than anything.

"It's not for sale, man!"

The smile faded from Smyth's face. "I understand that that property's location in the town center is a highly desirable commercial spot.

However, I'm sure that having a church building on that property is inconvenient for you and greatly diminishes the commercial value of the land. It is the perfect location for another Starbucks or Dunkin' Donuts. I don't need the land, so why don't you just sell us the church building itself? We will move it from its current location, making that property available for commercial development. I think $100,000 is a fair price for that small building, don't you?"

Don felt he was talking to a high-pressure salesman, an experience he would avoid if possible. "It ain't for sale, man. I kind of like it the way it is. It's got a cool vibe. So I'm hanging on to the building."

They paused, trying to determine whether this was a negotiation tactic or whether Don actually wanted the church building.

Smyth leaned in toward Don. "I'm sure there is a figure or other terms we can come to that would motivate you to reconsider your position on selling the building. What do you think?"

Don leaned in towards Smyth. "Maybe you could start by returning the big Jesus you ripped off from the church building, man!"

Reed spoke up, trying to deflect the negative away from Smyth. That is one of his primary jobs, protecting Smyth's public image. "You have no use for that cross, Don. Do you?"

Don was getting irritated, and his voice was getting louder. "That's not the point, man! You don't take a big Jesus that doesn't belong to you. That's stealing, man! Isn't there a rule or commandment about that? I mean... what the fuck?"

Smyth smiled and slid a business card across the table to Don. "Perhaps if you take some time and consider our offer. Maybe ask Ms. Gilman her thoughts on..."

"No, man, it's not for sale. End of story. That's all she wrote. The fat lady has sung, man!" Don waved his hands in the air to emphasize his point. "Understand, man?"

"Donny me boy; you appear to be a bit browned off, mate. These wankers taking the mickey, are they?" John stood at the end of the table, looking at Smyth and Reed.

Folding his arms, Don leaned back. "No, man, they're just buying what I'm not selling."

"Okay, lads, you've got his answer." John gestured toward the door. "Come on now, sod off, the pair of you!"

Smyth turned to John, his face contorted in disgust. "Listen, freak; I don't know what your fucking problem is but do us all a fucking favor and…"

Don sat and pondered whether Smyth saw the punch from John coming or if he believed she would hit like a girl. Either way, it solidly connected with his nose and knocked him back.

Blood ran down his crisp white shirt as a horrified Reed collected the cocktail napkins on the table to assist Smyth.

"I will have you arrested for assault, you psycho! Look what you did to me! You fucking weirdo!" Smyth was going to continue his rant but decided against it when John raised her fist again.

"Come on, Donny, let's give these gits a proper send-off. I'll take the vicar; you take the tosser."

Don reached up and gently took John by the arm. "That's enough, man, no fighting in my bar." He then turned his attention to the bloodied pastor. "And nobody's calling the cops. Do you want it in the news that you started a bar fight, pastor? That's probably undesirable publicity in your line of work, man."

Reed helped Smyth to his feet and hastily walked toward the door. Despite the bloody nose and their rapid exit, Smyth again yelled back to Don to consider his offer as the door to the bar slowly closed behind them. The room grew dark again. A few of the bar patrons giggled softly amongst themselves.

John looked at Don, smiled, pushed her glasses back up on her nose, and returned to her bar stool. "All that has left me thirsty. Kelly, me love, a pint of the usual."

Don smiled and told Red to "put that one on the house. And John, stick to the peace and love thing, man!" John nodded in agreement. "As sure as Bob's your uncle!"

Chapter 11 - I honestly think that we are a little weird
April 3rd 3:36 p.m.

"I'm not winking at you, dumbass! Lime juice squirted in my eye!" Jane set the hand juicer down and picked up a bar towel.

"Would you like me to take a look at it?" Without hesitating, Jane replied that she had it handled. She knew that if she let Pete, who she refers to as *pervie Pete* or *PP*, assist her, he would try to touch her.

Pete, a 37-year-old freelance computer programmer, works odd hours, so he is at the bar at different times during the week. His social skills are awkward at best, and he has difficulty relating to women.

Pete visually tracks the backside of nearly every female who enters the bar. He isn't subtle about it, and that's where the pervie part comes in. While he never touches a customer, Pete has a history of being a little handsy with Jane and Red. They are experienced at putting Pete in his place.

Red came over to assist Jane. "Here, try my eye drops. They're for my contacts but should help wash the juice out."

Jane quickly put several drops into her irritated eye and gently wiped the streaming water off her face. "Oh...that feels so much better! Thank you!"

Red looked at Jane's face and laughed.

"What? Did I mess up my mascara?"

"You know that one-eyed raccoon that hangs out by the dumpster at night? The one that Don named Sketchy? Well..."

Jane sighed. "Great, I have weird raccoon eyes! You think I would have figured out that stupid hand juicer by now."

Red paused in thought. "Didn't you do something similar in the apartment a couple of weeks ago?"

"Oh, my god! You mean the great nacho incident. It was way worse than citrus juice in my eye."

Red folded her arms. "Oh Jane, what did you do this time?"

"Okay, don't laugh! I was in our apartment making kalua pork nachos on our day off. I had just finished piling on the hot diced jalapeno peppers and quickly ran to the bathroom to pee. I guess I didn't wash my hands well enough and accidentally touched my lady parts while wiping. The stinging from the jalapeno essence sent me scurrying to the refrigerator to find something to neutralize the burning sensation. Don walked in to find me in the kitchen, pants around my ankles and massaging cold yogurt onto my inflamed lady parts. He never said a word; he just turned and left the apartment. He returned a few minutes later and said it looked like I needed some alone time."

Red, now wiping tears from her eyes, composed herself as Jane returned the eye drop bottle. "You two crack me up. There's always something slightly odd going on with you guys."

Jane nodded. "You know, I used to be offended when people would say something like we are weirdos or crazy shit always happens to us, but with this church building thing now, there's no denying it. I honestly think that we are a little weird!"

Red slipped the eye drop bottle into her pocket. "So, what's the deal with that church thing? I heard someone this morning talking about it at Dunkin's. They said they were going for the Sunday service there tomorrow."

"Seriously? What service? Don was hanging out with a couple of people there last Sunday, and he agreed to hang out again this Sunday morning before work. There is no churchy stuff going on! Who said they were going this Sunday? Do you know them?"

Red smiled. "Yes, and you know them too. They are here every Thursday after their D.A.R. meeting."

"Do you mean the old ladies, Lily, Doris, Millie, and Ginny?"

Red nodded. "Them's the bitches!"

Jane laughed. "I'm not sure what they expect, but they aren't going to get any Jesus preached at them. Don't tell Don; let it be a surprise. This should be entertaining!"

Chapter 12 - That old broad and her posse
April 4th 9:44 a.m.

Jim Reed and Ashley, the young assistant overseeing after-service refreshments, interrupted Smyth in his office as he previewed his sermon for Caruso. "I think you need to hear this, George. Ashley, tell Pastor Smyth what you heard at the donut shop."

Smyth paused the Teleprompter and smiled at the young assistant.

Ashley nervously cleared her throat. "I'm sure it's not like a big yikes, but yesterday, when I was at Dunkies placing the order for the after-service refreshments, I heard…"

Smyth interrupted. "What's Dunkies?"

"Oh, it's what we call Dunkin' Donuts. It has several different nicknames around here. I call it Dunks or Dunkies. My sister calls it DD's. Are you from Massachusetts?"

"No, I'm from Rhode Island."

Ashley slowly nodded her head. "Oh, Rhody, that explains it. If you know, you know. Right?"

Smyth was growing impatient. "You had something to tell me?"

"Oh, yeah! Anyway, I heard some old lady spill the tea about going to Sailers Church tomorrow. You know, the church that you preached at before this one."

Smyth smiled. "I wouldn't be overly concerned, my dear. We do have to accommodate the elderly and be patient with them. They likely forgot that we moved to this beautiful new church and will find their way here shortly."

Ashley smiled and appeared relieved. "My grandmother gets super confused occasionally too. I'm sure that Lily Snell and her squad will find us."

Smyth nodded in agreement. "I look forward to meeting Ms. Snell and her friends."

"But Pastor Smyth, you know Lilly! She lives in that huge house near Sailers Church in the center of town. The place is dope! She and her late husband, Mr. Crymble, have lived there forever. Well, I guess not for him since he did the big adios a couple of years ago."

The smile on Smyth's face froze. "Are you saying Lily Crymble is Lily Snell?"

"Yeah! Snell is a way-old family name around here. Very dusty! She is related to some Mayflower guy."

Maintaining his frozen smile, Smyth told Ashley he was familiar with the stately home but didn't know that Snell was Lily's maiden name. Reed sensed Smyth's mood quickly changed and escorted Ashley out of the room. He thanked her for helping to care for their church community members. Ashley felt pride in Reed's thank you and flowing comments as they walked back to the kitchen area.

Quickly returning to Smyth's office, Reed found him deep in thought. Caruso gestured to Reed to close the door.

Smyth was thinking this through. "I had no idea that Lily Crymble was the heir to the Snell estate or that her family was well off. That's the downside of not being from here. We don't have deep knowledge of the locals. On the other hand, if we can figure out her pain point, there may be a sizable donation to the church here. She needs to want to give in a big way, and we need to start working on her now. At her age, who the hell knows if she will be around much longer?"

"But George, she isn't coming here on Sunday. She's going to hang out with the bartender at his…what exactly would you call it?"

Smyth ran his hand through his hair. "A circle jerk, I guess."

Both men knew he would only touch his perfectly styled hair like that when frustrated. "We can't have the hippie wanna-be preacher getting in the way and fucking this up. I know that old broad and her posse hangs out at his bar drinking after their flag-waver meeting on Thursday afternoon. I want somebody in Sailers Church tomorrow and the bar on Thursday to watch them. I want to know if Lily has any relationship with that dipshit that could be a problem."

Reed was uneasy. "Do you think that's necessary? What if we get caught?"

"We are simply taking care of church interests." There was sarcasm in Smyth's voice.

"Listen, I want someone in that pissy little church and in that freak show bar with eyes on the prize. I want to know everything that old broad says and what is said to her. I don't trust the hippie bartender or his girlfriend. So who do we have that we can send?"

The list of potential spies was short. Smyth decided that Paul Caruso would be the one to go. Don and Jane hadn't met him yet. And being from Rhode Island, Caruso had no local connections. Smyth's circle of trust is very small. Caruso will be in Sailers Church this Sunday and the bar on Thursday.

Chapter 13 - An oasis from reality
April 11th 10:51 a.m.

The old aluminum chair squeaked as Don settled into it. He took a sip of iced coffee and set the extra-large cup on the floor. Looking around the room, Don counted 48 attendees, far more than the week before.

Karen and Kathy sat in the same place. Jane sat on the stage, leaning against the wall on the far-right side. Handyman Ed and his wife Cindy chatted with fishing boat skipper Lars Van der Berg. Roger and Brad were looking at a car magazine that the hot rod guys brought. Shakemaster Sam was talking with little Lisa from Rudy's Clam Shack. Geezer was snoozing in the front pew. The D.A.R. ladies sat in the back row for easy exit. Also, in the back sat a man in a dark suit. No one seemed to acknowledge him, so he must be a new face around town.

Wally finished setting up his video camera on a tripod in the front row of the pews. He was trying to record higher-quality videos of the get-togethers for his social media accounts. Finally, he signaled to Don that he was ready.

Don nodded his head and smiled. "So, did anyone see the streaker on the common Thursday night? It's like the 1970s again. What would prompt some guy to run naked down the street, man? No judgment; I'm okay with it, just curious as to why. What say you, fellow citizens of Brite Rock?"

Roger started to speak only to be interrupted by Brad, who reminded him to raise his hand first to be acknowledged. Don chuckled to himself as he thought about these people wanting to follow the rules for civil discourse.

"The aluminum chair recognizes Roger. What can you tell us about this uninhibited gent?"

Roger stood, uncomfortably collecting his thoughts. "Well, it, um, you see, it was the Town Manager's nephew, Andrew. I heard he was thrown out of BU for running naked around their campus."

Don looked perplexed. "I'm guessing the big brains at BU didn't find his expression of freedom refreshing."

"No, Don, they did not! As a BU alumnus, I expect that type of behavior from a Harvard student but not one from Boston University. Andrew was arrested twice for this while in college and cited for it during his senior year of high school. As a recovering alcoholic, I assume his need to run around naked is part of his addiction. Or he's just a fucking weirdo."

Roger sat down as the laughter subsided.

"Thanks for the update, man. As long as we know the weenie waver isn't some deranged sexual predator, just misguided youth with the need to be naked, the citizens of Brite Rock can rest easy." Don paused for a moment. "I think it was Mark Twain that said man is the only animal that blushes or needs to. I wonder if it's embarrassing for that young man when he gets arrested and is carted off naked. Has anyone here ever experienced anything that embarrassing?"

D.A.R. lady Doris raised her hand. "The aluminum chair recognizes Doris."

It took Doris a moment to stand with the assistance of her friend, Lily. "I have experienced something that embarrassing, dear. Well, I got over most of the embarrassment from my mental lapse of last week. At least, I think I have. At my age, I'm not sure. Anyway, I went to the doctor last Tuesday for my checkup. I was early, so I sat and waited for them to call my name, but they didn't. Finally, after the longest time, I went to the reception window and asked about it. It turns out that I had the wrong day. I was a day early."

Don smiled." We've all done things like getting dates and times mixed up. I'm sure they understood."

Doris shook her head. "Oh, that wasn't the embarrassing part, dear. I'm as forgetful as can be. It's when I turned around to leave, I misjudged a fart and shat myself. I didn't dare look back to see if I was leaving a trail. I think shitting your knickers is far more embarrassing than that young man purposely running down the street with his thing flopping around, don't you?"

Don sat waiting while the others tried to contain their laughter. "Thank you, Doris, for sharing. That was… enlightening."

Doris started to sit down but stood again and raised her hand. "Since this isn't a real church, I can say shit my knickers without offending you know who, right?" Doris points up.

"That's between you and whoever you're pointing at, Doris." She smiled and sat down.

Don looked around the room. "Who would like to offer up a story here on self-embarrassment Sunday? The aluminum chair recognizes Shakemaster Sam. What's up, Shaky?"

Sam lowered his raised hand and slowly stood as little Lisa giggled. "Well, little Lisa bet me I wouldn't tell everyone here why you nicknamed me Shakemaster. When Don and Jane first hired me as a bartender, I was too slow and had no bartending game. So, I watched the old Tom Cruise movie *Cocktail* and tried to use some of his showy moves with the cocktail shaker to impress a cute customer. She was not impressed when the top slipped off the shaker, and I bathed her in ice-cold sticky booze. Don stared at me in disbelief. Then, he said *hey, Shakemaster, are you done with the bar tricks, or should I install a shower in the ladies' room*? I was done with the bar tricks. And that's how I became the Shakemaster. I wear my shame as my name, and she wore my cocktail failure. And that movie is pretty bad."

Lisa waited for the laughter to subside before tugging on Sam's arm. "Hey Shakey, what happened to the girl that you splashed?"

Sam smiled. "I married her. Valerie and I have a beautiful daughter named Sophia. Val's dad, Morton, own's Rudy's Clam Shack, and this pain in the ass that I made a bet with is Val's cousin, little Lisa."

Don leaned back in the aluminum chair. "So, Shaky, what was the bet with little Lisa?"

"If I publicly told how I earned the Shakemaster name, little Lisa would have to watch the Tom Cruise movie Cocktail, including all the credits. If I chickened out, I would have to watch the Mel Gibson movie What Women Want, including all the credits. So it looks like it's crappy movie night for little Loser!"

Jane looked around the room. "Shakes, where is Val today?"

He sighed. "Well, that's a different bet I lost to my wife. She is home, having a quiet Sunday morning all to herself. Our daughter is with the grandparents, and I had to escort Val's annoying little cousin here."

Jane laughed. "Do you see a pattern here, Shakes? Maybe betting with the ladies isn't a good idea?"

"Jane's right, man. Even if you win the bet, you lose. So give me the matches and stop playing with fire." Little Lisa took Sam by the arm. He sat down as Lisa fought to contain her giggles.

Don scanned the room as another hand went up. "The aluminum chair recognizes the gent in the burgundy sport coat. I don't believe I know you, man. What's your name?"

"I'm Owen McCarthy, I live in South Boston, and I'm studying Behavioral Science at college."

"Welcome, man. Do you have a self-embarrassment story, general question, comment, or advice for Shaky?"

"I have no additional advice for Sam. You summed it up with the comment that even if you win, you lose. However, I do have a general question. I have noticed serious discussions on cars, food, friendship, love, and even death. Yet the firebrand topics of the day, such as politics, race, guns, religion, political correctness, and so on, aren't addressed in this forum. Yet, fart jokes, nudity, profanity, and other topics bordering on juvenile or immature behavior are common.

I understand from your rules for social discourse that some topics aren't open for discussion. My question is for the attendees in this room. Do you feel the rules limit your first amendment right to free speech, and do you want to discuss these topics here?"

Roger raised his hand.

"The aluminum chair recognizes Roger. What say you on this question?"

Roger stood. "Well, Owen, I don't know you, and I'm not trying to come off as disrespectful, but as I understand the First Amendment, it says Congress shall make no law abridging the freedom of speech. That means the government won't limit free speech in a public forum. Don isn't the government, and this isn't a public forum, so I am good with those topics being off the table.

I come here precisely not to listen to people drone on about the hot-button issues you listed. Those discussions just make people angry and foster hate. It's winner take all. There is no middle ground. I can't...no, I won't do a 24-hour-a-day diet of conversation on those topics. I come here to escape the world for an hour. I'd rather laugh at a fart joke than be hurt by those realities of life every moment of every day."

Owen waited for the applause to subside. Then, "Don, is your intent to create a space free of the angst often triggered by firebrand topics by limiting their discussion here?"

Don leaned forward in his chair. "Yes, exactly! Jane and I intend to provide a relaxed and enjoyable environment for people to reconnect with themselves and the others around them, man. Maybe they want to blow off steam from a hard work week or laugh with a few friends. Maybe they need to talk about a relationship problem or ask for advice on something very personal to them. Sometimes they need someone to listen to them. Maybe they need to belong. To be acknowledged, man. Our bar is an oasis from reality for most of our patrons. This Happening is an oasis too. It's as simple as that, man."

Owen thought for a moment. "Are you trying to create a utopian reality by doing this?"

Don laughed. "No, man. We only want to soften a few of the sharp edges of daily life for an hour or two for people. That, and rum, can make everything better if only for those few hours. So come by the bar and check it out."

Owen scribbled a quick note. "I believe I will, and thank you for the discussion. I learned something interesting today. I had not considered a social microenvironment like this. I'm going to ask my professor about it."

Don smiled. "Anytime, man! So, before Jane and I head over to open the bar, are there any other topics for the group? Anyone? Last call – that's all. See ya round town."

As everyone got up to leave, Don noticed the man that sat alone at the back of the church quietly slip out the front door.

Chapter 14 - Call him A-Wall since he's evolved
April 11th 12:56 p.m. ~ Continued

Don finished changing the keg in the beer cooler as Red installed the new beer tap handle. The Boston Beer Company had sent over a sample keg of their new *Sam Adams Island Lager* craft beer. It's to compete with Long Board, one of the best-selling beers at the bar. Red tasted the Island Lager and thought the delicate aroma of hops and the malty flavor profile should help it to sell well this summer.

Aside from a few beer and rum purveyors advertising signage, most product displays that the bar received don't fit the tiki/island motif. But Sam Adams Island Lager beer came with a large, framed print of an 1802 sailing ship, the Mary Adams, delivering wooden beer casks to a tropical island with palm trees. Don liked the *Set SAIL with Sam Adams Island Lager* advertising line on the print. This will have a home on the wall once Don finds the time and space to hang it.

As is the tradition at opening and closing time, Red rang the Kauai rooster bell that hung on the wall three times and announced, "all is well." No one knows who started the tradition or why, but no one dares stop doing it, particularly Jane. Then, keys in hand, Red unlocked the door to welcome the customers. She expected to see the usual couple of locals for a Sunday opening. Instead, she was surprised to find just over 20 people waiting to come in, with only two locals, John Lennon, and PP, at the end of the line.

"Aloha! Come on in and grab a seat. The bar is open, the beverages are tasty, and the staff is skilled. If this is your first time here, our cocktails are handcrafted fresh to your order, so it may take a few extra minutes. Thanks in advance for your patience. If you so desire, you can order food from our bar menu or have food from the Mariner's Shanty restaurant delivered to the bar. Place and pay for your food at the takeout station in the Shanty. Please place the plastic table number tent they give you where your waitstaff can easily see it for food delivery. Mahalo!"

Red held the door as the people filed in. A rather well-endowed petite blonde in 1950s style pink polka dot dress, one arm covered with tattoos, stopped in the doorway. She, and her boyfriend, dressed in 1950s-style jeans and a mint green and black vintage bowling shirt, could hardly contain themselves. The blonde excitedly asked, "is he here today?"

"Is who here?" Red gave the couple a questioning look.

"The man that's the bartender and has the crazy church show on the Internet. You know, Don!"

Red slowly nodded her head. "Yeah, Don is here today. I'm sure he'll be behind the bar soon." The couple slowly surveyed the room to find the best seats to observe everything happening. Finally, they settled on a couple of stools mid-bar.

PP entered, scurrying past Red, and went straight to the bar to secure his favorite stool and one for John.

"Kelly, me love. This is an odd-looking lot now, isn't it?"

Red laughed. "Are they all that different from the usual odd-looking crowd, John?"

"Ah, Kelly, us usual lot are upright citizens compared to these drunkards and masterbaters, particularly that dodgy-lookin' one." John points at PP.

Red nodded. "You're probably right about that one. As to the others, perhaps your opinion will change once you have a pint in your hand. I'll make you the first customer." John smiled as he walked to the bar to join PP.

Red watched a few more new people enter the bar as she poured John's beer. She expected the typical handful of usual locals and a few tourists until around 4:30 P.M. when happy hour started, and the dinner crowd would begin to show up at the Mariners Shanty restaurant.

Since Sunday afternoons were notoriously slow, Don and Red are the only two bartenders needed on the floor. Jane had the day off and was at the new house washing curtains and cleaning the floors in anticipation of moving in this coming week.

Red stepped into Don's office as he finished the weekly payroll paperwork. He could tell by her impish grin that something was going on. "I could use a little help out front. Your fans are dying to see you."

"My fans? What are you talking about, man?"

"Why don't you come out front and see?" Red followed Don to the bar.

"There he is! He looks the same as he does on the show!" Don looked over to see a blonde in a pink polka-dot dress pointing at him. She was loud and caught everyone's attention.

Don looked around the bar. There was an extraordinary level of giddy excitement. The last time he saw a rowdy group like this was when the Shriners passed through on their way to Cape Cod for some annual event last summer. They were very fond of Jane.

Don looked suspiciously at Red.

"Don't give me stinkeye, Ticky! I have nothing to do with whatever this is. Now, go wait on your adoring fans. I'll take care of the normal people... if there are any."

Don grabbed two cocktail menus and handed them to the blonde and her companion. "See, he looks just like he does on the show."

"Me? What show are you talking about, man?"

"You know, the show on the internet where you give cool advice to some very different people. It's way better and more real than those other reality shows. On your show, there's a church but no religion. How absurd is that for a church!"

"No religion? Can you imagine?" John smiled, proud about adding her Beatles reference to the conversation. Don found that amusing but had no idea what to make of the rest of it.

"So, what will you have?" Don pointed at the cocktail menus that he was holding.

"Oh, we don't need the menu. We went online and looked at it already. I'll have a Hemmingway daiquiri, and my boyfriend wants to try a Jane's Jungle Juice cocktail. That's the one you picked, isn't it, baby?" The blonde's boyfriend agreed.

"What do you mean you looked at the menu online? Jane's Jungle Juice isn't on our bar website menu, and that cocktail is unique to this bar." Don was perplexed. Some dots seriously needed to be connected for him.

"There is something trippy going on here, man. So, where exactly is this menu you saw on the internet?" Don stared blankly at the blonde.

"It's on your Church of Don website, see!" A tap of her fingers on her smartphone brought up a website that Don had no idea existed. It's where Wally posted the Church of Don videos. She handed Don her cell phone.

There were photos of Sailers Church and the bar building with directions to each. There was also a detailed map of downtown Brite Rock with important locations in the town highlighted. In addition, each bar staff member had a photo and a biography. There was even a photo of Don's hot rod Jenny. He was stunned at what he was seeing.

"Red, do you have Wally's phone number? I need to talk to him about this website thing." Don kept scrolling page-to-page on the blonde's cell phone. The pages included the bar's hours of operation, a complete food and cocktail menu, and a page containing Don's quotes.

Red was busy making cocktails. "Which Wally?"

"What do you mean which Wally? How many are there?"

Red paused for a moment. "There's four. Jane's dad is Wally, and there's white Wally and gray Wally and Asian Wally who goes by Wally or A-Wall."

Don was surprised at Red's comment. "Wally is Asian Wally or A-Wall? Isn't that like a racist thing to say, man?"

She laughed. "No, that's what he calls himself. Something about owning his identity and making a statement. He says to call him A-Wall since he's evolved beyond stereotypes and labels, and the rest of the world needs to catch up. I get it; people call me Red because of my hair color. I'm fine with that as long as it's done with respect and not in a derogatory manner."

Don knows Red's sharp wit and sense of humor. He once watched her convince a couple of overly entitled tourists that they shouldn't swim near the jetty because sea weasels hang out there, and they are known to bite during mating season, which is now. The tourists believed Red's fanciful story."

Don thought he should confirm with Wally his naming preference. So that leaves the other Wally's.

Don could instantly picture Jane's dad and Walter White, but not the other. "So, who is Gray Wally?"

"Gray Wally is the old guy with severe emphysema. He drags the little oxygen bottle on wheels wherever he goes. He's got that gray skin tone. His granddaughter brings him here on the first of every month. They do the fish and chips takeout. He has a gin and tonic, and she has a Suffering Bastard." Red delivers two cocktails and takes an order from another table.

"No, it's Wally, the internet guy I'm trying to find. Do you know how I can find him?"

Chapter 15 - What's up your skirt
April 11th 3:02 p.m. ~ Continued

"Are you looking for me, boss?" Smiling, Wally had found standing room at the bar. He looked around. "Big crowd for a Sunday. Looks like a lot of out-of-towners."

Don nodded as he silently picked up a clean glass and started making a Jane's Jungle Juice cocktail. He placed the cocktail in front of Wally and stared at him for a moment.

"What is your name, man?"

"What? It's Wally! I've been coming here for a couple of years. I thought you knew my name."

Don looked down the bar at Red, who quickly surmised that Don thought she was tricking him into saying something stupid again. Two weeks ago, Red said, "there goes Freddie Flatwallet," as Fred exited the bar. The next time Fred was in the bar, Don asked him about his unusual last name. Fred indignantly assured Don that Flatwallet was not his last name; it was Baxter. It turns out that Fred was cheap when it came to tipping yet drove an expensive car. Red figured no money, flat wallet!

Red waved to Wally. "A-Wall, how are you doing, baby? I see you are getting your Jane's Jiggle Juice on!" Wally smiled, nodded, and held up the cocktail.

Don studied Wally's reaction to Red's comment. "So, you are good with people calling you A-Wall, man?"

Wally took a sip of his drink. "Yes, absolutely! That's me! That's my brand! I am proudly Asian! Well, Chinese, to be specific, but I wanted to cast a wider net for my media consulting business, so the Asian name works for me. So, I hybridized Asian and Wally into A-Wall. It sounds like a rapper's name. Is that why you asked me what my name is?" Wally took another sip of his drink.

"Yeah, I wanted to be sure about the name thing, man. No disrespect shall be given within the walls of this tropical oasis from reality."

Wally smiled. "Thanks for caring; that means a lot to me. You know, in school, I had to put up with a lot of crap. Very racist shit, but I'd laugh along to get along. It hurt since some of them were friends but didn't understand that what they said was insulting. Then I saw the disrespect happen to my grandmother at the gas station convenience store. This twentysomething jackass purposely bumped into her and started yelling some pretty dark racist shit. I thought to myself fuck it; I'm not putting up with this for the rest of my life. So I ran directly at him, and he took off. He was okay roughing up an elderly lady, but when it came to a fair fight, he was a pussy. Most bullies are."

"Is your grandmother okay?"

"Oh, yeah! She wanted to get in the car and chase him down. She wanted a piece of him. I never thought I would hear my dear, sweet grandmother say *you catch him; I'll fuck him up*! That's when I decided to either own who I am or let them define me. A-Wall was born! My new identity became my social media and marketing brand. I'm kind of a communications bridge between East and West cultures. My website is A-WallMedia.com, and I'm on a dozen different platforms. Business is good!"

Don shook his head. "Are you sure the name thing is a good idea, man? There's no shortage of ignorant jackasses out there looking for a fight."

"You know, I can do nothing about the mouth breathers except stay clear of them. As to the A-Wall name, most people are amused by my business name. Some Asian friends think I am asking for trouble, and others admire my testicular fortitude. There are always going to be haters."

"Those are true words, man! You can't stop small minds from thinking small thoughts. While we are on the name thing, are you named after someone in your family, or was it a random choice?"

"Both! My actual Chinese name is Yŭchén. That's my dad's name too. However, it was my grandfather that gave me my Western name Wally. I could have picked one myself, but he was firm that he would decide my western name."

"So why Wally for a Western name?"

"Well, my family immigrated to the US in 1958. My dad was just a young boy. My grandfather watched a lot of TV shows to help him learn English. He thought the family in the show *Leave It to Beaver* was the wholesome model American family. The show's father, Ward, and his oldest son, Wally, portrayed the ideal father and son relationship to him. The youngest son on the show was nicknamed Beaver for some weird reason. Bad dental work, maybe. Anyway, my dad was given the Western name Ward, and when I came along a few years later, I was given the Western name Wally. Thank god he didn't give me the name Beaver! Can you imagine what Google would display if my website were A-Beaver instead of A-Wall?"

Don nodded. "You dodged a lifetime of humiliation on that one, man. So what was your grandfather's Western name?"

"He was a huge fan of the Western TV series Maverick and Jack Kelly's portrayal of Bart Maverick. So in the late 1970s, when the taking a Western name thing started, he took the name Bart. You know that name energized him. So I think it was a bold choice and a perfect fit. Kind of like A-Wall for me."

Don nodded. "I get it, man. Names can be empowering."

"That they can. It's kind of like a superhero persona for me. By the way, what did you want to see me about?

"Ah, the name game got me off-topic. This website and video about the gathering at the church building you did are freaking me out a little All these people showed up here because of the video and stuff about the bar you put out there. I don't know what to think about this, man?"

Wally was excited. "I know! Isn't this awesome? The site and social media are trending. I wouldn't say it's gone viral, but you are popular.

Don, you have over 40,000 followers and approaching 100,000 views per episode online. You're a somebody!"

Don shook his head in disbelief. "But I haven't done anything, man!"

"That's the point! You've connected with these people without putting anything on them. You provide space, sort of a mental sanctuary. It's about respect and acceptance. Toss in a freaky cool hot rod-driving guy that runs a retro tiki bar as the MC and his smart, attractive, and entertaining girlfriend, and you have magic. Look around; it brought them here!" Wally enthusiastically reached toward Don expecting a fist bump. Instead, Don slowly looked away, scanning the crowd of new customers as a few more entered the bar.

The loud blonde in the dress leaned across her boyfriend to join in the conversation. "A-Wall is right; this just looked so awesome online that we had to come and check it out. It's a long drive from Connecticut, so we missed the church hang-out part, and I am seriously bummed about that. You are a rock star. But this bar, oh my god, it's so up my skirt!"

"What's up your skirt?" Don glanced over at Wally.

"That means she likes it. A lot!" Wally turned to the loud blonde as she continued.

"Oh, yeah, this is great! And rum makes me horny, so me and my man will have to knock one out before driving back to Connecticut." She kissed her boyfriend as she glanced at the opening door. Brad entered, surprised at the full house so early on a Sunday.

"Oh my god, it's the guy that yells out random porno shit!" The loud blonde was motioning to Brad to join her. "Over here, baby!" She patted the bar stool next to her. Even though the bar was crowded, the seat was empty since she was seriously annoying to sit near.

Brad reluctantly took the bar stool and ordered a double Appleton Estate Old Fashioned. Don knew that potent cocktail was Brad's have-one-and-done drink when he felt uncomfortable. Being around all these new people made him nervous, and his condition was more prevalent when he felt that way.

The blonde took Brad's arm and leaned into him as she took a selfie. Her right breast pressed firmly against his arm. "So, cutie, why do you yell out random fucked up shit?"

Don picked up a glass and turned to find Jane talking with Red. Jane smiled. "Darlene called me and said you were slammed, so I came in. Did a bus dump these people here?"

Don continued to make the cocktail while explaining to her about A-Wall's website and social media and that the folks came to check things out at the church and bar. He downplayed that he was the main reason for them being there. Don was uncomfortable with the thought of being in the spotlight. He handed Jane the drink. "Here, please give this to Brad; you will take some of the attention off him."

Jane didn't know what that meant until she set the drink in front of Brad.

The loud blonde lit up. "Oh my god, it's Jane. You are so much hotter in person. And shit, girl, they aren't kidding; you do have a nice rack. It's hard to see that online." Jane smiled and politely thanked her.

"Hot tits!" Brad winced as he was doing well until he let that one fly. "Sorry...."

Jane smiled and rested her hand on Brad's. "It's okay, sweetie, and thanks for noticing." She winked at Brad.

The loud blonde was delighted. "This is so much better seeing it live."

A-Wall smiled broadly at Don. "It looks like the website and social media are good for business!"

Don reluctantly agreed. "I guess it is, but don't let it get out of control." Don glanced up to see the man that was sitting in the back of the church exit the bar. He fit in with the rest of the odd crowd today.

Chapter 16 - Gary from high school
April 18th 8:30 a.m.

Don turned off the alarm clock and gently nudged Jane. "Time to get up, babe." She snuggled up against him and sleepily whispered in his ear. "No!"

Don tried again. "Come on, babe, my fans await my arrival, and you are part of the show, so please get that cute ass of yours in gear." She again whispered in his ear. "No!"

Finally, Don climbed out of bed and slowly walked toward the shower, pulling the covers off Jane and the bed as he went. Jane grumbled – "stupid alarm clock." She slowly rolled out of bed and went to join Don in the shower.

For as long as Jane could remember, Sunday morning was the only workday she could sleep in an extra hour or two. The Happenings put an end to that. The attendance had rapidly increased, and the internet exposure brought many more people to Brite Rock. Business had increased significantly for the bar and the Shanty, which was welcome. But there was also a growing sense of pressure. It wasn't just that the bar was busy; some of these strangers acted like they knew Don and Jane. Being asked to pose with them for a photo or sign an autograph is now common. Jane pondered the benefits of this alternate reality as she stepped out of the shower.

Don was deep in thought as Jane gently moved him out of the way so she could use the mirror as she brushed out her wet hair. Don studied the contents of his closet carefully. Picking the right aloha shirt wasn't just a fashion choice; it was also a mood enhancer. What shirt would feel right for the day was the challenge. Jane would usually voice her opinion on his choices. If his clothing choices clashed or were a serious fashion faux pas, this was her opportunity to correct it. Once he left the apartment, whatever he wore was legal for the day.

Jane looked to see Don admiring her as she zipped up her jeans. "Are you checking me out again?"

Don smiled. "Maybe. You're kind of cute, you know."

"Awe, I love you too, babe. You are my everything. But you know what I don't love? That shirt with those shorts. Please pick a dark shirt, something less clashy, and get dressed quickly. I'm starving."

Besides the early wakeup time, the new Sunday morning routine was breakfast at the Shanty before heading to the Happening. Don would have the usual Hawaiian Loco Moco breakfast. Jane thought the plate of white rice, topped with a hamburger patty and a fried egg covered in brown gravy, was unappealing. She was a traditionalist, having her usual eggs benedict, country potatoes, and coffee – the trinity!

The Shanty is famous for its rich, dark roast coffee. It began with Darlene's parents buying coffee roasted in Boston's Italian north end in the 1950s. The Shanty still buys its coffee from the same supplier today. Running late, they ate a quick breakfast and took two large coffees to go.

Jane laughed as Don's hot rod sharply turned onto Main Street on the way to the church. Holding a to-go cup in each hand, she clenched her butt to keep from sliding across the seat as the car cornered. Don pulled into the open parking spot next to the church, gazing up at the sign that once said, "Reserved for Pastor," but had been less than expertly painted over to "Reserved for Jenny." Ed Mattie's work, no doubt.

As they approached the church building's main entrance, they were greeted by several excited people waiting outside. Don invited them in only to learn that there wasn't room. The place was crowded – not even standing room.

Rather than wading through the crowd, Don and Jane used the rear entrance. Don settled into the rickety aluminum chair while Jane sat on the stage to his left. He took a long sip of coffee and looked around the room.

"So, what's happening, man? You all look well." He took another sip of coffee and set the cup on the floor. "I see a lot of new faces here.

Whatever your reason for coming, welcome aboard. So, who would like to kick it off today?"

Several hands went up, and Don looked around the room to pick someone. "Let's start with someone new this morning. The aluminum chair recognizes the young man in the green paisley shirt. Cool retro look, man. Tell us about you."

"Hi, I'm Aaron Leland. So, I was listening to NPR on the way here this morning, and they said that the French consider the tomato the love apple. It's supposed to have aphrodisiac powers. You know, get you horny and stuff. What's your experience with this whole aphrodisiac thing? Does it really work?" Aaron sat down.

"You know, man, I've heard long lists of foods, drinks, and herbs that are supposed to up the desire for sex. I honestly have no idea. I've been with Jane since high school, and one look at her gets my motor running. But if there is an aphrodisiac thing in my life, it's Jane's scent. Maybe it's her pheromones that does it for me. And she says she digs my aroma too. So, I guess we are a chemically compatible match, man. Would anyone like to add to the what makes you horny conversation or change the topic?"

Several hands went up. Don spotted a new yet vaguely familiar face. "The aluminum chair recognizes the gent in the yellow shirt."

The man stood and started to speak. "Hi Don, my name is Gary…"

Before he could finish, Jane was on her feet. "Gary Berman! I haven't seen you since you left for California after graduation." Gary smiled. "Hi Jane, good to see you again."

Jane looked at Don, and a sense of excitement filled her. "You remember Gary from high school? He was in our senior English class."

Don thought for a moment. It was slowly coming back to him. Don and Jane had split up the day after high school graduation. Neither knew why; it just happened.

Chapter 17 - A sure thing with easy Lana
Flashback to Don & Jane - Recent High School Grads

With a freshly minted high school diploma proudly displayed on the mantle over the fireplace at home, Don departed on the trip to Kauai that his parents gave him as a graduation gift. Don's summer on the island wasn't what he expected. He enjoyed Friday afternoons when the locals took over Po'ipū Beach Park for the weekend. It was a two-day luau. Sleeping outdoors in the park in a lawn chair was accepted behavior. It had the makings of a perfect beach bum summer, except that he deeply missed Jane. She was more than his girlfriend; she was also his best friend. He missed sharing things with her, particularly the sunrise, as they had done at Brite Rock beach and several of the Cape Cod beaches numerous times.

Jane's summer wasn't going any better back in Brite Rock. She missed Don to the point of grieving. If they had only fought and had harsh words, it would've been easier to take, but they didn't. Jane wondered if they got swept up in all the change and teenage angst that came with high school graduation and starting their adult lives. Was it the pressure? Was it her? What if Don wanted to date other girls? She didn't understand how they got to this place and was heartbroken. She didn't know that he was too.

It was July 4th, and Don had been gone for three weeks. The town was crowded and deep into the tourist season. Jane's friend Sue had been asked on a date by one of their high school classmates, Stephen, to watch the fireworks. Sue begged Jane to make it a double date since Stephen's best friend and classmate, Gary, was being abandoned by him for the night so Stephen could take out Sue. Jane's heart wasn't in it, but she went along anyway.

The weather was perfect for July on the Massachusetts coast. Early afternoon thunderstorms had come through, pushing the hazy, hot, and humid weather out to sea. A slight breeze stirred the warm air as stars began to appear in the sky. Several campfires popped up in the fire pits on the beach as night settled in. Like many coastal tourist towns, Brite Rock puts on an extravagant fireworks display as part of the attraction to bring tourists to town. It worked, and like most every July 4th, the town was packed.

Conversations were interrupted by the resounding thud of a single aerial shell launching skyward. A small flash and thunderous bang followed. That signaled that the fireworks were about to begin. A spectacular show lit the night sky over Brite Rock beach for the next half-hour.

After the fireworks, the four walked across the street to Rudy's Clam Shack for a bucket of fried clams, clam cakes, fries, and Rudy's homemade root beer. Then, food and drink in hand, they returned to the beach, where they ate and talked until nearly 1:00 a.m.

Jane and Gary had a good time. They talked about everything from high school to what lies ahead in their future. Gary had already applied and was accepted to attend the University of California. His grandmother lives in Encinitas, a beach town just north of San Diego. Gary decided to leave a few weeks before college started to help around the house and settle in.

Jane and Gary went out a few more times before he moved west the first week of August. She found him to be funny, intelligent, and good-looking. But he wasn't Don, who Jane longed to hold. Finally, out of frustration, she momentarily let Gary get to second base. That was a dream of pretty much every boy in high school. But in a way, he could tell that it was a hollow victory. It was clear to him that Jane's heart wasn't in it, and despite the raging hormones of a teenage boy, he just knew nothing would come of his romantic efforts.

Jane assured Gary that she would be interested in him if she were available, or at least felt that way. But that isn't the case; she still has a lot to sort out in her life. After all, it has only been several weeks since she and Don split up.

Don returned from Kauai the first week of August, two days after Gary had left for California. He had been accepted at Emerson College in

Boston and returned early to help at the bar and spend time with friends before everyone scattered to their new lives.

Don was up early and spent all day at the bar cleaning, helping his dad do the inventory count, and placing weekly purveyor orders. After dinner, he decided to go for a walk to clear his head. The long day and the six-hour time difference between Brite Rock and Hawaii left him physically, mentally, and emotionally exhausted.

It was a few minutes before 8:00 P.M. The sun was setting behind him as he sat on the beach. It's the same place where he and Jane sat a thousand times before. It's their spot.

Don had never felt so empty. If this is his last summer before he officially becomes an adult, it sure had a shitty start. He replayed the situation with Jane in his head, which still made no sense to him.

Was it high school ending and going away to college? How did he become separated from Jane? Maybe the fear of Jane becoming pregnant? He wasn't ready for marriage but wasn't prepared to give up Jane either. He felt no firm ground under his feet. They always communicated freely and in-depth. Then everything stopped.

He decided to get a much-needed good night's sleep, visit her tomorrow, and apologize. He had no idea what to say. But he had nothing to lose and everything to gain.

He hadn't been lost in thought for more than a few minutes when a familiar voice asked if she could sit down. Don looked up and was momentarily jolted by his emotions. He reached up and took Jane's hand as she settled beside him in the sand.

Neither spoke, unsure of what to say. Don put his arm around her. She leaned into him. He breathed in her scent, causing his heart to race. She saw the pain in his eyes. He rested his forehead against hers. She softly kissed his lips. They pulled each other close and held tight. They sat motionless for several minutes.

Don had never seen Jane truly cry. He was deeply saddened by the trembling of her body and the staccato sound of convulsive gasps as she tried to catch her breath. His shirt collar was soaked from her tears.

Jane took a deep breath as she tried to compose herself. "I don't know what did this to us, but I can promise it will never happen again. We are so good at talking to each other. I have learned to open up and trust because of you. I fully accept and embrace all the quirky things about us. We are a really good "us," and I want that back. So, I am picking you, and it's for keeps. It's for life. You are mine! Do you understand that? You are fucking mine! No backsies! I love you completely, and I can't do life without you! And when I ask you for words, you will give them to me."

Don cradled Jane's face in his hands. "I don't know what happened either. I think maybe I just freaked out, man. Everything was changing all at once, and I didn't separate us from that change. I think I shut down. It's been a hard lesson, but I have learned that I…we…need to share everything, not just the good or fun stuff. If something freaks one of us out or one of us is going through something, we need to share it so we can work it out together. There will be glitches and screw-ups. That's just life. But life is just better and makes sense when we share it. I need you. You are mine. You have to be. We need to be us again. Can we be us again?"

Jane wiped her face with her hands. "So, you are all in?"

"Yes, I'm all in! I love you and am yours. I fully commit to you and us! No backsies! You are my one and only, my partner in all things. I will tell you everything. And thank you for loving me. So, can we seal the deal with a kiss? I'm exhausted!"

"Oh, I think we can do better than just a kiss. But before we seal the deal, all cards on the table. I need to tell you something. It's not horrific or a moment that I'm proud of.

I went on a double date Sue set up so she could be with Stephen Harrington on July 4th. I was set up with Gary Berman from our high school. We walked along the old train tracks and talked several times after that. I must have walked those tracks a thousand times thinking about you. Anyway, one thing led to another, and Gary and I kissed a little, and he got to second base for a moment before I shut him down. I told him it wasn't working because my heart was someplace else." Tears started to well up in Jane's eyes again.

Don sat for a moment, processing what he had just heard. "So, you two didn't…."

Jane shook her head. "No, nothing below the belt. No dry humping. No tongue wrestling. I touched nothing of his, nor did I want to. It all adds up to some talking, a little kissing, and a momentary titty touch. I don't feel great about that titty thing. But know it doesn't mean anything to me because Gary doesn't." Jane looked at Don, waiting for his reaction.

He cleared his throat. "Thank you for telling me. I'm glad to hear nothing happened with Gary and that you didn't give up on us."

"Of course, I didn't give up on us. I went to see your parents the day that you left for Kauai. Your dad told me you were just being a dumb 18-year-old hormonally charged male whose body is little more than a life support system for his penis. He also told me to give you a little time and that you would come to your senses and return to me. Your mom said she considers me a mature and positive influence on you. I think they like me more than you at the moment."

Don smiled and nodded. "You may be right about that. They both grilled me about what happened to us. When I said I didn't exactly know, they gave me some sage advice – get my head out of my ass and fix it! My parents are wise!"

"Yes, they are wise. So, what happened with you over the past several weeks?"

Don sighed. "It's been a horrible summer. My heart has been in neutral too. I've been missing you in a big way. There I was, in paradise, being a serious buzz kill, man. And for some reason, a local gal named Lana took a liking to me and asked me to be her summer romance. It didn't go well."

Jane's heart sank. "What do you mean it didn't go well?"

Don took a deep breath and slowly exhaled. "Well, Lana kissed me and asked me back to her place. I told her she was very attractive, and I appreciated the offer, but I couldn't do that. Lana then asked if I had a girlfriend or wife, and I said no. I told her that I had a girlfriend, but she wasn't that at the moment, but I wanted her to be my girlfriend again. Lana got pissy and said if I didn't have a girlfriend, then why not her now? So I started to tell her about you again, and that's when she got wicked pissed and stood up, called me a very long list of bad things, some in Hawaiian, and kicked sand in my face. Who does that? Then she flipped me off and left. And that's why I think that it didn't go well."

Jane smiled and hugged Don. "I'm glad you turned down a sure thing with easy Lana."

Don gently kissed Jane. "My heart was with you! It always is."

'I'm glad to hear that. Now, where is your car parked? We have a deal to seal!" Jane stood up, took Don's hand, and headed for his car.

Chapter 18 - That's just human nature, man
April 18th 11:17 a.m. ~ Continued

Don caught himself as if in a daydream. "Oh, sorry, man, I zoned out. High school flashback. So, what brings you back to our fair town, man?"

Gary looked over at Wally with his video camera in hand. "Well, I've returned to say my goodbyes and see a few friends. Two months ago, I was diagnosed with stage four pancreatic cancer."

Jane stared at Gary. She silently mouthed the words *oh my god*.

It took Don a moment to comprehend what Gary was saying. "Oh man, so sorry to hear that. How are you doing?"

"I am managing the pain with meds. I've decided not to continue chemotherapy when I return to California in a few days. In my case, that would be pointless, and the chemo messes with my head. Horrible brain fog and memory issues."

"Is there anything we can do for you, man?"

"Not really. I'm here to let my family and friends know and make peace with what is about to happen. In a way, I'm lucky to have time to say my goodbyes." Gary looked down at the floor for a moment.

"There is one thing, but this is hard to ask. So, here goes. Would it be okay to ask Jane to meet me for one last walk along the tracks? I just need to talk to someone who won't sugarcoat things. I don't need sympathy right now; I need honesty. I promise nothing will happen. Actually, on the meds, nothing can happen."

All eyes shifted from Gary to Don.

"I thank you for the courtesy of asking, man, but no need. This is Jane's decision, and I support her choice, whatever it is." The aluminum chair squeaked as he moved.

Jane walked over and hugged Gary. "Of course, we can go for a walk and talk. Just tell me when."

Gary was relieved. "How about this afternoon, around 2:00? Does that work for you?"

A faint smile came to Jane's lips. "Perfect! Pick me up at the Bar. You know the place." Jane squeezed Gary's hand before returning to sit on the stage. Her eyes welled up.

Gary looked at Don for a moment. "I have to thank you. Not many guys would let their girlfriends meet with another guy under any circumstances. That's very gracious of you, Don."

"Of course, Jane can do this, man. She is her own person, and we mean it when we say we support each other's decisions unless it's me making a bad fashion choice. Is there anything you would like to talk about now? These folks are good listeners and usually have pretty good suggestions."

Gary shook his head. "No, not really. But I would like to remind everyone what a special place Brite Rock is and how wonderful the people living here are. It's easy to forget that."

"Tits, Tits, Tits, Fucker, em-em!"

Gary was stunned. "What the...."

Brad looked at Don and then Gary. "Sorry."

In unison, and with the familiar drawn-out cadence that the bar patrons reply with, all in the room responded, "it's okay, Brad!"

A loud whisper was heard from the back pew. "This is so much better in person than online." Quiet laughter spread through the room.

Gary slowly sat down, confused by what had just happened.

Don smiled at Gary and looked around the room. "So, who's next? Does anyone have a question or need to share anything?"

Pete raised his hand and stood.

Don was surprised to see Pervie Pete. This was the first time he had attended a Happening. "The aluminum chair recognizes PP. So what's up, P?"

"So, this guy comes to town and asks Jane out on a date, and you're fine with that? Aren't you the least bit jealous? No offense, but he is better looking than you." Pete shifted his gaze to Jane.

The aluminum chair squeaked as Don sat back. "First of all, P, it's not a date. It's a walk and talk. Second, I don't do jealousy, man. That's one of those senseless things that people do to themselves. And while Gary is a handsome gent, Jane says I'm cute, and that cute works for her." Don looked over at Jane. She nodded in agreement.

Pete raised his hand again. "So, you won't be there on this…walk and talk. How would you know if Jane gave it up and did the dirty with cancer guy?"

"Cancer guy? His name is Gary, P!" The look of disapproval on Don's face was obvious to Pete.

"Sorry, that was insensitive of me. So, how would you know if Jane did the dirty with…Gary?"

"You know, P, serving the public as a bartender is often a lesson in humanity. People will tell their bartender things that they won't tell their friends or significant other. We hear it all, including infidelity and the different reasons why it happens. It changes the person that cheats. They feel different about themselves, and it often shows. Maybe it's guilt. Fear that they will be found out. Knowing that they destroyed the trust that someone put in them. Karma. Whatever it is, they act differently. I would know, as would Jane, that something big has changed in our relationship."

Pete raised his hand again. "So, what should somebody do if they did screw around and wanted to make things right?"

"It's like the sign at the hardware store, man. *You break it; you own it.* I think the only way to fix it is to be honest with yourself and your mate. Voluntarily tell them what happened. Take responsibility for your actions. If you don't, be prepared for the possibility of the relationship ending."

The wheels were turning in Pete's head. "So, if Jane did cheat, would you forgive and forget?"

Don thought for a moment. "I'm not going to answer your hypothetical question, man. I would have to presume that Jane has done something wrong to do that. But I will say this about forgiving and forgetting.

I believe we do forgiveness for ourselves, not the person who wronged us. It frees us from the anger, pain, and stress caused by holding onto a grudge. What happened can't be undone. Focus on the good in your life and stop agonizing over past mistreatment. And forgiving someone doesn't mean you must reconcile with them or continue the relationship. So, we can choose to forgive or not. It can be the end or a new beginning.

As to forgetting, I don't think it's genuinely possible to forget a painful wrong committed against us. That's just human nature, man. The memory of being wronged and the pain stays with us like an emotional scar. How we handle it depends on our willingness to acknowledge it and move forward. Keep the relationship going or toss in the towel. I guess that's my take on the forgive-and-forget thing, man."

Don took a sip of his coffee and looked around the room. There were a lot of quiet conversations and affirmative shaking of heads.

"So, is there something you want to tell us, P?"

PP sat down. "Nope!"

Chapter 19 - The seeds of uncertainty and doubt
April 19th 8:00 a.m.

Jerry Palmer looked up from the stack of papers he was sorting when Pastor Smyth and Paul Caruso entered his office. It was just after 8:00 a.m. on a Monday. Smyth displayed his trademark smile as he extended his hand. "Hello, counselor; how are things in our fair community?" Smyth stood in front of Jerry's desk, waiting for his reply.

Jerry's first thoughts were about their expensive tailored suits and Smyth's insincere demeanor. "Things are well in Brite Rock. We're a small town with typical small-town opportunities and problems. All rather repetitive and mundane. That said, what brings you to the town offices today?"

Smyth pulled up a chair and sat down. "I am here on behalf of the members of our faith-based community. I didn't know where to start, so I thought you, as Town Counsel, could provide guidance. As you may know, I began serving the community out of the little Sailers Church in the center of town two years ago. Fortune smiled upon us, and we were able to build a new larger church to serve the ever-growing community. But …I'm afraid our good fortune has created a problem at our original church. My heart aches just thinking about it."

Jerry gazed up momentarily at Caruso, who was standing behind Smyth. He wondered what Caruso's role was in this.

Jerry focused back on Smyth. "Can you be more specific? What's the problem?"

"As you may know, the bartender in town is holding Sunday service at my old church. As I understand it, it's a non-denominational service. In fact, I hear it lacks any relationship to any religion whatsoever. That makes sense since the building was desanctified upon my moving out. It's just a building now. But I'm afraid his Sunday service may be a big scam and that he's taking advantage of some of the members of our faith-based community, particularly the elderly and afflicted. Very sad, indeed. As leaders in our community, isn't it in the best interest of all to rescind his tax-exempt status and put an end to his so-called Sunday service?"

Jerry didn't understand where Smyth was going with this. "I'm not a tax attorney, but in this case, the religious tax-exempt status resides with the religious organization, not the building. That would be you as the religious leader and your congregation. I assume your tax-exempt status is the same in your new church as when you were operating out of the Sailers Church, yes?"

"Well, yes, but I'm not speaking of my tax-exempt status. It's those people that we are concerned about."

This was starting to feel like a fishing expedition to Jerry. "As far as I know, neither Don nor his partner Ms. Gilman have applied for or received any tax-exempt status. So, what is the complaint about people being taken advantage of?"

Smyth was trying to pick his words carefully. "I'm sure that as you investigate, you will find that he is collecting weekly cash contributions that he's not declaring on his taxes. I hear he also puts undue pressure on the elderly and afflicted to contribute beyond their means. Then there is the streaming of the service, which I'm sure brings in more undeclared contributions. He's using those poor people in his videos. He invades their privacy in such a demeaning way. He needs to be stopped for the good of the community and that church building placed in capable and loving hands."

Jerry didn't know much about Don's Sunday get-together, but he did know that none of this applied to his office. "To begin with, pastor, the only time this office may get involved with a tax issue is if it relates to an abandonment of property and unpaid related property tax. And I can't comment on the video that people willfully appear in. But, if there is coercion or other illegal activity, you must take that up with the District Attorney."

Smyth appeared to be deep in thought for a moment. "You know, counselor, perhaps it's in the best interest of our community to remove the old church from the bartender and put an end to his sacrilegious and demeaning actions. Now, my Brite Rock Cathedral by the Sea is willing to help by being a curator of the old church building. We, of course, don't want to place a financial hardship on Don or the lovely Ms. Gilman, so I propose that the town take just the old church building by eminent domain and leave the property in his hands as it is today. Our church would bear the financial burden of relocating the building to a site next to our new church and maintaining it at our expense. It's a win for everyone, don't you think?"

Jerry now understood what Smyth and Caruso were after when they entered his office. He just didn't know why.

"Well, pastor, I have to say this is one of the strangest eminent domain requests I can recall. The likelihood of this moving forward is rather slim. However, I will look into the Sunday gathering at the old church and let you or the District Attorney know if something needs further attention."

With that, Smyth and Caruso said their goodbyes and were on their way. Jerry couldn't figure out why Smyth wanted the old church building bad enough to devise a bizarre scheme. Jerry needed to talk to Don.

Smyth and Caruso exited the town office building and paused on the sidewalk. He had done what he set out to do, framing the conversation about Don's Sunday gatherings as something undesirable in the community.

"Paul, that couldn't have gone better. Sow the seeds of uncertainty and doubt. That's all you need to get people worked up and start rumors. They're a pack of sheep! We are one step closer to owning our legacy!"

Caruso smiled broadly. "You are right; rumors of him ripping off old ladies and the disadvantaged is a good start."

Smyth laughed. "Ripping off little old ladies is my act, not his! But, you know, we may have to get a little more aggressive with the bartender, or better yet, maybe we go after his girlfriend. She is so fucking hot when she is angry. Standing all straight and defiant, I'm getting hard just thinking about it."

Caruso laughed. "I bet she's an animal in bed. I don't get how the bartender scored prime pussy like that. What a waste. That crazy Beatle broad is more his speed."

The expression on Smyth's face changed to anger. "Oh, I still owe that bitch for hitting me in the face. I don't care what her fucking problem is, hit me, and I'll hit back twice as hard. I wouldn't feel bad if she was put under a public microscope so everyone could see how fucked up she is. Outing her crazy ass may be more fun anyway."

Caruso nodded his head and paused. "As much as I would love to see Jane all sexy angry, and the fucked-up Beatle bitch put in a fetal position, neither of those will help us get the church building. We need to stay on point with the rumors about the bartender ripping off his followers. Ramp that up on social media too. Make that church building a toxic liability to him, and he will pay us to take it away."

"You're right, Paul; cooler heads shall prevail. We must stay focused!" Smyth got into Caruso's Mercedes, and they slowly cruised by the Sailers Church building. If Sailers Church were a person, Smyth would be considered a stalker.

Chapter 20 - You want me full of lust, don't you
April 24th 4:47 p.m.

The unseasonably sunny, warm, and humid spring afternoon was a treat. It was the perfect weather for a walk on the beach before dinner and drinks. Olivia was waiting for Jerry at the beach when she noticed the towering storm clouds rolling in from the west. She sniffed at the sweet, pungent aroma of ozone in the air. Olivia had heard Don say in one of the online Sunday Happening videos about being able to smell a thunderstorm coming. She googled it and found out it was true. So Olivia paid close attention to the smell the next time a thunderstorm happened. She wondered how she had missed that reliable predictor of a thunderstorm all her life.

The beach walk would have to wait. Everyone on the beach or casually strolling through town will soon be seeking a place to get out of the weather for the next half-hour. Liv texted Jerry: "change of plans, meet me at the tiki bar."

Olivia heard the first rumble of thunder as she opened the door to the bar. The place was full of locals and tourists. Her favorite seat at the end of the bar was opening up as a hungry patron got up and left for the Shanty. When Jerry entered, Olivia was settling into her usual spot. He made his way through the crowd. She stood and gave Jerry a hug and kiss before sitting back down.

Jane set drink coasters in front of them. "Welcome to the Friday night springtime madhouse. Before I take your order, Don wanted me to tell Liv about eight new songs on the jukebox to check out. So there, I can cross that off my to-do list. Now, what can I get you?"

Olivia thought for a moment. "I'm in a lustful mood. I'll have a Pagan Lust, please."

Jane giggled. "And what about you, Jerry? Are you feeling lustful too?"

"Why yes, I am! But I'll have an original Mai Tai first. And before you go, is Don here tonight?"

"Yes, he's in his office."

"May I go back and speak with him?"

Jane's playful side-eye gaze was thinly veiled curiosity. "Is this business or pleasure?"

"It's business, and I don't want to discuss it publicly. Nothing bad, I just need some information."

"Well, if it's nothing bad, I guess you can talk to him. Come on back." Jane escorted Jerry to the office. She wanted to stay and hear the conversation but needed to return to work.

Don finished signing a check and handed it to Bootleg Bobby, the wine and spirits delivery driver. "Thanks, Bootleg. A pleasure doing business with you, man. Don't forget to ask Tony about those two rums. I would rather get those through you than Albert's company. That guy is harsh on pricing, man."

"Yep, Albert will pick your pocket if given a chance. I'll check with Tony and let you know. He may also stop by with the brand ambassador from Nicholas White Rum out of Mansfield next week. White is the last name of the guy who built the house in 1703 that this new boutique small-batch distiller operates out of. Tony said rum making in New England was very popular in the mid-1600s and 1700s. I can tell you; they never taught that in high school history class!"

Don looked deep in thought for a moment. "I didn't pay too much attention in history class, man. I was preoccupied with staring at Jane and trying to come up with a plan to ask her out. I guess I did!"

Bootleg laughed. "Yeah, I guess you did! Oh, and please tell Red that I was asking for her. She's a hottie!"

"I'll pass along your words to Miss Kelly Rose, man. Take it easy, Bootleg, and I'll see you next Friday."

Don turned his attention to Jerry. "How goes it, man? What brings you to my inner island sanctum?"

"Don, I had a strange visit from Pastor Smyth and his shadow, Paul Caruso. They came to my office to air a laundry list of complaints about you and your Sunday morning gatherings at Sailers Church. They said you are soliciting donations from old and less fortunate people. Is there anything I can help you with? Maybe the tax code application for religious donations?"

Don was confused. "What is Smyth talking about, man? I don't take donations of any kind from anyone. It's just a happening. The people are guests of Jane and me."

"So, to be clear, you don't take donations, offerings, or any income from the events you hold at the old church?"

"No, not a penny. Jane and I pay the bills on the place out of pocket."

Jerry was putting the pieces together and suspected the start of a smear campaign might be taking place. "Have they said anything to you about the Sailers Church building?"

Don rubbed his face, clearly frustrated. "Yeah, they came here a couple of weeks ago and offered to buy it from me, man. I told them I wouldn't sell. They pressed the issue. Things got loud, and bar regular John Lennon punched Smyth in the nose. I knew those guys weren't cool when they stole the big Jesus from my church. I never did get that back, man."

"John Lennon, the Beatle? Ah, he's dead. Is there another John Lennon?"

Don laughed to himself. "Yeah, I could have picked my words better, man. Of course, it's not actually John Lennon; it's Alexandra being John Lennon. She has some form of personality thing and sometimes walks, talks, and resembles Beatle John. She can answer any Beatles question. She knows every lyric to every Beatles song. It's trippy, man. Spooky too! But when she's on her meds, she's this gentle soul in a sundress. I like both of her, man."

Jerry smiled. "You do have an eclectic clientele in your bar. Why do you think that is?"

"I don't know, man. We run a pretty accepting establishment. As long as people treat everyone with respect, check their harsh views at the door, and don't be a dick, they are welcome. In this bar, it's island time all of the time, man. So step away from the everyday hassle for a little aloha. Speaking of the bar, I better get back at it."

"Yeah, and I better get back to Liv. Oh, and I have a feeling that this Smyth thing is far from over. I'll let you know if I hear from them again."

Jerry followed Don back to the bar just as Jane served their drinks. Olivia grinned. "I have been looking forward to this all week."

As is customary in the bar, when someone orders a Pagan Lust cocktail, the server shines a handheld spotlight on the served drink as the opening part of the song Pagan Lust by Don Tiki blasts out of the bar sound system. Bar staff and patrons sing along.

Whatever you do to help you make it through
Whatever you do, do what you must
But whatever you do, don't drink
Whatever you do, don't drink
Whatever you do, don't drink – that Pagan Lust

Olivia holds the drink high before taking a sip. A short round of applause follows. She likes the cocktail but could live without the theatrics every time she orders one.

Jerry laughed. "Did you know your drink came with a song and dance, Liv?"

"Yes, I guess it's the social price I pay for ordering this tall cup of lust. I'll have to eat before I have another one. Two of these on an empty stomach will knock me on my ass."

Jerry pointed to the Shanty pass-through door.

Olivia smiled. "Yes, my boyfriend should go next door to the Shanty and bring back a fried fisherman's platter with two forks. Oh, and extra Ipswich clams and tartar sauce. Please?"

Jerry took a long sip of his drink before leaning into Olivia for a kiss. "Boyfriend… I like that. So, if anyone's looking for me, I've just stepped next door to get my smoking hot girlfriend some food. By the way, what's so special about Ipswich clams?"

"It's the taste of the sea, baby! Now, go get us food while I sit here and soak up this lust. You want me full of lust, don't you?"

Chapter 21 - All day long and into the night
April 25th 11:09 a.m.

A-Wall's live streaming of what he had titled the *Church of Don Happening Hour* had found an ever-increasing audience. The Sunday morning Happening attendance had grown to well over ten times the capacity of the little church building. Those unable to get inside sat outside and watched the Happening on their phones and iPads under the trees, on blankets, or on the lawn chairs they brought. A few of those chairs were artfully modified to look like Don's chair, including the deformed back leg with a broom handle taped to it. It didn't matter that they weren't inside; it only mattered that they were part of the Happening.

The atmosphere was a mix of interpretive tiki and island-themed decorations. Someone had easy listening Hawaiian music softly playing as two young women practiced their version of hula on the lawn. Aloha shirts and tropical wear were typical, as was food. Many brought coffee, doughnuts, take-out food from local restaurants, and what appeared to be homemade Mai Tais in tiki-decorated cups. One regular attendee, Musubi Mike, brought a tray of Spam musubi to share with his Outside the Happening Ohana.

A television news crew from Bay State Sunday Morning waited in front of Sailers Church to broadcast a live news segment. The reporter repositioned her earpiece to hear the director's countdown cue better.

"Standby, Ella. Weather will be throwing it to you in ten. He said it's a nice day where you are. And in five – four – three – two..."

"You are so right, Matthew! It is a perfect spring morning here in Brite Rock. There's not a cloud in the sky, and the crowd is enjoying the festivities outside the old Sailers Church. In this small building, sixty-two people are attending the unconventional Church of Don Happening Hour that streams live on the internet every Sunday morning. You may ask, what's unconventional about this event? Well, pretty much everything!

Don and his girlfriend, Jane, host the Happening Hour. This often humorous duo tends bar at their Don's Tiki Cocktails & Lounge here in Brite Rock. A bartender by trade, Don often shares his bartender advice and philosophy on numerous topics. From hot rods to cocktail recipes to relationship advice, any subject is up for discussion except politics. And what do people think of that specific limitation? Let's ask an attendee."

Ella approaches a nearby couple. "May I ask your name and where you are from?"

"You sure may! I'm Tim Binkman, and this is my wife, Ophelia. We're from Woburn."

"It's good to meet you. So, what do you think of Don's limitation on discussing politics in The Happening?"

"My wife and I love it! It is so refreshing to escape the mindless talking heads telling us their opinions on politics every minute of every day. And the ones making the most noise aren't experts; they're just overly opinionated. I can live without the lot of them!"

"So you are fine with not discussing your political beliefs in the Happening?"

"Absolutely, Ella! This isn't the place for that. You wouldn't expect deep discussions about politics at a Red Sox game, would you? There's enough hate at Fenway Park already with the Yankees in town. Go, Sox!"

Ella laughed. "I see your point, Tim. I also see a lot of Hawaiian shirts and a few lawn chairs that resemble the famed battered chair that Don sits in during the Happening. Is this like a cult thing?"

Tim shook his head. "It's no more of a cult thing than dressing like your favorite movie star or wearing the shirt of your favorite sports team. Well, except for the Patriots. I'm pretty sure Coach Belichick's Patriot Way could have been considered a cult back in the day. Did you know Bill created Tom Brady in his basement, and Tom escaped to Florida because that's where retired people go? True story!"

"OK, Tim, now I know you are pulling my leg! It was nice meeting you folks and Go Sox!" Ella turned back toward the church and continued with her live report.

"Well, this may be the only place in New England where you can go to escape the hot-button topics of the day, but not Hawaiian shirts. And be prepared for the large Sunday crowd here in Brite Rock. And it's not just the Happening at the old Sailers Church and Don's Tiki Cocktails & Lounge that enjoys the extraordinary number of Sunday visitors. The local restaurants, coffee shops, gas stations, hotels, and other Brite Rock businesses also enjoy the added visitor traffic. The Chamber of Commerce has started tracking these visitors as the "Sunday Surge" to serve this new demographic better. And judging by this crowd, good Mai Tai's must be nearby!

I'm Ella Nguyen reporting live outside the Church of Don Happening Hour for Bay State Sunday Morning. Aloha, New England!"

Inside Sailers Church, Don looked the crowd over and acknowledged a nicely dressed young man with short hair and a rather full yet styled beard. "The aluminum chair recognizes the gent with the killer beard. What's your name, man?"

"My name is Ethan Roberts, and I have a rum question. I want to set up a home Tiki bar and want to know more about Navy rum. I've researched it online, and it looks like something I should have. So what do you think?"

The aluminum chair squeaked and leaned slightly to the right as Don sat back. "Yeah, you want a bottle of Pusser's Navy Rum, man. That, with Coco Lopez cream of coconut, pineapple juice, orange juice, and nutmeg, makes a tasty cocktail called a Pain Killer. It's easy to make, even for beginners. We serve a lot of those at the bar. We also use Navy rum in our Admiral Vernon grog cocktail."

Ethan took notes on his phone. "Why is it called Navy rum, and what is grog?"

"You see, man, in the 1600s, the British Royal Navy started giving their sailors a daily ration of French brandy. The problem was that the brandy turned bad in hot tropical climates. So when the British colonized Jamaica in the mid-1600s, they switched to rum, which improved the longer it aged in the barrels. That's when sailors began receiving a daily ration of 1/2 gill of rum, about 2 ½ ounces, called a tot.

In the mid-1700s, Admiral Vernon watered down the rum and added lime juice to prevent scurvy, a common dietary problem for sailors back then. The British Navy stopped the daily rum ration for its sailors in the summer of 1970. Oddly enough, we have an authentic Royal Navy rum pitcher from the late 1700s on display at the bar. It was used during rum ration time on an HMS Ship.

As to the name grog, Vernon wore an old grogram coat well past its fashion expiration date. The sailors would bust on him with the nickname "Old Grog." His rum, water, and lime concoction became known as grog. His original recipe has been greatly improved over time."

Ethan paused his notetaking. "Who was Pusser?"

"Ah, common misunderstanding, man. The Brits like wordplay and would call the purser "pusser" just to be funny. Since the purser gave out the daily tot of rum, it became known as pusser's rum. Does that answer your questions, man?"

"Yes, Don, it does, and I appreciate you taking the time to answer my questions."

"That's what we come here for, man. Now, one last thing. Making cocktails may mean that you are serving them to friends and family. As a home bartender, your job is to help your guests manage their mellow without getting knee walking, snot hanging drunk."

Ethan smiled. "Manage the mellow. Good tip!"

Don took a long sip of iced coffee. "So, who's next?"

Roger raised his hand. "The aluminum chair recognizes Roger. What's on your mind, man?"

"Well, Don, I would like to know if you remember the words to that sea shanty that your dad would sing in the bar from time to time. Can you lead us in a sing-along?"

Don scratched his head. "I don't know, man. It's been a while and…"

Jane laughed. "Yeah, baby! Lead us in song! If you don't, I will, and you know my singing voice sounds like a raccoon mating with an angry house cat."

Don nodded. "Good point, Jane."

He reluctantly stood. "I'm sure most of you remember the words to Poor Captain Greg. So, the gist of this sea shanty is that Captain Greg spent almost all his money building a fancy dock and didn't have much left to buy a boat. I expect you all to sing along except for Jane, of course."

Don proceeded to sing the sea shanty. Most of the people inside and outside Sailers Church sang along.

Captain Greg (An original Sea Shanty)

Captain Greg was a water man
Oh, Captain Greg was a water man
Captain Greg lived by the sea
But that was not his folly

Captain Greg built a mighty dock
Oh, Captain Greg built a mighty dock
T'was grand and strong and hard as rock
Tis the envy of his neighbors

Captain Greg had spent all his money
Oh, Captain Greg had spent all his money
Captain Greg didn't own a boat
His neighbors thought that funny

He could only afford a tiny dinghy
He could only afford a tiny dinghy
T'was old and wood and past its peak
T'was also a wee bit leaky

Captain Greg set out to sea
Oh, Captain Greg set out to sea
He soon returned with his trousers wet
His dinghy sprung more leaks - three

Word spread through the village now
Oh, word spread through the village now
Captain Greg had a soggy bottom and a tiny dinghy
Captain Greg had a soggy bottom and a tiny dinghy

Don, mildly embarrassed by his less-than-professional crooning, returned to his aluminum chair as laughter and applause followed his odd performance.

Jane wiped tears of laughter from her face and pointed at her watch.

"My lovely assistant has informed me we have time for just one more question, complaint, accolade, or observation." Before Don could ask who would like to speak next, a young man, maybe 16 years old, slowly stood and raised his hand.

"The aluminum chair recognizes....what's your name, man?"

"Kyle, sir. My name's Kyle."

Don studied the young man for a moment. "I think I've seen you around town, man."

"Yes, I work at the Dairy Queen. I've waited on you before."

Don's face lit up with that look of sudden recognition. "That's it! You do the extra dip on the cone. Superior product and superior service. I dig the coneage. So, how's it going, man?"

"Good, sir. Um, can I ask sort of a question?"

"Sure, man. What's on your mind?"

Kyle was uncomfortable speaking in public. "Well, there's this girl that I'm friends with. We always hang out together in a group at the beach and around town. I want to ask her on a date, but I don't want to risk killing our friendship if it gets weird. I'm not sure if she likes me in that way. Some high school jocks have already asked her out, but she turned them down. I love her, but she's like a total ten, and I'm like a four on a good day. Since you're also a four kind of guy, can you tell me how you got Jane? Wait, that didn't come out right! You're way better than a four! I don't know how to rate guys; I'm not into guys!" Kyle's face turned crimson as laughter filled the room.

Don smiled and leaned back in the chair. "No offense taken, man. I can't argue with your ranking. I work hard to maintain my averageness. And yes, I think Jane is a ten too. But that's all just looks, man. It's the wrapper. I dig Jane's looks, but I love who Jane is. I first fell in "like" with Jane, and love followed."

Kyle recovered from his faux pas and asked, "so what did you say to her? It must have been very convincing. What was your line?"

Don looked over at Jane. She smiled and winked, allowing him to discuss their personal life publicly.

"Okay, the first thing to know is that there wasn't a line. Jane and I started as friends in school too, man. We were just like you and your lady. We hung out together all the time. We were inseparable. Most everyone thought we were a couple, and I guess, in a way, we were. But we weren't romantic, not yet anyway.

Now, her being hot attracted many boys that seriously wanted into her pants. Don't get me wrong, I wanted that too, but there was the usual teenage fear of what to do. What if I frightened her off? She was my best friend, and I didn't think I could risk losing her by making a play for her. Sound familiar?"

Kyle looked at Jane. "Is that true?"

Jane nodded. "Every word of it."

Kyle felt a connection. These people understood his situation. "So, what happened next?"

"I could always make Jane laugh. It just came naturally in our relationship. One silly night she said that she found me funny and that girls love guys that can make them laugh. I wasn't ready to sign up for that theory since I couldn't imagine that circus clowns get laid a lot. I also didn't think she was referring to me when she said girls love guys that make them laugh. I totally missed the clue."

Don leaned forward in the chair. "Well, then came an end-of-summer trip to the Cape. It was a beautiful day at Chapin Beach in Dennis. I couldn't take my eyes off Jane in her bikini. She looked like a woman, not a schoolgirl about to start her senior year in high school. She had filled out in all the right places over the past year, and it scared the shit out of me, man.

We walked the beach and talked for hours. Most of the guys at school have no idea how smart Jane is. I'm talking about Honor Society smart. I was proud to have such an intelligent and gorgeous girlfriend. On the way back from spending the day on the beach and exploring the dunes, we stopped for pizza and a shared beer at Joe's bar. I ordered the pizza, and Jane ordered the beer. They didn't check her license, so we got away with it.

As we were leaving the bar, Jane asked me if we could stop at a no-name motel mid-Cape. I nervously counted the cash in my pocket, and we had enough to pay for a room. Anyway, the sun was starting to set when I checked us in. It was a down-market establishment but within my financial situation. I remember the musty smell of a closed-up room on a warm, humid day on the Cape when I opened the door.

Jane slowly looked around the room; her eyes settled on the king-size bed. She trembled as she started to unbutton her shirt. I then realized that she was more nervous than I was. My heart sank, man. I put on my best smile and told her that we didn't have to do this, but she shook her head no and said that she wanted to; she had to. I asked her why, and she said she didn't want to lose me to another girl who would sleep with me. I didn't see that coming because there weren't other girls lining up to do that, and we hadn't gotten much past second base.

I took Jane in my arms and held her. I told her that we would take it at her pace. She wasn't ready. The weight of the world was off her shoulders. She then kissed me as I had never been kissed before. She asked how do we get comfortable enough to be intimate. I said that we need to learn each other on a new level. We talked about everything, no secrets. She asked if she could see my body. Soon we were both naked and studying each other. We touched and talked for a couple of hours. I have to tell you that conversation greatly improved my understanding of the female anatomy. All week long, random questions would pop up for both of us. Finally, when we talked the topic out, Jane declared that she was ready to try. That was an understatement. The following Friday night, we made love and still do regularly. We are connected for life in that way, man."

Kyle looked over at Jane. "Is that true?"

Jane smiled. "Absolutely. With all the talking, we got to know each other deeper. He didn't rush me. There was no pressure from him. He put me first. Our mutual trust in each other grew. I fell deeper in love with Don. He was my first and my only. We still talk…and never run out of things to say."

Kyle looked a bit puzzled. "You still talk about sex? So what's left to talk about?"

Before Don could reply, Jane spoke up. "Of course, we still talk about sex and everything else in our lives. If you want to get to that place with your mate, you have to love and trust each other. Words are the foundation of that. I use words if I want Don to do something at work, around the house, or in bed. Feed the soul with words and the body with passion.

Look, you're young and just getting started. You learn, love, and respect that girl, and don't rush her; she may be your Jane! And as to Don being a four, maybe he isn't movie-star handsome, but he is cute as hell all day long and into the night! He is my favorite human being!"

Kyle thanked Jane and Don for their honest answers.

A-Wall commented to himself as he live-streamed Kyle sitting down. "I hope there's an Academy Award classification for shows like this!"

Chapter 22 - The bartender is a cultural leader
April 26th 1:53 p.m.

Smyth looked up as Paul Caruso set a file folder on his desk. "I met with the marketing team, and we are up 16% on viewership and 9% on donations. However, we are significantly behind the revenue plan, and if we want to be in the top fifty megachurches in the country, we have a hell of a lot of ground to make up. Are you sure you want to stick with your *From Humble Beginnings* pitch? The marketing team can test other phrases to see if they score higher. What do you think?"

As he thought, Smyth tapped the large ring on his right hand on the desk. He liked that sound. It made the statement that he was in charge. And when he stopped, there was anticipation. "I was scanning YouTube for preaching material and came across this guy that talked about starting with nothing and becoming balls to the wall successful. So I wrote it down."

Smyth flipped through several pages in his notebook. "Got it...*Bible verse Job 8:7... Your beginnings will seem humble, so prosperous will your future be*. That's what I'll sell. Everyone can be wealthy if they believe in the message and give. I am the shining example of that prosperity. I started with nothing in that shitty little church, and look where I am today!"

Caruso slowly nodded. "I do have to admit, George, that is a pretty good angle. But do you think that's our strongest play?"

Smyth laughed. "Of course! Everyone holds out hope for that easy win. Hitting the lotto, or some unknown rich relative dies, leaving them a fortune. That is the true American dream – easy money and lots of it! I tell you, Paul, *From Humble Beginnings,* plays well. People buy that kind of positive bullshit. And not just the unsophisticated ones; many well-educated people will be happy to buy our Humble Beginnings story. Hell, they elected Obama president years back on his pitch about hope. He sold them hope! Prosperity is hope! Anyway, let's run with the From Humble Beginnings pitch which brings us back to the little church building. Where are we on that?"

Caruso exhaled. "We are no closer to getting the building. Actually, it's getting worse. That bartender is getting more press than we are, and we buy ad space in the religion news feeds every week." Caruso hands Smyth an iPad. "Check out page one of the religion section of the Boston Globe."

Smyth's eyes narrowed as he stared at the picture of Don standing in front of Sailers Church. He studied the favorable article on the bartender and his odd flock, reading it three times.

Smyth set the iPad on his desk. Caruso watched as he worked up a head of steam. "How does someone that is not a religious leader get on page one of the religion section? The article says the bartender is a cultural leader. So what the fuck is a cultural leader? And why aren't we on page one, Paul? He's a nobody!"

Caruso cleared his throat. "Somehow, he has become a media sensation. Bay State Sunday Morning did a live broadcast segment from Sailers Church yesterday, and I hear that the late-night comedy shows want to book him as a guest. This thing is getting bigger, making getting that church building all the harder."

Smyth slowly picked up the iPad again. "And let's not forget that rich little old lady that is spending her Sundays with the bartender now and not with us. We have to step up our game, Paul. Enough fucking around. I want that pissy little church!" Find Jim Reed; we need to talk.

Chapter 23 - Beaver in the pond
May 1st 1:16 p.m.

Red picked up the phone and cradled it on her shoulder while mixing a drink. "Aloha, Don's Tiki Cocktails & Lounge, exotic drinks for exotic people." Red listened for a moment. "I sure will, and remember to turn before you burn." Red hung up the phone and relayed the message.

"Jerry, Olivia said she found a prime spot on the south end of the beach. She has your cell phone and said to remember to get the condiments."

Jerry nodded. "Thanks, Red. I'm on it!" He took a sip of his Pain Killer.

Jerry had become a regular at the bar since he started dating Olivia two months ago. He was aware of his growing fondness for tiki music, exploring the flavors of more exotic cocktails, new foods, and friendships with people he thought he had little in common. He was especially fascinated with Olivia's desire to own a vintage car and was grateful that Jane and Don were schooling her on the ins and outs of owning and driving such a vehicle.

Jerry took another sip of his cocktail and checked his watch. Five more minutes, and he had to check on his to-go food order. He knew Olivia would be starving. She always was a couple of hours after morning sex. It was nearly noon by the time they finally left Jerry's house. Saturday afternoon on the beach sounded wonderful to both of them on this warm and sunny mid-spring day.

He looked around the bar. Mostly regulars at their usual tables or bar stools. PP was at the end of the bar checking out Red. John and Brad were in deep discussion in one of the booths. A-Wall was talking with Benny the bear, a large muscular man sporting a baseball hat with a bear logo and the inscription Provincetown on it. A.J. and Millie were at her favorite table without the other D.A.R. ladies. A budding romance, perhaps? Several other folks he recognized from the bar or the Sunday morning Happening were scattered around the room. As he started to look at his watch for a time check, he paused on a vaguely familiar face but somehow was out of place. He knew that face but from where? It bothered Jerry for a moment, but he had to pick up lunch and get to the beach.

Jerry settled up with Red, said goodbye to Jane and Don, and walked into the Shanty to pick up lunch. Jerry handed his credit card to Darlene as his food order was being bagged. He remembered the condiments needed for cheeseburgers and fries. Mustard, mayo, and catsup should… Jerry froze mid-thought. "Oh shit – Darlene, I'll be right back." Jerry quietly walked back into the bar and casually asked Jane to have Don come over.

"Did you forget to settle up with Red or something, man?"

"Don't look now, but I'm pretty sure the guy in the blue shirt in the corner booth is from the State Alcoholic Beverages Control Commission. After graduating from law school, I worked on liquor license prosecution cases. It could be nothing, but I think you may be about to have an underage decoy try to be served. He likes to use out-of-state licenses in his sting since they are harder for most bartenders to validate."

"Thanks for the heads up, man. We are pretty good at sifting out the underagers, but this one may be a pro. I'll spread the word to Jane and Red." Jerry nodded and turned to see Darlene in the doorway with his credit card and a bag of food.

A few minutes after Jerry left, a young woman entered and sat on the right side of the bar. Red called out to Don and Jane, "did you see the beaver in the pond this morning?" That was Red's code phrase for a suspected underage female at the bar. Both answered yes.

Jane looked at Don and grinned. "Let's see if she is real. Jane walked over to wait on the woman. From her appearance, she looked to be in her mid-twenties.

"Welcome to Don's Tiki Cocktails & Lounge. What can I get you?"

The young woman exuded confidence. "I'll have a Guinness."

Jane smiled. "What's your name, sweetie?"

"What? Oh, Samantha. But my friends call me Sam or Sammy."

"I'm sorry, Samantha, but we serve several craft beers, wine, and hand-crafted cocktails here. You'll have to go a couple of blocks up the road to McCabe's Irish Pub for a Guinness. They're equipped and trained to pour you that perfect pint of ebony nectar."

Samantha's confidence was shaken. "Oh, I'll have any beer, I guess."

"Any beer it is, but first, let's discuss your age."

"Of course, I have my license right here." Samantha was holding the New York driver's license in her hand. Jane took it, placed it face down on the bar without looking at it, and put her right hand over it.

She locked eyes with Samantha. "What brings you to Brite Rock, Samantha?"

"Well… I…um. Shopping and drinking."

Jane held eye contact. "Shopping and drinking. I see. What's your full name, Samantha?"

"It's Samantha Davis."

Jane still held eye contact. "Your name is Samantha Davis? Your friends call you Sammy? So you're Sammy Davis?"

Samantha was flustered. "Yes, that's my name; I mean nickname. May I have my…"

How do you spell your name, Samantha?"

"The usual way. Why do you ask?"

"Have you ever noticed the typo on your license, Samantha?"

"No, it's… I mean, yes, but… I don't feel good." The young woman pushed Jane's hand aside and grabbed the license. Then, she hastily exited the bar. A moment later, the man in the corner went as well.

Red laughed as Don walked over and hugged Jane. "Babe, was her name really Sammy Davis, and was there a typo on her license?"

Jane shrugged her shoulders. "Maybe."

"And is there a reason she suddenly didn't feel good?"

"She could feel her lies were failing, and her anxiety made her want to throw up. She won't come back."

Don nodded. "Well, that was amusing, but we need to be extra sharp for a while. I'll make a few calls to the other bars in the area so they don't get stung.

Chapter 24 - I have your back; may I have your heart
May 1st 1:47 p.m. ~ Continued

Olivia ate the last bite of the cheeseburger and washed it down with a sip of Mai Tai. It was against the law to drink alcohol openly on Brite Rock Beach. The key word in Olivia's mind was *openly*. She made the Mai Tais at home and put them in used sports energy drink bottles. From looking at it, it was impossible to tell that it wasn't an authentic flavored energy drink. She also felt she was getting away with something by providing beach cocktails to her town lawyer boyfriend.

Jerry took a sip of Olivia's homemade mai tai. "You are getting the recipe down, babe. This is good! Will you be serving these in prison when we get arrested? My defense is that I had no idea that you spiked my sports drink with alcohol. Your defense, well, it doesn't look good for you, now, does it?"

Olivia laughed. "Oh sure, throw the black girl under the bus for corrupting the white town lawyer. Of course, you can't be with a convicted felon after I get out, which means what we did in bed this morning was the last time you'll be getting any of this goodness!"

Olivia thought for a moment. "Am I the first black girl you have dated, or is this your thing?"

Jerry laughed at the question. "Can you clarify? Does dating you make it a thing?"

"Jerry, I'm serious!"

"Okay, you are the first and only. And this isn't my thing, as you put it. You started this when you offered me a taste of your drink when I didn't know what to order when we first met. Plying me with alcohol before we were properly introduced. My mother warned me about fast women."

Olivia laughed. "Oh, now you're just being a little shit!"

No, Liv, it's true. Your act of kindness broke the ice, and I was quickly enamored by your engaging conversation, intellect, and the coolness factor of you and the tiki scene that I knew nothing about."

"So, it is my intellect and being into the tiki scene that caught your interest? Not my ass when I stretched across the bar to get you a straw? You know that was for you, right?" Olivia looked over the top of her sunglasses to make a point.

Jerry was caught off-guard. "No, I didn't think…so you were interested in me? I thought I was chasing you!"

Olivia pushed her sunglasses back up. "Men never seem to figure that out. We chase you until you catch us. You must be some kind of lawyer to get outsmarted by little ol' me."

"Well, we guys can be challenged when it comes to the object of our affection. So when I think of my love for you, I guess I…."

Olivia nearly choked on her sip of Mai Tai… "Wait, did you just say my love for you?"

"Well, yes, I guess I did! I like talking with you. I learn from you. I deeply care for you. You keep me on my toes. The sex is fantastic. I like holding you as we fall asleep at night. I think of you a hundred times a day. Cooking together and making breakfast on Sunday morning warms my heart. The list goes on. So, that feels like love to me. But if that isn't what you want, please don't run away. I'm pretty confident I am falling in love with you, and I couldn't take that pain."

Olivia studied Jerry's face. "You know love for me is a serious business. And me being black and you being white will be an issue for some people on both sides of the color line, right? So this won't be easy at times."

Jerry took Olivia's hand and looked into her eyes. "Liv, I know there will be people that will take issue with our relationship. I also know I'm a white guy who knows nothing about being black or being a woman, especially a black woman. There's a lot I don't know, but I….

Olivia shook her head. "Jerry, you can never truly know what it is like to be me, and I get that. I think the best we can hope for is for you to understand and support me when things happen, and they do every day. For example, the other morning at the donut shop, I paid in cash, and the owner, Kevin, put my change on the counter in front of me. He handed the change to every patron before me but not me. He didn't want to touch my hand. It's been that way since I started going there when I was seven. I like Kevin and accept him as he is. But you need to know I can't have you react when you see those things happen to me. It's just the way life is for us. You have to be good with that for this to work long-term.

And it would help if you read Carol Taylor's Little Black Book. It's a guide for black males growing up in America. My dad said it applies to me too. It's part of *the talk* every black parent should have with their child on how to survive in the world. The book will help you understand why I do or don't respond in specific circumstances."

Jerry didn't hesitate. "I accept those challenges. I'm not saying I won't unintentionally fuck things up once in a while, but I learn from my mistakes, and it won't happen more than once. And I would love to talk with your parents so I know their perspective on what's out there. Whatever it is, we will deal with it all. The good and the not-so-good. Liv, I would like you to be my official girlfriend."

Olivia laughed. "Your official girlfriend… well, since it's official, I should probably consult my lawyer before answering. You know, the party of the first part and all that legal babble and fine print."

Jerry feigned desperation. "Come on, say yes. I have your back; may I have your heart?"

"Wow, that's a good closing argument, counselor." Olivia slowly started nodding her head yes. "Thank you for asking for my heart. I trust you will be gentle and attentive to it. And I'm glad that I'm not in this love thing alone. I love you, Jerry."

"Then it's official, you are my girlfriend, and we are in love. You gave me your heart. And if you play your cards right, someday, I just may be asking you for your hand. That's my plan. To acquire you one part at a time."

Olivia smiled, kissed Jerry, and handed him the sunblock. "You are a goofy bastard at times. That's one of your more adorable traits. Now, be helpful, and please do my back and legs. Slather it on heavy."

Jerry poured sunblock on Olivia's back and legs and worked it in, taking care to get it under the lines of her bikini. "Since we are on the topic of you being black, I have a question. Do dark-skinned people get sunburns?"

Olivia looked up at him. "I assume you are being serious, so I will answer the question. Yes, most dark-skinned people can get sunburn. I think the darker the skin, the longer it takes. One of my cousins is very dark and never uses sunblock. She really should. Although less common for people of color, we can get skin cancer, and the survival rate isn't great for us. It was skin cancer that killed Reggae great Bob Marley. So, being lighter-skinned, I use a strong sunblock. I turn a bit darker than I am in the winter, and that's fine. But being judged for my skin tone, even by black people, is so weird. Colorism is another thing that you will need to come up to speed on."

Jerry's brow was wrinkled in thought. "So, some in the black community judge you by your skin color, how dark or light you are?"

Olivia made that; *how can you not know this* face? "Yes, of course. We live in a super judgy world. Everybody gets judged for everything. I get judged on my lighter skin tone, petite nose, thin body and small ass, natural hair, love of tiki music, and hot rods. I'm sure I can add a successful white lawyer boyfriend to the list. I even got called out at the church this week, although I still can't figure that out. It could have just been a hater."

Jerry was perplexed. "I don't recall anything negative at the Happening on Sunday!"

Olivia shook her head. "No, it wasn't at the Happening. It was at the big new church on Tuesday. I was there to help the techs balance the sound system my team installed using our new products. It's a killer system. Great use of our arrays with background and foreground, and…sorry, I just nerded out. Anyway, the guy sitting in the back by the door at the Happening on Sunday was there. He approached me all cop-like and asked what I was doing there. I had to show my company ID to get him to calm down and back off. I was just about done, so I finished and left. I gotta tell you, babe, he clearly didn't want me there."

"Liv, could it have been a racial or a woman thing?"

Olivia thought for a moment. "That's the weird part; it didn't feel like either. It didn't feel personal. Have you ever been dumped on for something someone else did, and they know it wasn't you but dumped anyway? It felt like that, a by-association thing. But who and why? I don't know; maybe it was a racial or a woman thing after all."

"It may not be who; it may be what." Jerry took Olivia into his confidence and told her about Pastor Smyth making a play to get Don's Sailers Church building. "He wants to move it next to his new church for some reason."

"That's it!" Olivia had figured it out. "We needed to test all the audio sources, so their media guys played a video clip for us. It opened with an illustration of Sailers Church and had this story about Smyth and how he got his start there. Something about humble beginnings, I think. I was busy analyzing the sound quality and ignored the infomercial message. But Smyth did come off as charismatic in the propaganda piece. I do have to give him that."

Jerry smiled. "It's a marketing prop! That's why he wants it so badly. It's his story, his legacy. It must piss him off that Don has the building and won't sell it to him."

Olivia nodded. "He's also probably wicked pissed about Don getting all the media attention too!"

Chapter 25 - What's this, trouble in paradise
May 2nd 9:48 a.m.

It was a clear and warm Sunday morning. Jane woke to the smells of springtime, the ocean, and the first flowers on a nearby Linden tree drifting through the window. She was a bit cranky, typical for her when she is hungry and needs morning coffee but doesn't want to get out of bed.

She could hear Don in the shower and knew she needed to get up. But instead, she sprawled out, taking up as much of the bed as possible. A good morning stretch didn't improve her disposition, nor would the quarter-mile walk to the Shanty to get breakfast. Jane missed the convenience of having the Shanty just a few steps away when they lived in the apartment above the bar. But she wouldn't trade their new home for that convenience.

Jane decided that she needed to hurry things along, so she joined Don in the shower, nudging him out of the way. "I'm hungry, babe, so let's get a move on. It's my turn to shower."

Don offered to wash Jane's back, which she enjoyed, along with a good back scratch.

"Don, babe, that's not my back, and I can reach that to wash it. Now go get dressed before I bite you. I'm starving!"

Jane finished her quick shower while Don went through the daily ritual of picking out his aloha shirt. Pin-up girls in grass skirts and tiki totems on a black shirt had the right feel for this Sunday. Jane threw on underwear, jean shorts, an aloha shirt, and sandals and headed for the door. "Let's go, Don!"

The town was busy with tourists and locals as they made their way down the picturesque Main Street. Don greeted everyone they passed. Occasionally he would pause for a quick chat, a trait that Jane could live without at the moment.

"Hey, Mayor Aloha, come on! I'm not waiting for you!" Jane kept walking.

Don excused himself from the conversation with Been Dead Billy and quickened his pace to catch up to Jane. She knew he was a social creature that was easily dragged into conversations. She swears he could talk a hungry dog off of a meat wagon.

As they rounded the corner onto Brite's Jetty Road, Jane moaned as she spotted a long line waiting to get into the Shanty. Waitress Stephanie was taking names at the door for the list to be seated.

Stephanie glanced at her list when Don and Jane arrived. She smiled as she motioned them to come forward. "Where did you wander off to? I called your name a while ago." Stephanie moved Don and Jane past the line of waiting customers and seated them.

Jane smiled. "Thank you, Stephanie. Your kindness will be rewarded."

Don slid into a booth and ordered iced coffee for the both of them as Darlene brought Jane a copy of the Sunday Boston Globe newspaper. Jane loved the Sunday Globe, but since the Happening started, she hadn't had time to read it cover to cover.

"Shall I get you the usual?" Darlene held her pen over the order pad, waiting for an answer.

Jane looked at the pastry counter. "Yes, for Don, but I want one of those gigantic cinnamon rolls. They smell incredible and are the size of a baby's head. I may eat two." Jane rubbed her hands together in anticipation.

Darlene paused. "Two? Aren't you the least bit concerned about your figure?"

Jane smiled. "Nope, I've lost 6 pounds running around that big house. My jeans are getting too loose. My ass dimples have dimples! Bring on the tasty!"

Darlene wrote down the order. "Okay, one Hawaiian Loco Moco plate, light on the gravy, for Don and one straight to your ass cinnamon roll for Jane. Anything else?"

"Yes, two large, iced coffees to go when we leave and another cinnamon roll to travel. I'll also have a large OJ, and Don will have a large POG juice with breakfast."

"Got it! Drinks will be right over, but food will take a few minutes. The kitchen is slammed this morning, partly due to you two. Sunday's sure are busier now!"

Don couldn't resist commenting. "You are right, Darlene; all of this is Jane's fault."

Jane stopped pulling the sections of the newspaper apart. "Wait, what? What did I do?"

"You told me to meet the two ladies at the little church building and talk to them. It couldn't hurt, you said. Just chat with them, and that will be the end of it, you said. Now, look at where we are. Brite Rock is crowded. The restaurants and bars are overrun with your groupies. And we don't get to sleep in on Sunday mornings anymore. Your fault!" Don sat back and smiled.

Jane gave Don her mock death stare. "I am so going to hurt you when I am awake, over-caffeinated, and jacked up on sugar."

"What's this, trouble in paradise?"

Don and Jane looked up to see Pastor Smyth standing at their table. He had the same phony smile you see in his church advertisements.

"You know, we have couples counseling weekly at our new Brite Rock Cathedral by the Sea. It looks like your relationship could use a tune-up. Perhaps the stress of all this attention and the burden of owning Sailers Church is taking its toll. Deacon Reed would be happy to sign you up for counseling." Smyth was baiting Don.

"Hey, wanker, do you fancy another go-round?" John Lennon approached Smyth. She was in an exceptionally cocky mood. Brad followed closely behind for moral support.

Reed stepped in front of Smyth to protect him. "You need to back off!"

"I have no quarrel with you, tosser. It's the cheeky vicar that's bothering me friends. He needs to bugger off."

Smyth squared off with John. "Listen, freak show; I'm ready for you this time, so take your best shot. Just be ready for.."

"Motherfucker!" Brad looked around the room, knowing that one was extra loud. "No, I meant to say it this time!" The room erupted in laughter. Brad had inadvertently defused what was about to be a brawl between John and Smyth.

That gave Darlene a moment to wedge herself between the two of them. "Okay, boys, that's enough. Take it outside if you want to continue acting juvenile. And who starts a bar fight in a restaurant anyway? Well?" Awkward silence. Reed starts to point at John but thinks better of it and lowers his arm.

Smyth smiles and takes Darlene's hand. "You are so right, and I apologize for these young people and their crude behavior. That kind of talk, particularly on a Sunday, is just appalling. Let's put all this behind us so I can thank you for another wonderful breakfast. And your coffee puts the other local establishments in town to shame."

Smyth quickly glances at his watch. "Oh, look at the time. I've got to get to my church for service, but I will return soon to try one of those incredible cinnamon rolls Ms. Gilman is raving about." Smyth gently squeezes Darlene's hand. "Now, you take care and have a blessed day!"

Darlene slowly pulled her hand back. "I will."

Smyth glanced down at Don and Jane. "You two have a blessed day as well."

"Yeah, you too, man. Have one of those days." As Smyth and Reed left, Don sipped his iced coffee and looked up at a puzzled Darlene.

She sighed. "Smyth says the right words, but he comes across as insincere. I can see why people want to punch that man." She started to turn to walk back to the kitchen when a young woman immediately interrupted them to take a picture.

"It's you! Oh, just a quick photo op. I am such a huge fan. You two sit there." She directs John and Brad to join Don and Jane in the booth. She hands Darlene her phone and asks her to take the picture as she squeezes in next to Jane. "Okay, everyone, look at the waitress and smile. Say sleaze!" She immediately took the phone back from Darlene. Then, thrilled with her picture, she hurried back to her table to show her friends.

Darlene shook her head. "This is quickly becoming a peculiar day."

John stands and announces his departure. "Sorry, mates, but I've got to visit the loo. It feels like I waited a bit too long; I think I'm crowning. Ah, it could be touching fabric. No time to dawdle." John hastily exited the Shanty. Brad spotted A.J. sitting alone at another table and excused himself to join him.

Jane sighed. "Darlene is right. There's a seriously weird vibe happening this morning!" Before Don could comment, Jerry and Olivia slid into their booth and sat down.

Jerry spoke in a hushed tone. "Liv and I were talking, and we think we figured out Pastor Smyth's angle regarding your Sailers Church building. It's where he started preaching, and he sees that as the keystone to his marketing pitch. So, Liv, tell them what you saw."

Olivia leaned in. "I was working on the sound system at Smyth's big ass church, and they played a video promo to test the system. The video showed your church building and a story about how he started small but is now leading his big new shiny church. The video drove the message of his humble beginnings hard. It was heavy on him and light on religion, at least the type of church I grew up in."

Don sat back and thought for a moment. "Well, he did start at the little church. And I understand where it would make a cool marketing prop for him, but it's not for sale, man. So why won't he take no for an answer?"

Jerry sighed. "I don't know. His massive ego, maybe? I have seen people go the extra mile to screw themselves over to prove a point or for some other self-aggrandization. I will be surprised if Smyth backs away from this."

Don nodded in agreement as Jane picked up her fork in anticipation as Darlene served them their food. "Here you go, enjoy! I'll have your to-go order ready with the check. Oh, and Sarah from McCabe's Pub said if I saw you thank you for the warning regarding a beaver in a pond. She said you would know what that meant. I don't want to know!"

Chapter 26 - He and that chair belong together
May 9th 9:51 a.m.

Jane was chattering away as she and Don walked back home to the little church building for The Happening. Don had to quicken his pace to keep up with her. He wasn't sure if an overdose of caffeine and sugar had her walking fast or if she had to pee. She did have the habit of waiting until the last moment to go. He considered that an example of poor pee management by Jane. Jane quickly handed Don her coffee cup when they arrived home and bolted for the house.

Don carefully balanced Jane's coffee cup on top of his as he awkwardly opened the back door of the little church building and entered. He was surprised to find the room full since it was over an hour before the scheduled Happening start time.

An easy-listening blend of tiki and Hawaiian music played through a new sound system that A-Wall and Olivia put together that serves both inside and outside the building. A-Wall felt it would improve the overall experience of the live-streamed "Church of Don Happening Hour" show. The Happening Hour had over 352,000 live and replayed views last week.

There was a spontaneous round of applause for Don when he walked across the stage. He smiled and went to set his coffee by his old aluminum beach chair, only to find a new high-end leather chair in its place.

Don looked around, perplexed and a bit upset. "Does anyone know where my aluminum chair is? That's like a part of my thing, man! I can't do this without it."

A well-dressed middle-aged man quickly walked up and introduced himself. "Hi, Don. I'm Andy Milner from Milner's Fine Furnishings in Boston. I'm a big fan and thought you would enjoy this. It's a Stickley mission-style chair made of natural oak and rich leather. It's yours!"

Don slowly smiled. "Thanks for the kind gesture, man. This is a pretty awesome chair, and I appreciate it, but it's just that the old aluminum beach chair and I are comfortable with each other. It's a vibe thing, man. We belong together. Now, while I dig the style and that new leather chair smell, I need to stick with what works for me. Can I get my aluminum chair back, man?"

Andy was embarrassed. "Of course, and I'm sorry. I should have asked first. And I see what you mean about the aluminum chair. I'll be right back." Andy passed Jane as he headed out the back door to his van. A round of applause and a few playful whistles greeted Jane as she stepped onto the stage. She smiled and curtseyed to acknowledge her fans. When Andy returned with the aluminum beach chair, Don was telling Jane about the chair incident.

"Sorry again, Don. I didn't even consider that this was part of your…" Andy paused, not sure what to call it. "Identity! That's the word that I was looking for. This aluminum beach chair is part of your identity."

Don smiled as Andy handed him his vintage aluminum beach chair. "You know, it's a survivor, man. It could have been tossed out many times over the years, yet here it is. I honor that longevity, man. Now, the new chair that you brought is very nice. I can tell by how Jane is staring at it and stroking the leather that she likes it. Can I buy it from you?"

"No, but I would like to give it to Jane if she wants it. It's a gift for both of you." Jane didn't hesitate; she graciously accepted the offer and, with Andy's help, moved the chair far over to the right side of the stage, her chosen spot to heckle Don and interact with the people in the room.

Jane settled into the chair, her fingers again stroking the leather. "This feels so elegant!"

Andy smiled. "This chair suits you, Jane. It speaks to your importance and prestige. You look good sitting in it. Well, you always look good; the chair doesn't…you know what I mean." Andy blushed a little.

Jane smiled. "I do know what you mean, and thank you. So, Andy, this chair is pretty old-school looking."

Andy told her about Stickley and his hand in the American arts and crafts design movement in the early 1900s. "Stickley's designs reflected his ideals of simplicity, honesty in construction, and truth to materials. Those ideals reminded me of Don as I've watched him online, so I brought this chair. I didn't think he would see those same values in the old aluminum beach chair, but he does, and he's right! He is so in tune with his surroundings."

Jane agreed. "That's Don; he sees the value and history in things. Somebody made that aluminum beach chair in an old factory. Somebody owned it and used it. When the leg was damaged, they didn't throw it away; they patched it with a broom handle and tape. And that old chair was here when Don needed a place to sit. He meant it when he said he and that chair belong together. The same could be said about his old hot rod Jenny, the bar, and this building. You know, over a hundred years ago, Don's family built this little church as a gathering place for the community. Now it's a gathering place for the wonderful universe of people surrounding us."

Andy was fascinated. "Is that why Don does these Happenings? Is it to continue the family legacy to keep these community gatherings?"

Jane thought for a moment. "No, it's not a legacy thing, at least not on purpose. This all started when someone walked into this building and needed help. They needed to talk out a situation. Don listened. Sometimes that's all people need, just to be heard. He gave a little bartender advice, and this Happening thing grew from that moment of kindness. He is a genuinely kind man."

Andy glanced over at Don. "Wow, I didn't know that. I'm even more impressed and now clearly see my error with the chair."

Jane touched Andy's arm. "Oh, this chair is in no way a mistake, Andy. I am very grateful to you for your kind gift. You know, men so often miss the point about kindness. Women like that quality in a huge way. Your girlfriend or wife is a lucky gal." Jane stood and gave Andy a big hug.

Andy's smile faded. "I'm single, a…widower actually."

Jane was stunned. "Oh Andy, I'm so sorry. I shouldn't have…."

"It's okay, Jane. It's been almost two years since my wife Rebecca died of cancer. My son says enough time has passed, and I need to take off the ring and get back in the game. I think I may be ready to try. I'm thinking of signing up for one of those dating websites. You know, just to see what happens."

Jane studied Andy for a moment. "What are you doing after the Happening today? Are you available for lunch? There's someone I would like to introduce you to."

"Yes, I'm free all day. Lunch sounds good!"

Jane hugged Andy again. "Excellent, we'll do lunch after the Happening."

Chapter 27 - Make it look like it was an accident
May 9th 11:01 a.m. ~ Continued

There wasn't an empty seat. Smyth smiled as he looked out across a full house. The church band, the Brite Rock Revivers, began softly playing *Here Because of Him,* one of their rock originals. Then, the worship team fanned out with offering plates for cash, checks, and mobile payment devices for debit cards, credit cards, and digital payment contributions.

Smyth stood at the front of the stage. His white suit appeared to glow in the multiple spotlight beams. In a gentle parental tone, he addressed the parishioners. "I've been talking for almost an hour now, and I want to leave you with one last thought. In Corinthians, it says whoever sows sparingly will reap sparingly, and whoever sows generously will reap generously. Now, I don't just believe that... I live that! Yes, I tithe too! You see, I give my tithe and offering as an act of honor, gratefulness, and love. I put the Lord first in my life, and I believe I have seen an abundant return. I know that to be true, for, from my humble beginnings, I stand here today, prosperous in heart and soul, doing the Lord's work. I am... here because of him!" On cue, the band takes over and rocks out as Smyth leaves the stage amid a light show, loud music, and the lyrics " Here Because of Him " fill what now feels like a rock festival venue.

Paul Caruso hands Smyth a towel and a chilled bottle of Perrier water as he exits backstage. They start to walk to Smyth's office. A production assistant stops him and removes his microphone and transmitter. They continue down the hall.

"There, now it's safe to talk. The last thing I need is to be caught on mic saying I don't give money to the church; I take it. Or commenting on Billy Bob Mecker's hot wife, Beverly. She sits in the front row in a short skirt with her legs wide open. It's very distracting. Ask Jim to look into seating them a row or two back." Smyth took a long drink from the Perrier bottle.

"I'll ask Jim to speak with Steve from the worship team. I'm sure we can seat her elsewhere, although they typically tithe $200 per week and $1,000 at Easter and Christmas." Caruso waited for a response from Smyth.

"All good points Paul. Okay, leave them where they are. I'll try to ignore her…offering. Now, what's the status of the trademark approval on the band's name? And where are we on the song copyrights as well?" Smyth settled into his chair behind his desk.

"The lawyer said the review went well with the Patent and Trademark Office. He expects to have approval for the Trademark in a few months. We have completed all negotiations with the band, and we did well. They agreed that for all recorded music and use license revenue, you and I would get 30%, the band would get 45%, the church would get 15%, and their manager would get 10%. They also agreed that for revenue from live performances, you and I would get 25%, the church would get 10%, and the band would get 65%, and they are responsible for any expenses not covered by the concert sponsor. We also have the rights to sell their music along with t-shirts and other merchandise sold through the church gift shop and website, royalty-free. So they pretty much agreed to all of our requests."

"You have done excellent work here, Paul! I think there is serious money to be made with that band. These people love them. We deserve that healthy cut since we put them in front of a large audience every week. I know I could always use a few extra dollars, and I'm sure your wife won't mind another trip to the Caribbean. What's her favorite island, Aruba?"

"Yes, and she would live there if she could. I have to tell you, she still looks good in a bikini, so it's a win for me too!"

Smyth laughed. "Good for you, Paul. You know, you should book a trip there soon. Take ten days and bill it to church travel. And don't go cheap; you two deserve it."

"Thanks, George; I will take you up on your offer. Maybe we'll go the first part of January after we're done with the big money-making Christmas and New Year's programs."

Smyth hands his white suit coat to Caruso. "Here, hang this up. You know, January is a good time to go. When you get back, we'll need to cook the books for the year-end accounting. We have to pay income tax, but the church gets..." His attention shifts to the footsteps outside his office door. Head down and reading numbers on his iPad, Jim nearly walked into the doorframe as he entered Smyth's office. Smyth giggled as he sat down in his chair.

"I tell you, George, this new collection app for reporting electronic donations from credit cards on the floor is great. Our electronic collections this morning are currently just over $16,000 and climbing. They are still working the floor. We will have a cash and credit card contribution count in a few hours. A rough guess for today's floor take would be in the $35,000 to $45,000 range, with an additional $110,000 to $120,000 coming in from broadcast and streaming viewers. Our total seven-day take last week was just over $156,000. That was a 4% growth over the previous week. So the numbers continue to trend up."

"That's great! The revenue looks good! What about marketing? Where do we stand on getting that little church building? Do we have any positive news there?" It was apparent to Caruso and Reed that Smyth's tone and body language had changed.

Caruso glanced at Reed before answering. "I'm afraid not. He has refused all offers, so we are at a standstill."

Smyth silently looked at Caruso. As he thought, he began tapping the ring on his right hand on his desk. The slow, methodical tapping sound was unsettling to Reed. It reminded him of the methodical drip, drip, drip of Chinese water torture that he saw in a movie as a kid. What may have been a moment felt like an eternity to him. Reed excused himself to check on something. Neither of them acknowledged his departure.

Smyth exhaled in frustration. "OK, we need to change our tactics if we are ever going to get that building. That serving a minor thing didn't pan out at all. We have uncovered nothing we can use against him. Not dodging taxes or illegal assembly… nothing! How the hell is he so squeaky clean? And nothing on her either. This is ridiculous. Even my grandmother was caught cheating at bingo. Who the hell cheats at bingo? Do you have any ideas at all, Paul?"

Caruso shrugged his shoulders. "Our only legit play is to offer more money, but that's not likely to motivate this guy."

Smyth dismissively waved off the idea. "No, this isn't a money thing. I think this is personal. He's like a kid with a toy. He probably doesn't really want it but doesn't want me to have it. How's that for a juvenile mentality? I hate that asshole!"

Caruso hesitated. "Well, maybe we start one of those rumors like he's into weird porn or something. Once a rumor like that gets started, it does a lot of damage before it gets quashed."

Smyth's face showed that he was not impressed with Caruso's suggestion. "No, we aren't pros at managing the social media rumor mill. Besides, that Asian guy who streams the bartender's Sunday shit show looks pretty sharp and could trace it back to us. That's too risky. And we've got nothing on the bartender for any kind of violation, building or otherwise. And to top it off, the town lawyer is now friends with the bartender. I also hear that the lawyer is screwing the black chick that put the sound system in our church. Those two are also sharp. We need to steer clear of all of them. Whatever we do needs to be off the books."

Smyth got up and walked around his office, noting how elegant walking on the thick wool carpeting felt. He paused to admire the craftsmanship of his office door. He always appreciated the deep sound of an expensive, elegant door being closed. That was the sound of money.

He settled into one of the designer chairs in front of his desk. Smyth never could remember the designer's name but thought the furniture looked good. He had earned this opulent lifestyle. Smyth focused, drew in a deep breath, and sighed. He motioned for Caruso to sit behind his desk, a momentary reversal of roles.

"Paul, think like you are running the show. Getting the Sailers Church building from the dipshit hippie bartender is going nowhere. He won't play nice, and we can't figure out how to get him to give up the building. We've made a couple of offers to buy it, but he won't budge. And now that he is popular with the media and is attracting a large number of idiots to town every week, the risk of…well…things need to be managed."

Caruso lit a cigar and thought for a moment. "So, here's my take on it. Our goal is to get the building and move it here to support your message of humble beginnings. We can up the offer again, but if he doesn't budge, and I don't think he will, we would have to find his pain point and press on it hard. As you pointed out, that's too risky as there are a lot of eyes on him now, and the town lawyer is his shadow. So, what if we build a replica of the Sailers Church building here? We can market that as your legacy."

Smyth shook his head. "No, it would just be a copy. The original would be right down the street. It would make me look weak."

Caruso admired his cigar for a moment before shifting his gaze back to Smyth. "Of course, that would look weak unless the original building no longer existed. There would be nothing standing to compare our replica to."

Smyth had not contemplated this scenario. He wasn't sure how he felt about the destruction of the Sailers Church building. "I don't know, Paul. To purposely destroy the very thing that we are trying to own…"

"George, do you think you need that specific building to support your humble beginnings pitch? You don't! It's just part of the narrative, and we control that. It's a facade. It's part of the con.

Try thinking of it like it's Texas justice. This prisoner goes before a judge. The judge asks him why he shot the mass murderer in the back, killing him. The prisoner replies *well, your honor, he needed killing!* The jury agrees and lets the prisoner go. The killing wasn't legal, but it was justifiable in the jury's mind. It solved the problem. Having your copy of the building means the original has to go. It's justifiable, but only to us."

Smyth weighed the options, and the pros started to outweigh the cons. He was coming around to the fact that something would need to happen to the Sailers Church building. He could justify that sacrifice and is willing to make it happen. Paul was right; it's justifiable.

"I like this plan, Paul. I want you to head up the research. Let's start gathering building plans, photos inside and out, the building materials they used, paint colors, stained glass window designs, and measurements. Everything needed to make an exact copy of that building. And we will call it the founding church. I don't want to hear it referred to as a copy or a replica. That cheapens it. We need to be public about our plan to build a representation of the founding church so we can do this in the open. The part about getting rid of the original church must be kept quiet. Only you and I need to know about that." Smyth watched Paul's face for a reaction.

Caruso tapped his cigar on the rim of Smyth's coffee mug. The falling ash hissed as it landed in the last sip of coffee. "I can do that for you, George. I only need an architect and contractor to help gather building information and someone to make the original building go away when we have what we need. I know a guy who can get rid of the building for a reasonable price. He's good, and he keeps his mouth shut."

Smyth leaned forward. "I agree that you, an architect, and a contractor should get all of the building information and get the cost numbers to Jim Reed, but I don't want someone I don't know involved with the delicate part. We have one shot at getting rid of that building. I know every inch of that place. So I'll do that myself, and don't tell Reed that the building is going away."

Caruso wasn't happy with that part of the plan. "I don't know, George. Plausible deniability is the best way to keep you out of this. Once we have everything we need, you should go away for a few days while we finish. Visit friends in Florida or maybe take a trip abroad. You can't be involved if you aren't here."

Smyth leaned in. "I get where you are going with this, but it looks too contrived if I am not here when things happen. And to repeat myself, you and I are the only ones in the know on this — no outside people. I can make this look like it was an accident. I will be the only one involved with eliminating that building, so there aren't any stories to coordinate. So, are you with me on this?"

Caruso snuffed out his cigar in the coffee mug. "Yeah, of course, I'm with you. We need to be careful, no fuck ups, nothing that can be used to point the finger at either of us."

Smyth smiled. "Paul, I will be shocked at the loss of the original Sailers Church building. My sermon the Sunday after will be about that very topic, how we often must lose some things to gain other things we desire. The town will be happy that we took on the burden of constructing our founding church, a historically accurate representation of the original Sailers Church building. And it will be done through our parishioners' generous hearts and hands. I'll devise a good generosity sermon to get the extra ask for this project. Let's also see who the tradespeople are in the flock. We can lean on them for discounts and free labor. If we do this right, we should be able to construct my founding church and make a nice profit on the side."

Chapter 28 - Something classy for my sassy chassis
May 9th 12:24 p.m. ~ Continued

The smell of bacon, burgers, and freshly baked cinnamon rolls hung in the air. It was a few minutes past noon when Don, Jane, and Andy entered the Shanty. The line to get in for Sunday brunch was long. Jane motioned to Darlene to come down to the end of the counter.

Darlene was happy to have a momentary diversion. The restaurant had been busy all morning. "So, how was the Happening? A good one?"

Jane had a mischievous grin. "Yeah, I think it went well — good group of people. Great conversation. And Andy here made my ass happy today!" Darlene's eyes darted to Andy and then to Don, back to Andy, and finally to Jane.

"Do I want to know about this happy-ass thing?" Darlene cocked her head slightly to the right, a trait that Don once compared to his cousin's perpetually confused Golden Retriever.

"Yes, you do. Darlene, this is Andy. He was super kind enough to gift me a very cool designer leather chair I now sit on during the Happening. No more sitting on that cold hard stage floor. I now have something classy for my sassy chassis!" Jane did a brief happy dance.

Darlene laughed as she reached to shake Andy's hand. "Andy, it's a pleasure to meet you. I'm Darlene Rogers, owner, and operator of this place. So, how do you know these two?"

"Well, my son was researching home tiki bars for our store and came across Don and the online Happening videos. I watched a couple of shows and found them to be refreshing. It wasn't like… it felt like a group of friends hanging out. There was something about it that I had to see for myself."

Darlene nodded. "Yes, that's how I see the Happening too! It's like an open house for people to meet and hang out. I would be there if I didn't have the brunch crunch on Sunday. So, about the tiki bar research, are you in the bar business like Don and Jane?"

Andy chuckled. "Oh no, I wouldn't know the first thing about running a bar. I own the Milner's Fine Furnishings business. It's seven stores throughout New England, with the headquarters in downtown Boston. One of our product lines features home bars, bar stools, and other pieces. My son would like to add a quality tiki or island-themed grouping. I plan on him taking over running the business someday soon, so bringing up a new product line is a good experience for him."

"Wow, that's impressive. Does your family live in Boston?"

"My son lives in Cambridge with his fiancé, Caitlín. She's a fiery Irish redhead from Glendalough. She is brilliant and top of her class at Harvard. She and my son work well together. I'm very fond of her. As for me, I have a place on Beacon Street in Boston. I just sold my summer home in Hyannis Port. The traffic to get there is horrible in the summer. I have to say, Brite Rock looks nice!"

Darlene agreed. "It is! You and your wife would find this town much easier than being on the Cape in the summertime. It gets busy, but not insanely so."

"Oh, it's just me, Darlene. My wife passed away a few years ago. That's another reason why I sold the Hyannis Port property. Too many memories there."

Darlene felt awkward. "I'm so sorry. I saw your wedding band; I shouldn't have assumed…"

Andy smiled. "It's okay; you didn't know. Besides, show me someone with the right words to say in situations like this, and I'll show you someone with a career in sympathy card writing."

Darlene smiled. There was kindness in how Andy took the awkwardness out of the conversation.

"While I love my wife… former wife, I've decided enough with living in the past. The ring needs to come off, and I must get on with my life.

But, as I said, I have a home in Boston and am ready to make new memories."

Jane spoke up. "Andy told me he is considering signing up for one of the dating websites. Didn't you say you were thinking about doing that too, Darlene?"

"Well, yes, I was wondering about those dating sites. People say they work, but I don't know if they're for me."

Andy agreed. "I'm not confident a computer can find a good match for me either. You know, I was thinking, I know we just met and all, but would you consider maybe going out with me sometime? Show me around Brite Rock, maybe?" Andy watched Darlene's eyes.

She blushed a little. "Yes, I believe I would, Andy."

Before Andy could reply, Jane took his hand. "Good, now follow me. There is one seat open at the other end of the counter. You sit there, and you and Darlene can discuss the date details. Oh, and you should order the Grand French Toast. There's a splash of Grand Marnier in it, and it's served with real maple syrup. When you are done here, stop by the bar. It's through that door right there."

Jane led Andy to the other end of the counter while Darlene and Don watched.

"So, Darlene, it looks like Jane is playing matchmaker again, and you are her latest... what would you call it? Client? Target? Victim?" Don was enjoying this.

"Jane might be onto something this time. You know, he's sort of cute, and he seems to be kind and gentle. He also runs a successful business, so he should be able to understand my restaurant lifestyle and what it takes for me to run this place. This one has possibilities!" Darlene hugged Don.

"You two are the best. I love you both. But I have to get back to work. So, place your order with Stephanie, and I'll deliver it to the bar.

"Thanks, Darlene, that sounds great. Oh, and about Andy, just don't get swept off your feet and give up the Shanty. I'm too old to break in a new best friend since childhood."

Darlene laughed. "There is no way I am giving up the Shanty, my favorite bar, or my favorite people that run it. Andy did say that he liked Brite Rock. Let's see how much!"

Chapter 29 - Jane obliged
May 18th 10:12 a.m.

Monday morning was the start of their weekend. Jane lounged in bed as Don took on the hunter-gatherer role and brought back breakfast and coffee from the Shanty. After eating, he went outside to start his usual Monday chores. Jane remained in bed, nibbling on the remains of her breakfast. She was making mental notes of things to do on their day off. Having done the big shopping last Tuesday, Jane thought a quick run to Trader Joe's the next town over for fresh produce, and a couple of bags of their frozen Mandarin Orange Chicken would do it. She has been jonesing for that orange chicken, steamed broccoli, and brown rice with a drizzle of fina'denne', a salty, spicy, sour all-purpose condiment Don's friend from Guam turned him on to making.

Don's ringing cell phone on the nightstand interrupted Jane's imaginary feast. She answered the call. Bob Chartley from the Brite Rock Building Department called to say he sent a couple of people over with questions about the Sailers Church building. Jane thanked Bob for the heads up and said they would expect the visitors.

She threw on shorts and a well-worn Cape Cod tank top, pulled her hair into a ponytail, and slipped her feet into a pair of sandals. She found Don in front of the church building. He had just finished mowing the lawn. Because he spent so much time in a dimly lit bar, he enjoyed being outdoors and looked forward to yard work. Jane thought it was weird that he considered lawn care to be exercise. But then, he thought she was a bit odd for sprinting the length of the beach several times a day to keep fit. Running in the sand did keep her body toned. Don mowing the lawn to tone his body, not so much.

As Jane relayed Bob Chartley's message to Don, three people came up the walkway to the church building. Pastor Smyth smiled as he greeted a wary Don and Jane. He then introduced architect Brian Franklin and builder Leo Kingston. Don invited them into the church building. Jane led the way, and they followed. Don couldn't help but notice that Jane skipped wearing underwear and went commando. He was sure the guests noticed too.

Don settled into the aluminum chair. Jane decided to forego her new chair and sat directly in front of Don on the stage. The three guests were seated in the first pew.

"So, what can we do for you, man?" The aluminum chair squeaked as Don leaned back.

Smyth smiled with the confidence of a used car salesman. "We are here to pay homage to this fine church and the historical impact that it has had on our community. As you know, this church has provided comfort and guidance since your ancestors generously built it for the community in 1920. For over one hundred years, it has served the people well and…"

Don leaned forward. "It's not for sale, man."

Smyth paused. The salesman's smile returned to his face. "Oh, we don't want to buy it. No, that was just a passing thought. A poor suggestion, really. But after careful consideration and reflection, I have come to the realization that this church building continues to serve a new and different kind of community. It provides much-needed comfort and guidance. So, I want to build an identical copy of this building over at my new Brite Rock Cathedral by the Sea complex. It will show my historic rise from my humble beginnings to the large and growing congregation I serve today. Think of it as a museum replica.

Jane was skeptical, and Smyth's constant smile creeped her out a little. "So, what do you want from us?"

"Great question, Ms. Gilman. We need your permission for Brian and Leo to have access to the building to create architectural drawings and building material lists. We will take measurements and lots of photographs. It will only take three or four days to gather the needed information. We could do it much faster if we had a copy of the original building's architectural drawings. The town doesn't have them on file and doubts they exist. Have you seen the original drawings for this building?"

Don thought about each paper he went through in the stack of documents that Jerry Palmer gave him. "No, man, sorry. The only drawing was of the position of the church and house on the land. You know, a plot plan."

Brian Franklin told Smyth that he could develop building plans to help make an excellent visual representation of the church.

Jane interrupted. "Wait, I think I know where I saw a copy of the building drawing. It was in one of those wide flat file cabinets in the library basement. It had some big architectural drawings of a few of the historic buildings in town. That may be worth checking out."

Smyth was hopeful. "Ms. Gilman, I hope you are right. If it is there, that will save us time and expense. However, we will still need to take measurements and pictures, if that's okay.

Don agreed. "I think we are cool with you guys doing your picture and measurement thing. If you want to make a copy of this building, have at it. Oh, and I assume you will return the big Jesus you took from here?" Don pointed to the outline on the wall behind him where the cross had hung.

Smyth had a momentary look of confusion. "I must apologize for that. You see, my team borrowed that to make a reproduction of it. It's such a pure, simple design. I guarantee that the cross will be returned as soon as they are finished with it. It won't be more than a few more weeks." Smyth knew returning the cross would never happen since Don's church building wouldn't exist much longer.

Smyth stood, shook hands with Don and Jane, and thanked them for their time and cooperation. "We are off to the library to check the historic building records. The boys will be back tomorrow morning to take photos and measurements if that's fine with you."

Don agreed to their return, and with that, Jane escorted them to the door and returned to Don, still seated in the aluminum chair.

"So, when did you see those building drawings at the library?"

Jane smiled. "Oh, in high school, I did my history paper on the Alden Williams house on Main Street. The Brite Rock Historical Society made technical drawings of the house in the 1950s when they renovated it.

Let's see…in April 1639, three men from the Massachusetts Bay Colony came to survey the 28 square-mile tract of land that they had purchased. They divided their purchase into three equal parcels of land, with the more desirable inland parcels going to farming brothers John and Edward Davenport. The coastal parcel, which included the beach, the shallow water inlet, and the natural rock jetty, went to sailor Adam Brite. The natural rock jetty that sticks out into the ocean just past the end of the beach was known as Brite's Rock on the old navigation maps. Alden Williams, who married Brite's daughter Abigail in 1642, was granted one hundred acres of land in exchange for helping to incorporate the town and designing and building the town's first meeting house. Williams built his house, which also served as a tavern when Brite's Rock was incorporated in 1643. In 1648 Williams started making rum on the property for the tavern and local townsfolk. When the first US Post Office was established in the town in 1811, the government mistakenly dropped the "s" on Brite's, and the town name Brite Rock stuck. See, I remember everything! I'm a frickin' genius!"

Don chuckled. "You can remember all that from all those years ago but forgot to put on underwear today?

"No, silly! I went commando to see if you would notice. If you hadn't, that tells me I need to up my game for you." Jane struck a playfully seductive pose.

"I think your game is doing just fine. Now, come over here so I can better appreciate your commandoness." Jane obliged.

Chapter 30 - Call me hot bronze goddess
June 11th 4:32 p.m.

Darlene stood in the doorway between the bar and the Shanty. It only took a moment for Don to sense something special. He smiled even before seeing Darlene or the warm slab of aromatic pineapple upside-down cake she was holding. This game always amused Jane.

Don excused himself from a conversation he was having with Best to retrieve the warm cake. He walked around the bar, slowly eating it. The aroma followed him, and within minutes Darlene had sold nearly 20 orders of cake.

Olivia and Jerry entered the bar to find the Friday happy hour crowd had filtered in earlier than usual. It was standing room only. Don was watching a group of tourists that had been there since lunchtime. They were getting close to the drink cut-off limit. He had made two passes by their booth with the cake. It worked as they discussed going to the Shanty for an early dinner. Don sent Red over to settle their bill and help get them a table at the Shanty.

Darlene was good about giving bar patrons needing a bit of sobering up priority seating as long as they behaved. Four people at the bar quickly left their seats to take the open booth. Olivia and Jerry claimed their usual bar stools as Jane approached to take their order.

Standing on the brass footrail, Olivia leaned over the bar and hugged Jane. "I need to thank you and Don so much for helping me to buy my first classic car. I am now the proud owner of a 1959 Chevy Brookwood 2-door station wagon."

Jane was thrilled. "That's great! I'm so happy for you. What made you decide on the wagon?"

Olivia was giddy. "Well, I loved the '55 Ford Fairlane, but the cat eye taillights and cool lines on the long roof wagon sold me. She feels, and yes, it's a she, feels sexy to me. Spider did a great job on the restoration and additions. The new 350 crate engine runs great. It looks factory new, and Don gave the work an enthusiastic nod of approval. And that Hawaiian Bronze with Sungate Ivory two-tone paint job that Pudsy did is spectacular. He said he would paint some tiki-inspired accents on the car for me too! It's the perfect beach and Cape weekend car. Now I have to learn how to parallel park it. It's over 17 feet long!"

Jerry couldn't contain his enthusiastic smile.

"So, Jerry, I guess you approve of her taking another step into the tiki and car culture?"

"Jane, I couldn't be prouder of Liv. This was her decision, and I agree with her choice. I like the car and believe Liv has successfully dragged me into the tiki scene. What else could explain me preferring an old station wagon over my new BMW?"

Jane smiled. "Oh, I don't know, Jerry. Could it be the hot bronze goddess behind the wheel of that hot bronze wagon?"

Olivia turned to Jerry. "Hot bronze goddess, I like that! So you have to call me hot bronze goddess from now on. Not in front of my parents, of course, but when we have sexy time. And I will call you my alabaster stallion."

Don delivered cocktails to Brad and John and greeted Olivia and Jerry. "How's it going? You two look more than your normal level of happy. What's up?"

"Don, I bought Spider's Brookwood station wagon. I'm an official classic car owner!"

"Congrats, man! This calls for complimentary adult beverages. Jane, set them up, please!"

Don stepped to the back of the bar, paused the juke music, and rang the rooster bell three times. "Here ye all, within the sound of my voice, Miss Olivia has purchased her first classic car befitting a tikiphile. She has gifted this fine establishment a superior sound system to bring good vibrations to all who enter. She has embraced the vintage tiki lifestyle. She has studied and speaks of tiki with great affection. She's inked with an island-themed sleeve tat and a tat of dolphins on her ankle. It is, therefore, my deepest honor, with the powers vested me by the great spirit – rum, that I hereby nickname you Kani, the Hawaiian word for sound. Welcome, my sister, to the way of the tiki."

With the sound system cranked up, the Polynesian's 1961 song Hawaiian War Chant rocked the bar. As is customary, the staff and a few patrons dance when this song plays to celebrate the event. Once the song ended, all returned to normal.

Olivia took Brad and John out to look at her new car. Officer Dillard and J.C. were already out there admiring it.

Jerry leaned in to talk with Don. "So, I guess you will also be celebrating now that Pastor Smyth has decided to build a copy of the Salers Church building at his place. He should stop bugging you now about buying your building."

Don sighed. "I hope it's that easy, man. The couple of run-ins I've had with Smyth and his boys leaves me cautiously optimistic. He's slippery, man. And the way he leers at Jane isn't cool. That dude's got a bent weathervane."

"A bent weathervane? What's that mean?"

"It means more than his moral compass is fucked up, man. He's off all the way around, as in not normal. It's like he believes rules and boundaries don't apply to him. I don't know; maybe I have a low opinion of him because he's a dick."

Jerry nodded in agreement. "Well, he certainly is a dick. Bob Chartley said Smyth's minion, Jim Reed, was a pain at the Building Department office a few weeks back. He had strongly requested a fast turn on all permits and the taking of some land to put in a parking lot on Pete Mitchell's property. Pete evidently wouldn't sell them the 5 acres they wanted, so they asked the town to take it by eminent domain and donate it to the church."

"Can the town do that, man?"

"Regarding the taking, it must benefit public use, such as a public parking lot. A church parking lot is considered private property and not for use by the general public. Smyth struck out on that one, but the Building Department expedited all other permits to get them out of their hair. Smyth is in a hurry. They poured the building foundation a few days ago."

Don tossed a coaster down on the bar in front of Jerry as Jane arrived with his Planter's Punch cocktail.

"It sounds like Smyth and his boys will have their tribute building built in a couple of months. Maybe I should celebrate too, man!"

Chapter 31 - The nickel and dime crowd
July 2nd 11:41 a.m.

Construction of Smyth's Sailers Church replica was quickly taking shape. The concrete foundation, side walls, and roof were up. The utilities were being installed, and a truck delivered the custom-replicated windows and doors.

The surveyor finished driving the last of the grade stakes into the ground. Smyth could now visualize how the founding church building would look next to his Cathedral. The grade stakes showed a nearly four-foot rise of the land on which the founding church building would sit. Raising the lot, and positioning the building at an angle, would allow them to add a stone retaining wall, lawn, wrought iron fence, and a sidewalk that would precisely recreate the side and front walkway of the original Sailers Church building in the center of town. It was to be identical in every possible way.

Leo unrolled the building plot plan and held it up for Smyth, Caruso, and Reed to see. Smyth appeared to study the technical drawings. But, in reality, he just wanted Leo to think he was fully engaged and observing the process. Smyth believed it is harder to con a person who pays attention to details. "This looks good, Leo!"

Smyth waved his hand in front of the plot plan as he addressed Paul and Jim. "See how the founding church is close enough to the front of the Cathedral to show the relationship. It's a relationship of size that illustrates where I came from. It shows my humble beginnings. It's a relationship of stature, the great heights of our achievement. This looks good!" Both agreed.

Leo pointed to the plans. "The site line matches up. We will cut the walkway to enter the founding church from the main right-side Cathedral walkway. The majority of people will pass that entrance when they arrive for service. Now, you may want to consider a small park with physical elements on the left side of the Cathedral to balance the view of the complex from the street. Perhaps a walkway with terraced elevations, benches, trees, a water feature, and a large stone with a dedication plaque. The landscaping will help define the people who use the space and provide a sense of place that differentiates one side of the Brite Rock Cathedral from the other. It's a matter of symmetry, of harmony."

Smyth was ecstatic. "Leo, I had not considered much past building the little founding church, but I have to say what you presented today is impressive. That big stone with the plaque, can we get one on both sides of the Cathedral? The one on the founding church side would have the story of my humble beginnings on the plaque, and we'll figure out what to say on the other. Please work with Paul and Jim on the details and cost. I want to get this going as soon as possible. I look forward to seeing the next round of plans for review."

Leo rolled up the plans. "Thank you for this opportunity. I'll be by tomorrow afternoon with the refined plans for the left and right side projects. Once you approve, we can start work on the changes and additions immediately. We will hit the mid-August completion date with additional guys on the finishing crew."

Smyth, Caruso, and Reed saw Leo off. Smyth watched as Leo got in his pick-up truck and drove away, not to be sure that Leo had gone but to see if there were any bumper stickers on the back of Leo's truck. Smyth believed that tradespeople who place political or controversial stickers on their vehicles show poor judgment and shouldn't be hired. Leo's truck was new and without stickers. Smyth smiled.

"Okay, Leo's touchy-feely comment about *the landscaping will help define the people who use the space* is borderline feel-good bullshit. But the guy is good. Let him run a bit on the designs for the park before we try to squeeze him on cost. Let's also pull a presentation together to pitch to some of our deep-pocketed A-list patrons. Do it as one of those help us name it pitches for the park and include a donation ask. We can then follow up with a couple more rounds of asks with the online and pass the plate crowd once we have momentum. The nickel and dime crowd loves to jump on board a project with momentum, so keep the pressure on the builder to get this project done fast. And one last thing for your task list, we need to focus more on that rich old lady. Figure out if there is a way to use this building project to get her on the hook."

Chapter 32 - We can be nudie buddies
August 3rd 8:56 a.m.

It was almost nine in the morning, and the sun was already hot on the skin. It was the start of another hazy, hot, and humid New England summer day, just the way Darlene liked it. Andy wondered if the years of working in hot restaurant kitchens gave her the love of steamy summer days. Andy put his arm around Darlene as they sat on the beach. The scent of her sunscreen reminded him of summer's past.

They had only been dating for a few weeks, and this was the morning after spending their first night together. They had stopped by the bar the evening before for a few drinks, watched the moon rise over the ocean, and walked the town, hand in hand, before heading to Darlene's house for the night.

They talked about being glad to have the awkwardness of being first-time lovers in a new relationship out of the way. Darlene discovered a sensuality that she hadn't experienced in a long time. Andy found his passionate voice to express his feelings as they made love. Both were surprised at their high libidos, something neither expected. Both discovered the start of their love story.

Darlene tilted her head to the side and closed her eyes. Andy gently kissed her neck, a sensation that made Darlene's toes curl and sent chills down her spine. Andy then….

"Oh my god, will you two get a room already!"

Darlene looked up to see an out-of-breath Jane. She had paused her run on the beach.

"Look who's talking! You and Don are always flirting with each other and playing grab ass. It's not natural for an old couple like you two to be all hot for each other like that."

Jane took a drink from her water bottle. "You are probably right about that. I have no idea why we still go at each other like a couple of horny high school kids, but I'm sure glad we do! Hell, I have to run up and down this damn beach every day to stay in shape just to keep up with him. Running in sand is a bitch!"

Darlene laughed. "True, but your legs and ass are in great shape, and it keeps you thin enough to overdose on my cinnamon rolls, French toast, and decadent desserts without gaining an ounce."

Jane took another sip of water. "That's the reward for torturing myself with these beach runs."

"It's paying off! Most of the sand in your hourglass figure is still stuck at the top."

Jane nodded in agreement. "My figure is still 37-23-34. But these big things bounce around no matter what sports bra I wear. And I'm a bit light on the opposite end, not enough counterweight for my tits. Oh, sorry, Andy, probably too much sharing there."

Andy smiled. "Jane, it is refreshing to be in the middle of these conversations. It's a different world than I have lived in, and I love it!"

Jane nodded in agreement. "Different certainly does describe us. Welcome to the typical restaurant and bar people and our lifestyle. We don't conform to the norm. And now that Don has his Happening following, it's even crazier, but in a good way, I think."

Darlene laughed and looked around. "By the way, where is Don? He's usually here when you run."

Jane rolled her eyes. "Whenever I think about maybe having a kid, I remind myself that Don has a 9-year-old inner child with that child-like curiosity. It's low tide, so he's just past the jetty looking for little sea beasties in the tidal pools. He can entertain himself for hours poking about."

Darlene agreed. "I've known Don all my life. Count your blessings that he entertains himself so you don't have to."

"Oh, I do! I appreciate my "me" time. Speaking of "me" time; this conversation has been mostly about me. What are you two doing for fun today besides making out on the beach?"

Darlene smiled and looked at Andy. "Andy put an offer on the big house for sale on Muhsachuweesut Camp Road. We are waiting to hear back from the real estate agent today."

"I know the house that you are talking about. Merle Freeman lived there before she retired to Florida. That house is gorgeous! My fingers are crossed for you, Andy."

"Thanks, Jane. I look forward to moving to town and becoming a local. Maybe even try one of every drink on the bar menu!"

"If you really want to jump into the tiki bar scene with both feet, join the bar's Alden Williams Rumbullion Society and sample all of the selected one hundred rums, an ounce of each. Membership is secret and limited to fifty people. I'm sure we can find a spot for you if you're interested."

Darlene's eyes spoke for her, pleadingly looking at Jane.

"Go ahead, Darlene, you can tell Andy, but he must keep your secret under penalty of being banned from rum cocktails at the bar until he completes the much dreaded Pele's gauntlet. Well, our bar version, that is. The real Pele...that goddess doesn't play!"

Darlene took on a serious tone. "Andy, you need to keep this secret. Pele's gauntlet is brutal. If you tell the secret, the Society members will flame your ass with insults and humorous name-calling for thirty minutes. It's all good fun, just not for you!"

Andy smiled and assured Darlene and Jane that he would honor their trust.

Darlene looked around to be sure no one could overhear her. "Okay, I'm a secret Alden Williams Rumbullion Society member. I've got four more rums to sample to make one hundred and achieve 100 Proof status. Of course, that comes with a few secret perks, including being invited to join the Rum Crawl trips."

Jane agreed. "That's true! We set up and host a 10 to 14-day tour every other year to some of the finest rum producers in the world and sample both commercial and exclusive distiller reserve rums. Society members may come along at their own expense, but we get some good travel deals. And Darlene, the next Rum Crawl is in the Caribbean. Barbados, Puerto Rico, Guyana, and Jamaica. There's even an optional upscale adults-only resort in Jamaica with a guest-only nude beach! I've gone topless on Nantucket, but never totally au naturel on a beach. I want to try it. It must be awesome to feel so free. Just us and nature."

Darlene laughed. "Are you seriously talking about being naked in front of strangers having sex on a beach?"

Jane laughed and shook her head. "It's not one of those creepy swingers' beach resorts. It's a private well-managed, upscale, clothing-prohibited beach. It's couples only, and resort security monitors the no-banging on the beach policy. That's what your room is for. Besides, getting sand in happy valley would ruin sexy time."

Darlene looked skeptical.

Jane kept pitching her idea. "I'm confident I can work up the nerve to do it. I'm even going to talk Don into it too! I want to experience the purest form of nature in a safe environment. Come on, Darlene, I saw you on the beach in a bikini last week, and you're looking good. And think, no tan lines! You have to try it at least once in your life. Please? We can be nudie buddies!"

Even though it was way outside her comfort zone, Darlene was intrigued by the thought. She trusts Jane's judgment. Jane was not one to rush into a situation without knowing all about it first. Darlene felt it would be safe if Jane could talk Don into it. Awkward but safe. Maybe a bit thrilling too!

"Well, if you and Don are both going to do it, I guess I will try it too. It's a little scary, but if I'm ever going to do it, that would be the time before things sag much further. I can't believe I just committed to being naked in public in front of you two and some total strangers."

Darlene turned to Andy. "I really want to travel with you on the Rum Crawl. You need to join and drink up, sweetie, so that you can be naked with me on the beach in Jamaica. Are you open to doing that?"

Andy silently looked straight ahead. Darlene started to get nervous, wondering if she had gone too far in this new relationship too soon. What if Andy found all of this offensive? What if he thought less of her for wanting to try it? Darlene was about to rescind her commitment to Jane when Andy turned and leaned in, and kissed her. "I think life with you will be a lot of interesting firsts for me. OK, I'll give it a try. Sign me up for the Society and point me at my first rum sample. I have some catching up to do. Maybe a few push-ups and sit-ups too!"

Chapter 33 - I will be honorable and gentle with Red
August 8th 11:01 a.m.

The old air conditioning system in Sailers Church struggled to cool the room. Don gently settled into the aluminum chair. The squeak sounded a bit louder than usual to him. Maybe his beloved old chair needed a safety inspection and more tape. He picked up his large, iced coffee, took a long sip, and looked around the room. He figured the attendee mix was about 60 percent regulars and 40 percent new visitors.

As usual, it was a full house, with a large group of dedicated Happening attendees outside watching A-Wall's streamed show online. The overflow crowd of attendees seems to grow in size weekly. Some sit in their cars, while others sit on benches under umbrellas that Andy donated from his store's excess inventory. Jane was in her special chair on stage, quietly chatting with Roger. Don gave her "the look." They stopped.

"Welcome to this showery Sunday morning. It's warm and muggy, and I'm in need of mass quantities of iced coffee. That three-in-the-morning thunderstorm last night was intense. Those that know Jane know that she is afraid of thunderstorms. It was hard to sleep with her cutting off the circulation in my right arm."

Jane looked indignantly at Don. "I don't like lightning. I'm not paranoid. I know it's out to get me."

Don laughed. "Is it because you're a witch?"

Jane gave Don the side-eye. "Would you like me to come over there and show you what I am?"

"No, sweetheart, you good – lightning bad!" Laughter floated around the room. This banter was endearing and entertaining to those who attended and watched online.

Don refocused his attention on the attendees. "Moving along, so what shall we talk about that isn't weather-related or likely to get me turned into a frog?" Several hands went up. Don scanned the room. "The aluminum chair recognizes Miss Kelly Rose, barmaid extraordinaire and first-time Happening attendee. Welcome, Red! And is that my favorite hooch peddler with you?"

Red stood up. "It is! Mister Bootleg Bobby, in person! I've been showing him some of the attractions around town."

"Are you one of those attractions, Red?"

"Why yes, I do believe I am, Don. Bobby, would you say I am one of the local attractions?"

Bootleg grinned. "I would have to say that you're the most attractive of the local attractions. You have my undivided attention."

Don smiled. "It's good to see you two out on the town, man. Bootleg, please return Red to us in good working order. Jane and I have the day off tomorrow, and Red runs the bar. She must be fully functional."

Bootleg nodded. "I will be honorable and gentle with Red."

Red gave him a dirty grin. "You can go light on the honor and gentle stuff. I'm not delicate."

Don was not surprised by Red's saucy comment. "I suggest you two have a safeword in case things get overly rambunctious."

Jane cracked up. "Yes, and pick a better safeword than Don did. Moor is not the best choice as a safeword, is it, baby?"

There was light laughter.

Don tried to explain his word choice. "It's nautical, as in moor your boat to the mooring buoy like the ones near the jetty. Okay, I can see that was not one of my better choices. Moor and more do sound a little similar. But, my second choice, which I thought was a generic term, was interpreted by Jane to mean more too! My word choice was fine until you applied dirty girl thinking to it."

Jane's mouth fell open. "Oh, come on. So you picked cowbell as your new safeword. Cowbell! As in MORE cowbell! Really? Didn't you see the connection to more cowbell? Classic SNL skit? Will Ferrell? Christopher Walken? Use the Google and look up more cowbell. Cowbell equals more, end of story."

The room lost it. It was the type of laughter that goes on for a while and dies down, only to be reignited. In this case, it was D.A.R. lady Doris who repeatedly lost composure. Laughter, being contagious, took a moment to get everyone quieted down.

Don shook his head. "Well, after that discussion on safewords, good luck, Bootleg, on your date with Red. Moving along, what shall we talk about that isn't safeword related?" Several hands went up.

"The aluminum chair recognizes Ed Mattie and his lovely wife, Cindy. How goes things, man? For those who don't know, Ed is the craftsman who painted my name on the church sign out front as a joke. He is responsible for naming this place The Church of Don."

Cindy gave Ed a firm look. "You've had your fun. Now you need to repaint that sign properly, Eddie."

Don came to Ed's defense. "No, I kind of like its rustic look, man. I'm a fan of the local avant-garde movement, and according to my media consultant, A-Wall, it's part of my brand. You can check it out on his website. So, Wally, what's your website address, man?"

Wally stepped from behind his camera and walked around in front. It was the first time he appeared on the Happening live stream. "Hi, I am Wally. I go by A-Wall, and you can check me out at a-wallmedia.com. That's my brand. Own who you are! I am available for domestic and international marketing and social media consultations. Thank you." Wally returned to behind the camera.

"Thanks, man, for being my marketing brand guy. It must be working; these fine folks are here or watching from wherever they watch from, and the bar is much fuller these days. Very cool. Now, Ed, you had a question, man?"

Ed started to speak but was interrupted by Cindy. She told him to stand to talk, and he did. "I have the contract to paint the replica of this little church being built over at Smyth's cathedral. They want the painting to start next week. Can I take a few paint chip scrapings from this place to have analyzed for the color match? I will touch up wherever I sample from and repaint the front door too. It's looking worn around the handle."

Don was impressed. "They are ready for paint next week? Wow, that was a fast construction job, man. Does it really look like this building?"

Ed grinned. "It does! It's an exact copy, flaws and all. Even the crack in the wood at the end of this pew has been recreated. The claw marks on the back door from Pastor Moreno's dog back in the 70s is there too. And get this; they put in an old heating and air-conditioning system that matches the one in this building. The attention to detail is incredible. You should come by and see it. The only thing missing are you and Jane. Oh, and your ratty squeaky aluminum chair."

Chapter 34 - Ally is my girlfriend, John is my buddy
August 11th 1:02 p.m.

Jane both loved and hated Wednesdays. It was the start of the work week for her and Don. She was happy about the social aspect of being with her bar family. However, she was not so happy that the typical twelve to fourteen-hour workdays could feel endless when the bar was slow. Even in the summertime, Wednesday was usually the slowest day.

The front door opened, letting brilliant late morning sunlight stream in as Jane and Red finished deep cleaning the bar top. It was momentarily blinding as the light reflected off the wet bar surface. Nevertheless, Jane recognized the silhouette in the doorway.

"Hi Brad, what are you doing here this time of day? Stop by for an early hydraulic lunch before returning to work?"

Brad smiled as he approached the bar. "No, I took the day off to take a friend to Boston for a doctor's appointment. Just a check-up."

"That was nice of you. You always think of others."

"I don't know about that, Jane. I guess I do. I try."

Jane picked up a fresh towel from the stack and dried the bar top in front of Brad. "So, what may I serve you?"

Brad sighed. "I don't want anything at the moment. Is Don here? I have a question that both of you may be able to help me with. It's personal."

"Yes, he's in the back shuffling papers. He will welcome the distraction from that task." Jane asked Red to have Don come out front on her way back to the stockroom.

Don didn't hesitate to set the paperwork aside and appeared from his office quickly. "Hey, man! We don't usually see you on Wednesday or before happy hour. So what brings you to our tropical paradise?"

"I took the day off. I had to help a friend. You know, stuff to do."

Don nodded. "Yeah, I get it, man. By the way, did the ladies offer you a libation?"

"Yes, and I said no, but on second thought, I would like to. I have this serious personal question, and a little liquid courage may help. May I have my usual?"

"Of course, coming right up." Jane started to make Brad's usual original Mai Tai.

Brad took a deep breath and slowly exhaled. "Okay, here it is. There's this girl, and I have a relationship question. PP said you would be a good person to ask, Don, since you scored Jane. He said that you're a pussy whisperer."

Brad looked nervously at Jane. "Maybe I wasn't supposed to say the pussy whisperer part out loud. Or in front of you."

Jane smiled. "No, you're fine, sweetheart. PP is a bad man. I'll deal with him later. Go on with your question."

Brad hesitated for a moment. "Well, there's this girl that I really like, but it's complicated. She has a condition that causes her to be different sometimes, like she is a totally different person. She is cute and into me romantically when she is one way, and we are good friends when she is different. The thing is, when she is different, she's kind of a guy, but not really. More like she's playing a character that's a guy but believes she is the guy. Are you following this?"

Don thought for a moment. "I think so. Are you talking about Alexandra DeCarlo, man?"

Brad sighed. "Yes. I'm not sure what to do since Ally is my girlfriend, and the other times' John Lennon is my buddy."

Jane set Brad's Mai Tai in front of him. "Wow, I guess I never thought about her life before. We, of course, know John from being here at the bar. Don and I have run into Alexandra at the grocery store and donut shop. You are right; she is cute and well-spoken too. Pretty long blonde hair. That's a wig, right?"

"Yes, it is. Ally can't be herself without it. The doctor said it helps her identify as Ally easier, and she is less likely to switch to her alter, John Lennon. Something about visual cues. I'm still learning about this."

"So, how does the switch work, man? Do you know when she will change to John and vice versa?"

Brad took a long sip of his Mai Tai. "From what her doctor told me, the dissociative identity thing is a mix of symptoms. For Ally, when she finds it difficult to cope or forgets to take her meds, she may become John. It takes an hour or two for her to switch. You can see it coming. Her cousin, Kimberly, told me what to look for. There's an hour or so of confusion, and then she's John. She can also wake up as John. That caused a problem last week when I spent the night with Ally. I woke up, and she was John. He wanted to know why we were snuggling in his roommate's bed. John now thinks I am bisexual and told me he isn't into me that way. But Ally is. She's pretty good in bed, I think. This is a lot to keep track of."

Don thought for a moment. "Wow, you are right, man. Lots of moving parts on this one. How is home life for her? Does she work? And why John Lennon?"

"Ally knows that John is her roommate. She doesn't know that she has become him. It's a two-bedroom apartment. Ally has one bedroom, and the other is John's. Oh, and John has a seriously great Beatles collection. I'm talking original stuff and lots of it. I think it belonged to Ally's parents. From the photos and posters, I'd say John was Ally's mom's favorite Beatle. So maybe being John has something to do with her mother's affection for him. I don't honestly know. Her parents died in a car accident when she was four, and an abusive relative raised her. That's where the doctor thinks the trauma came from that caused her condition. At least, that's what I understand.

As to working, Ally's family lawyer manages a trust that Ally's parents set up for her at birth. Her cousin, Kimberly, became her guardian when Ally turned sixteen. Kimberly lives in the apartment next to hers. Ally is very smart and relatively self-sufficient. She can afford not to work, and that's good. Work can cause anxiety, triggering her to switch."

Jane waited for a pause in the conversation. "Are you and she in love?"

Brad smiled. "I have never felt this deep hunger for any girl before. Woman, I mean woman!"

Jane laughed. "We call people girls and boys too. I'm Don's girl and have been since high school. He's my boy. When he's ninety, he will still be my boy."

Don smiled. "We don't get hung up on the title thing, man. It suppresses our inner child. So, is Ally on the love train with you?"

"We have talked a lot about this, me and Ally. We think of each other night and day. We feel stressed when we are apart, and that's not good for either of us. Her doctor said that falling in love is hard on the body. The brain releases stress hormones that divert blood away from our gut. Maybe that's why I feel like I need to throw up when I miss her. That's important since we both have challenges triggered by stress and anxiety. But we are so open and honest with each other. We talk about my Tourette's and her memory issues. That's the extent of her understanding of what's happening to her. I want to protect her, make her laugh, cook her breakfast, kiss her goodnight, and never leave. She's my girl!" Brad smiled as he thought of Ally.

"I know what it's like to feel that way about a girl, man. I still see Jane with those eyes."

Jane winked at Don. "Yes, you do, baby!"

Don thought for a moment. "So, what are you prepared to do, man? Have you gone public yet?"

Brad finished his Mai Tai. "No, we haven't. We will try the Shanty tonight for an early dinner and then a walk on the beach. We'll see how that goes before we expand our social circle as a couple. I don't think I can bring her to the bar. She can't drink because of her anxiety medication. That's why she doesn't come here. She's off her meds when she's John. Besides, this is John's hangout. It wouldn't be fair to him. I have to take care of my buddy in this relationship too!"

Don nodded in agreement. "That you do! So, when you came in, you said you had a question. Do you still have it, or have you talked it through to the point of clarity?"

Brad thought about his situation. "I guess I talked it through, but I still don't know if I am doing the right thing."

"Only you can answer if loving her is right for you both, man. You know what challenges you face and are going into this with eyes wide open. So my advice would be to take it slow, steady, and keep talking. Build your confidence in each other, and the anxiety and stress of the new relationship will lessen. You'll find your groove with each other, and it will become as natural as breathing. That's my take on it, man!"

Jane took Brad's hand. "In my relationship with Don, we appreciate the little things that show our love. Do the little things. And I agree with Don on talking. Knowing where you and your partner stand in the relationship is important. Make her your partner in all things, but never lose your individuality."

"I will, Jane, and thanks to both of you for listening. As I said things out loud, it all became clearer to me. I love this girl and want Ally and John in my life."

"That's cool, man. Well done for thinking it through and putting Ally first. Now, I have a question for you. This has been stressful for you today, yet you haven't had any motion or vocal tics. Are you on some kind of med right now?"

Brad hadn't noticed his Tourette's, or lack of it, either. "Yes, I am, and it is kicking my ass. Lots of minor side effects that make me feel like I am coming down with the flu. Very spacy. It can mostly alleviate my verbal and motion tics but isn't worth the long-term discomfort. I don't want my thing to be a problem on our date tonight if I can help it."

Brad put a twenty-dollar bill on the bar.

"No, man, the drink is on the house. Put that back in your wallet. Now, you need to tell us if you are on meds that could interact with alcohol. You are Ohana, and we don't want to put you at risk. Are you good with that?"

Brad smiled sheepishly. "Yeah, I shouldn't have had a drink. I know better. You know, anyone here can reality-check me anytime you like. It's good to have people care about me. I like being part of this family."

Jane and Don walked around the bar toward Brad. "We like it too, man!

Jane and Don hugged Brad and sent him on his way. The brilliant sunshine faded as the bar door slowly closed. Don fired up *Sweet Ōkole* by *Hoaikane* on the sound system and sang along as Jane danced. Jane loves to dance.

Chapter 35 - His humble beginnings pitch
August 15th 10:36 a.m.

Smyth stood in the middle of his founding Sailers Church building, admiring the new addition to the story of his humble beginnings. It smelled like new construction. Several wet paint signs and construction notes were randomly placed on walls, windows, and the floor. Many pointed out minor corrections to be made. One note on a baseboard said it needed to be distressed more and directed the carpenter to see the photo from the actual Sailers Church as a comparison. Smyth bristled at the note referring to the *actual Sailers Church*. He muttered to himself, not for much longer.

Smyth stepped up onto the chancel. He preferred that church-specific term over calling it the stage. There was an exclusivity to it. Any no-talent comedian or stripper could work a stage, but his performance took place on a chancel. That was power in his mind.

He smiled when he saw the pulpit, an identical original 1920s version of the one he first preached from at the Sailers Church. The restoration and reclaimed materials contractor bought it from a company that sells used and antique pulpits. Smyth found that amusing. He pictured a used pulpit salesman wearing a cheap suit, thinking he probably sold used cars the week before he got that job. But then, he thought, everyone has an angle in this game.

Smyth rested his right hand on the pulpit. Looking around the room, he started to tap his ring on the wooden top. He scrutinized every detail in the room, looking for things that were wrong or not precisely correct. But instead, it was all perfect, from the authentic 1920s brass door hardware to the opaque milk glass pendant lights to the width and finish of the worn oak floors. He had to give Jim Reed credit; he managed the construction project better than Smyth had expected. This building is identical to Sailers Church.

Lost in thought, Smyth was startled by the loud sound of the front door opening. Reed peaked in and then entered.

"For fuck sake, Jim, you nearly gave me a heart attack!"

"Sorry about that, George. That squeak is pretty loud. It's on the list to fix. So, we are getting ready to start the service."

Smyth looked at his watch. "Damn, I lost track of time."

He quickly walked out the back door of the founding church and headed toward the rear entrance of the Brite Rock Cathedral, spouting commands to Reed almost as fast as his brisk pace. "I need to change into my white suit. When we go live, have the band play the extended version of my opening song. I'm going to slowly walk the intro to do crowd contact before taking my start position. After that, I need to work up to the announcement of the dedication of the founding church."

Caruso greeted them as they entered the back door of the Cathedral. Reed excused himself and walked to the video production center to discuss the opening with the director.

Smyth entered his office and started to change into his white suit. "That construction job looks great, Paul. You can't tell our knock-off from the original. This is going to work out well for us. I can feel it! It's going to be a moneymaker."

"I agree, George. It's going to be a great prop and marketing tool."

Smyth paused for a moment. "Speaking of money, we need to get our hooks into that old lady, Lily Snell. Have Jim get her here for the founding church dedication so I can work on her. A stroll down memory lane will help get us closer to her money. She has to be worth millions!"

Caruso looked at his watch. "I'll talk to Jim about the old lady. You're on in 5 minutes. Get out there and sell like hell!"

Smyth laughed as he put on his white suit coat and adjusted his white tie. He loved the way his suit had an otherworldly white glow on camera. He could hear the Brite Rock Revivers church band getting ready to play his intro as he went backstage and waited for his cue.

A production assistant turned Smyth's microphone on and asked for a sound check. "Testing...testing... You getting me?" The production assistant gave him a thumbs-up.

The band started to play as the lights came up on the stage, and the announcer introduced the show.

"Live from the Brite Rock Cathedral by the Sea in the scenic shoreline community of Brite Rock, Massachusetts; it's an Hour of Reflection with Pastor George Smyth."

Smyth entered and walked toward the front of the stage, acknowledging the band with a salute as he passed by. He feels the warmth from multiple spotlight beams the moment they hit him. The applause continued as Smyth mouthed the words *thank you* several times. Then, he signaled the band to stop playing so he could quiet the audience.

Smyth points toward the band. "Aren't they something else, ladies and gentlemen? If I knew church music could rock like that, I would have started preaching years earlier! So, please, another round of applause for our Brite Rock Revivers. And remember, their original songs, including *Here Because of Him*, are available from your favorite faith-based music retailer and, of course, in our Faith Store after today's service."

Smyth was not subtle in his efforts to establish the band and grow its sales. What was good for the band was good for him.

"Today, I want to talk about being selfless. You know, being selfless means that we are acting from our heart and soul instead of our ego and pride. I once heard someone say that selfless people are weak. Weak? They are mistaken. Being selfless takes great strength. Our ego and pride are strong, so it takes greater strength to overcome them. Yes, it does! And that work is difficult. But like all good work, it has its rewards.

As I look out upon you today, those here in front of me, and our brothers and sisters watching from around the country, I have to say that I have witnessed incredible acts of selflessness. Acts of great personal inner strength. You know what I mean. You can feel it in your heart. It is your selfless kindness and giving that I speak of. And it has its rewards.

You all saw the founding church that we have been building over the past few months. Well, it is done. The workers have laid down their tools. Your selflessness turned a vision into a reality. Your acts from the heart have taken physical form. And now, we must dedicate this founding church. The founding church where our congregation started and where I first preached. From humble beginnings, here we stand today."

The congregation applauded. Smyth smiled and held up his hand.

"Next Saturday afternoon, we will have the dedication of the founding church. There will be food, music, events, special commemorative gifts, and a tour of our church's newest yet oldest member, both actual and virtual. Make no mistake, the founding church is 100% part of Brite Rock Cathedral by the Sea, and as such, we will hold a special Sunday morning program live from that building.

Now, I know most of you are thinking, but Pastor Smyth, there are thousands of us. It would take a miracle to fit this massive congregation into that little building. You are right, and I will not ask for such a miracle since the world has need for miracles for things far more important. So, sixty people will be selected from a drawing held at the Saturday dedication to attend this intimate event on Sunday morning, so please be sure to enter your name. This special Sunday morning program will be the first of many events to be held in the founding church throughout the year. Of course, our usual Sunday program will be held here at the regular time after this special event. The dedication will be streamed online, and the usual Sunday service will broadcast and stream live for your viewing. How are those rewards for your selflessness?" Smyth smiled at the thunderous applause. In his mind, this validated his humble beginnings sales pitch.

Chapter 36 - Jeanette should have one for the road
August 19th 2:18 p.m.

Red dumped a fresh bucket of ice into the last of the four bartender service bins as A.J. mixed drinks for the Daughters of the American Revolution crowd that had arrived. He has decades of experience bartending for the D.A.R. ladies. He smiles as he makes a Vodka Gimlet for Lily and a Tequila Sunrise for Jeanette, who is known to get unruly when drinking tequila. A.J. goes light on the tequila.

The D.A.R. open bar is an annual event. They hold some sort of ceremony for new members, and then the ladies come to the bar to celebrate with free drinks and light fare. Don's mother started the tradition when she was a member. Her other tradition was to hang a replica colonial New England Ships' Flag over the bar entrance to honor the legacy of the Revolutionary War era Massachusetts Navy and the current local fishing community.

New England merchants and ship captains in the late 1600s wanted their ships in the port to be easily identified as ships sailing to and from New England. Flying the red and white flag with a green pine tree was advantageous in a busy port where traders were looking for New England fish, lumber, or rum. Especially rum!

The Massachusetts Navy adopted the green pine tree on a white field with the motto *An Appeal To Heaven* as its flag in 1775 and flew it proudly as it fought the British. Don keeps the flag and D.A.R. traditions in memoriam to her, his colonial ancestry, and the ladies.

Red noticed Andy as he entered through the pass-through door from the Shanty. "Come on in, Andy! There is a seat right here at the bar." It took Andy's eyes a moment to adjust to the subdued lighting. The air held the scents of citrus, a blend of lady's perfume, and tuberose flowers from Red's lei. Red had several double-white bloom tuberose plants that filled her sunroom over the winter. They take over her deck in late spring and bloom by midsummer. Jane made leis for Red, Darlene, and herself from the fragrant flowers.

Andy settled on the bar stool in front of Red as she dried her hands. "So, Andy, are you here for the D.A.R. ladies or aloha Friday?"

"Definitely aloha Friday, Kelly! I have a few more rums to sample to get them checked off my list. I think I'll do five to start, and if I don't fall off the bar stool, I may try one or two more. May I have my rum-tasting list, please?"

Red retrieved Andy's Rumbullion Society 100 Rums List and set it in front of him with a large glass of ice water. "I take it, Darlene, is your designated driver?"

"Yes, mam, she's the one that said I need to catch up to her tasting list, so I better get to drinking. I'll try the next five on the list. Oh, and Jane said I should make the Kōloa Coconut Rum one of them today. It's supposed to have a true coconut flavor."

Red set up the rum sample cups for Andy. "It's my favorite coconut! But as Don says, we are all individual chemistry sets, and what tastes good to one person may not to another. This one is made on Kauai. Have you been there?"

"Yes, many years ago on my honeymoon. I want to go back. I wonder if Darlene would like Kauai?"

"I know for a fact that Darlene loves Kauai. You two should consider going when Don and Jane make their annual trip there. Maybe he can set it up so you and Darlene can join them for a rum factory tour. Ask him when he's done talking to Lily and her posse. I'll send him your way."

Andy was about to take his first sip and paused. "Does Don usually get access to the rum makers' facilities?"

Red laughed. "Yeah, Don's a geek when it comes to the rum-making process and the tiki scene. He's also pretty observant about what customers are ordering and asking for. Don, the distillers, and the blenders speak the same rum language. If they let him, he would go out in the field and talk to the sugar cane."

Red finished pouring the five rum samples and excused herself to tend to several of the D.A.R. ladies who had just entered the bar.

The song Midnight by The Shadows began to play on the juke. It's one of the few tiki songs that Andy knew the name of, only because it's the ringtone on Don's cell phone. Andy sampled and savored each of the rums and made notes on the back of his tasting list. Slightly tipsy, Andy giggled as he sipped the Kōloa Coconut Rum and paused. The coconut scent and flavor were pleasantly unexpected.

As much as he wanted to focus on flavor profiles and notes, his mind wandered. His eyes closed. Soft images of a long empty tropical beach accompanied the warmth of the consumed rum. Darlene walked just ahead of him on the sand. He was captivated by the soft swaying motion of her hips and the contrast of the white bikini bottom against her tanned skin. She looked back at him as a light trade wind gently stirred her hair. He saw that she was topless as she turned to take his hand. He became aware of his heartbeat. The breeze carried the scent of her to him. She turned to face him. Her skin was warm to the touch. She was….

"I'll have a raspberry lime rickey!" Andy was startled from his tropical mental vacation to find Jim Reed sitting beside him and ordering a drink from Jane. It took him a moment to recognize Reed. He had placed a big furniture order with Andy's Boston store months ago for the Cathedral by the Sea.

"Jim Reed – remember me? I'm Andy Milner from the furniture store."

Reed studied Andy's face trying to place him. "Yes! I'm sorry. I've dealt with so many contractors and vendors at the church that it all blurs together."

Andy nodded in agreement. "I sometimes have the same problem remembering customers, particularly if I haven't seen them in a while. I haven't heard anyone order a raspberry lime rickey in years. Does their version have alcohol in it?"

"No, it's the traditional old soda fountain soft drink. It's on the bar's no-alcohol mocktail menu. I have a lot of church business to work on later, so I need a clear head. I just stopped in to be social and say hello to a few of the D.A.R. ladies. I believe I see someone over there I should say hello to."

Jane set Reed's drink in front of him. He picked it up and took a long sip. "That's perfect!" He then stood, dropped a ten-dollar bill on the bar, and walked over to Lily's table.

Andy was baffled by Reed's abrupt departure. "Did I say something to offend him, Jane?"

"I don't think so, Andy. It appears he came here on a mission."

Jane and Andy watched as Reed worked the ladies at the table like a politician. He focused the majority of his attention on Lily.

Lily laughed at Reed's feeble attempt at a humorous greeting before she changed the subject. "I have to tell you that I so enjoyed when Pastor Smyth held Sunday morning service at the little church. Living across the street from it was perfect for me. I no longer drive, and the short walk from my house was good exercise."

Reed took Lily's hand. "You know, Lily, Pastor Smyth is holding a special dedication service at our new founding church this Sunday. It will be live-streamed, but you will want that true Sailers Church experience that only being there can provide. So the Pastor asked me to invite you to attend. It will be a very important social event, and we miss you at church."

Jeanette, now halfway through her second tequila sunrise, chimed in. "Lily, you said you were going to Don's Happening this Sunday with us girls. Are you considering ditching us for Pastor Slick and his shiny new Jesus stadium?"

"Well, no, Jeanette. I was politely listening to…I'm sorry, I was concentrating on stifling a fart when you said your name, so I don't remember it. What is it again, dear?"

Reed tried to maintain his compassionate smile. "That's all right, Lily. My name is Jim Reed."

"I am sorry for my lapse of etiquette, Mr. Reed, but you should never trust a fart at my age. Doris had an embarrassing experience just a few weeks ago. Doris, tell Mr. Reed about your fart mishap at the doctor's office."

Reed quickly tried to get the conversation back on track. "That's OK, Doris. I get the picture. So, Lily, we look forward to seeing you for the special founding church sermon this Sunday. It will be…"

Lily sighed. "I'm sorry, Mr. Reed, Jeanette is right. I promised the girls I would go to Don's Sunday Happening get-together. Please thank Pastor Smyth for the kind invitation and tell him that I watch his service on my iPad every Sunday to get right with the lord before I walk over to Don's Happening. The Happenings are quite fun. I wouldn't miss it for the world."

Reed had to force a smile. "That is perfectly fine, Lily. I'm happy to hear you watch the service and find it rewarding. Now that I think about it, I recall Pastor Smyth saying something about visiting you. Just checking in with the important people in the community, like yourself. Would you be open to a visit from the pastor?"

"Yes, that would be nice. Please have the Pastor call and make an appointment. I do have a very active social schedule, you know."

"I'll let the pastor know to call you for an appointment. It was a pleasure speaking with you and the ladies today. Ladies, have a pleasant day." Reed made his way to the door. His forced smile barely hid his disappointment.

Jeanette held her empty cocktail glass up to signal for a refill. Don made his way to their table through the crowded bar.

"Are you ladies ready for another round?"

Jeanette thrust her empty glass toward Don. "Yes, dear! You know, Don, you are a handsome man, and you look good in those jeans. They make your bum look very firm."

"Why, thank you, Jeanette. Is that you or the tequila talking?"

"Oh, it's the tequila and old age talking. At my age, I'm like the dog that chases the car. If I caught it, I wouldn't know what to do with it. And being an old lady, I can say the most inappropriate things, and people think it's quaint, except for Jane. I can't slip one by her. She just seems to know things like she has UPS or something."

Lily giggled. "I think you mean ESP."

"Yes, that's it, ESP! I wonder if she can read minds. Don, do you think that rumor about her being a witch is true? Does she dance around naked in the woods on a full moon?"

Don feigned a quizzical look. "Well, you can't slip anything by her, and she does know things, and she does dance around naked at home but not outside. Oh, and Jane turned Pervie Pete into a frog once, but only for a few hours. So maybe she is a witch. Lily, your thoughts?"

"I think Jeanette should have one for the road before you shut her off. Maybe a little food too. A pupu platter for four would do nicely."

Don made a mental note of the order. "So, it's another round and pup for four. I'll get your food order right in. It may take a few minutes. Is that okay?"

Lily motioned Don to come closer so she could speak privately. "That's fine on the food. These old broads have no place special to be Now, I assume that you saw Mr. Reed at our table."

"I did. Is there a problem? Did he say or act inappropriately?"

"No, he's just Pastor Smyth's lackey. Well, a putz, actually. We played with him a little before sending him on his way. He's not the sharpest tool in the shed, and it's easy to see they are sniffing around this old lady for her money. Anyway, he invited me to a special sermon the Sunday after next in their version of your church building. It's going to be live-streamed. That means there will be two very different programs streamed from identical-looking locations at the same time on that Sunday!"

It took a moment for what Lily was saying to sink in. Don laughed. "I guess no one will mistake us talking about rum, car parts, or PP's armpit rash with Smyth's preachy show."

Lily smiled. "No, they won't, dear."

Chapter 37 - Jane won't put up with our shenanigans
August 26th 11:51 a.m.

Light. Crisp. Well-seasoned. Fried to perfection. Don pondered, as he sat on the bench in front of Rudy's Clam Shack, how the owner was able to make his signature fried clams so tasty. It had to be something in the seasoning. Don pulled another fried clam out of the white cardboard pint box and studied it carefully.

"Forget it, Don. Rudy is like Colonel Sanders when it comes to the secret herbs and spices for his clam recipe. He's not telling. Morton also isn't telling how he got the nickname Rudy!"

Don looked up to see A-Wall standing in front of him. "How's it going, man? Want a clam?"

Don held the box up. Wally pulled one out and popped it into his mouth. "Damn, those are tasty! So, what has you sitting here besides the great weather and killer view of the babes on the beach?"

"Jane is off getting her hair done, and I was jonesing for Rudy's clams, so here I sit. What about you, taking a day off from…what exactly is your job again, man?"

Wally laughed. "For the nth time – I am a marketing and social media consultant serving North America and select Asian countries. I freelance to a portfolio of clients and handle all of their social media needs."

Don had a slight look of confusion. "Yeah, I still don't know what that is, but that's cool, man. I don't know what a theoretical physicist does either, but if it pays the bills and you are happy, what's not to like about it?"

"Yes, it pays the bills, and I love it. And yes, I skipped work to have a beach day with my date, Shūlíng. I came over to get us lunch when I spotted you loitering."

Don thought for a moment. "I don't think I know her, man. Have you been dating Shūlíng long?"

"No, and it's not from lack of trying. Shūlíng has been super busy finishing up her thesis paper. She's from Taiwan and is here studying computer science at MIT. She's super smart, and she won the looks lotto too. I'm a happy man!"

Don holds the clam box up for Wally to help himself. "So, how did you meet Shūlíng, man?"

Wally smiled. "She saw one of the Happenings online and sent me a message asking if it was legit or a put-on. I told her that it was one hundred percent for real and that she should come to see it for herself. She agreed. And along the way, it turned into a date thing. Shū's here today and will be back in town for the Happening on Sunday. We'll be at the bar for happy hour later this afternoon."

"That's cool, man. I look forward to meeting her. Speaking of the Happening, word on the street is that Smyth will do some special preachy thing in two weeks at their copy of the little church building. It's supposed to be streamed on that Sunday morning, so there will be two very different shows from what will appear to be the same place that weekend. Trippy, huh?"

Wally was not happy. "I didn't think they would stream from the replica church building. That visual location is part of our online brand. We will need to up our online game to fend off this blatant encroachment. Maybe a campaign to snag viewers to our stream. Shūlíng may have some ideas on how to spice up our messaging. I think I'll also have a chat with town lawyer Jerry too. I have a question about the original church name that may give us some leverage."

Don peered into the empty clam box. "Well, this online stream thing is outside my area of expertise, man. It's not within my purview. But whatever it is that you've been doing, it works. Jane thinks you have done great things with the Happenings, and we appreciate the uptick in the bar business. But she also reminded me not to let the Happenings get out of hand. She made it clear that the Happenings can stay or go. Jane won't put up with any of our shenanigans if it hurts the bar business."

Wally nodded. "Got it! This will be a mostly shenanigans-free effort. At least it will appear that way."

Chapter 38 - Okay, yes, please, taser him for me
September 6th 4:57 p.m.

It was the last day of Labor Day Weekend, the unofficial end of summer. Shadows were starting to grow longer as five o'clock approached. The beach crowd was thinning, and the tide was going out. The heat of the day was beginning to fade.

Jane and Don stood on the beach, side by side, looking at the calm ocean. Jane's left hand was in Don's left back pocket. Don's right hand was in Jane's right back pocket. Neither can remember why they started doing that back pocket thing in high school. Jane thought it was their sneaky way of playing grab ass in public. She still believes that.

Jane glanced over at Don. His eyes were closed, and he appeared contented. "What are you thinking about, babe?"

His eyes remained closed. "I'm not thinking; I'm sensing. The warm sun on my back. The barely discernible scent of your skin. The light onshore breeze out of the east. The changing smell of the ocean as the tide goes out. The occasional whiff of roasting garlic from the Shanty. A hint of smoke from a fire pit down by the jetty. You next to me."

Jane laughed. "You can feel me next to you because you have your hand in my back pocket and are holding onto my ass!"

"Well, yes, there is that. But I also feel connected to you on some deep level. Like part of me has melded with part of you and created something that is a shared us. I don't know what it is or how to explain it, but it is incredibly comforting."

Jane pulled her hand from Don's back pocket and turned to face him. Her kiss was soft, barely brushing his lips. "That's why we are still deeply in love after all these years. I don't have to try and remember what that desire was like to check you out in the shower. I did that this morning. And I don't have to remember your teenage optimism, where life is ahead of us. We live that every day. I don't have to try to remember you as the high school boy who would try to feel me up when no one was looking. You did that an hour ago. I love the perpetual teenager part of you. It keeps us young, and we play well together." This time Jane's kiss was firmer and more passionate.

Don smiled. "Can you live without our play time while I'm in Los Angeles for one night? It's not too late; they did offer you a free ticket!"

Jane slowly shook her head no. "Flying to the west coast for just one night and then back the next day is jet lag hell. The only part of the trip that sounds fun is your planned stop at the Tonga Hut bar after the show. So no, you do this thing, and I'll stay and run the bar. I know you don't like showing sports and stuff on the big screens in the bar, but Olivia will temporarily wire them up so we can watch your big-time TV interview. Your five minutes of fame will be good for our bar biz and the town, babe."

Don agreed. "That's the only reason to do this. I don't know what he will ask me, but it's HBO, so anything goes, I guess."

Jane looked over at the bar and sighed. "I suppose we have to get back to work."

Don reluctantly agreed and looked up and down Brite's Jetty Road to be sure no cars were coming. It was clear. He then looked over his shoulder at the ocean and asked, "what's that?" When Jane turned to look, Don pinched her on the ass and ran for the bar's front door. He made it halfway across the street when he noticed a police car pull out of the public parking lot and put its flashing lights on. Don stopped on the sidewalk in front of the bar. Jane waited in the middle of the road, laughing and pointing at Don.

"You're in trouble now, baby!"

The police car slowed, and Officer Jim Dillard rolled down the front windows. "Hello, Jane!"

"Hi, Jimmy. How is your shift going?"

"Well, Jane, it was going great until I observed that man appear to assault you. Do you want to press charges? Maybe I could taser him a little if you would like."

"That is a tempting offer, Jimmy. After all, he did assault me right there." Jane points to where Don pinched her. "Those are the actions of a scoundrel. I've even heard him referred to as a rogue!"

Officer Dillard looked at Don. "I can see what you mean, Jane. He does appear to be a rascal. Maybe a scallywag too! The offer to taser him still stands."

Jane put a finger up to her chin. "Let me think. Okay, yes, please, taser him for me!"

Don shook his head. "Are you two done?"

Jane coquettishly replied. "Well, maybe I can come up with a punishment more suited to the crime."

Officer Dillard agreed. "I'm sure you two can work something out when you get home. But please keep the shades closed and the noise level down when you do."

"Thanks, Jimmy! I think this intervention has put Don on the road to redemption. Will you be by the bar after your shift this evening?"

"I think so, Jane. But, you know, just to make sure he is behaving."

Jane looked at Don and giggled. "Okay, Jimmy, I think we have resolved this situation. You go protect us town folk, and later Don will serve you a tasty beverage. The first one is on him. That's how we do protect and serve in Brite Rock!"

"Roger that, you two. Now move along. Nothing to see here." Jim turned off the flashing lights and slowly drove away.

Jane sauntered over to Don. "Okay, baby, that pinch is going to cost you. I expect you to return to the scene of the crime and…

"Do you need a good lawyer, Don? I don't know any, but I'm sure we can find one." They turned to see Jerry standing in the doorway to the bar. "Red told me to tell you that she is slammed and has to pee, so hurry up, or one of you will be mopping up a piddle puddle. Her words, not mine!"

Jane hurried off to cover for Red. Jerry asked Don if he had a moment to talk.

"I just wanted you to know that Wally, the guy that streams your Happenings online, came by my office and asked questions about what he could and could not say about the name Sailers Church of Brite Rock as it applies to your building. I counseled him that Smyth evidently trademarked the name, but it is also listed in the town records as a historic site by that name. So, there is an argument to be made that referring to it as the "Historic Sailers Church of Brite Rock" is legitimate. That said, doing so will likely cause a cease and desist letter to be sent to you by Smyth. I can say, as Town Counsel, that the town will vigorously protest the letter based on the historic name. That may be enough to cause Smyth to drop the cease and desist, but you could be sued if you use the name after that. The town will protest the lawsuit if it happens but would likely not be part of it. Wally looked at it like the use of the Historic Sailers Church of Brite Rock name was fine until you were informed otherwise by the cease and desist letter. That's probably accurate."

Don thought about what Jerry had just told him. "So, what you're saying, man, is that Wally can use the Historic Sailers Church name until Smyth blows a gasket and sends the knock-it-off letter."

"That about sums it up, Don. Do you know what Wally is up to with all of this?"

"I truly don't, man. Something to do with the streaming Happening thing. I don't know the finer points of what A-Wall does with the website, but it has grown in a big way. He even sells t-shirts online with the bar sign, the Church of Don graphic, or printed photos of the bar staff. It's on a page with other stuff he calls merch. That brought in over three grand in sales last month. And the custom tiki mug he has in the works will be killer. It's got Jane, me, the aluminum chair, and the Church of Don sign on it. We sell custom collector tiki mugs at the bar, but nothing with us on it. Being on a tiki mug is weird now that I think about it."

Jerry got serious for a moment. "The merch sales sound like a sizeable business. So who is keeping track of the money?"

"A-Wall set this up with my accountant, Beansie. I would only agree if everybody gets a cut of their merch sale after expenses, and it is a legit business. So, let's say someone buys a t-shirt with Jane, Red, A.J., or whoever is on it. Then, from the net, that person gets 40%, Wally gets 20% as the merch designer and manager, the bar gets 15%, 15% goes into our community bar cookie jar, and 10% to Beansie to keep the biz running and legit.

"That's great, Don! Glad to see you spreading the wealth with your employees."

"Ohana, man! They are our family. A.J. has been bartending here for around fifty years. Geezer on occasion for thirty years. Red for maybe fifteen. J.C. for about six. Shakemaster for about two years. Oh, and Darlene is family too."

"You know, Don, Olivia said that you and Jane are two of the most caring people she has ever met. I know what she means now."

Before Don could respond, the bar door opened, and Jane leaned out. "If you two are done gossiping, I could use help behind the bar, babe. And Jerry, Liv said she wants drinks, food, and loving – in that order. So you better get moving; the woman has needs!"

Chapter 39 - I will do forever with Don
September 17th 9:07 p.m.

Jane had not seen the bar this crowded since the last luau party. Don being interviewed on national live television was a big deal for the town and the bar. Even the Chamber of Commerce members were in attendance. Jane was suspicious of their newfound support of the bar and the sign they were previously intent on having removed. It seemed everyone wanted to be associated with Don, Jane, and the Happenings. It was one of the downsides of publicity.

The live HBO show was on all three large screens. Excited conversations filled the air as Jane rang the rooster bell to silence the room. "Quiet! I think this is when it's Don's time." Jane motioned to Olivia to turn up the sound.

The host walked over to the opening interview set, two chairs facing each other on the part of the stage defined by the rug the chairs sat on. It was spacious yet intimate. Don had seen the set before. He and Jane usually streamed the show on their off time. The set looked surreal to him as he waited to go on.

"I'd like to welcome our first guest this evening. You may know him from the popular internet series the Church of Don Happening Hour or his Don's Tiki Cocktails & Lounge in Brite Rock, Massachusetts – give a warm welcome to Don!"

Don enters the set to robust applause and settles into the guest chair. "How's it going, man? It's a pleasure to meet you."

"It's a pleasure to meet you too, Don. By the applause, these people know you and your show. Now, I had not seen your show, but my staff, who are usually right, said I should watch it. So I did, and I have to say, I found it entertaining and nothing like what I expected. But the title, Church of Don, threw me. I expected something religious to creep into the show, but it didn't. Why not?"

'The whole Church of Don title thing is a prank gone awry, man. And the building wasn't a bona fide church when I took possession of it. It had been desanctified. Its mojo had left the building. So the bottom line is it's a nonchurch building, and I'm a nonchurch guy that hosts the Happening along with Jane. The Happening is just a bunch of people that get together to talk about what's happening in their lives. I guess people find that interesting enough to watch online or come and hang out for an hour or so."

'Why do you think that is, Don? I've watched The Happening Hour, and there are some colorful characters in Brite Rock, but it's nothing special. Yet I found it fascinating and look forward to watching it again. I don't understand the pull. Why are people following the Happening Hour and you?"

'I don't know, man. Like you said, it really isn't anything special. Maybe they relate to it, like hanging out at a friend's house. It's comfortable."

The host shuffled his note cards and nodded in agreement. 'Comfortable is hard to come by these days. That leads me to my next question – politics! I understand that topic is not open for discussion at the Happening. Why is that?"

'We prefer to avoid that topic since civil discourse isn't possible these days, man. Politics has become a team blood sport that tends to bring out extreme views and actions in people. People are pre-pissed off, so it takes little to light them up. That can harsh the vibe in the room, man."

'What about you? Which political team are you on?"

'None. I'm a middle-of-the-road kind of guy. I don't do teams or care about Republican or Democratic solutions. I only care about the right solution. We vote for someone, and they get the job. All I ask is that they do the job, but too often, they take up the party-over-country team position or play to some small base. That's no bueno, man."

"So that's a no on a political team. Circling back to religion, you've seen my show, so you know I am an atheist or whatever label they want to put on my nonbelieving ass. I find religion can be highly destructive. Are we brothers in this belief? As you said, you hold your Happening Hour in a former church building you own. Are you sure all of the mojo has left the building?"

"I'm pretty sure me owning that old church building is happenstance, not divine intervention, man. It sort of fell into my lap. And religion, like politics and masturbation, is a personal thing. There are so many unique aspects of each religion that it's easy to see where there can be conflicts between people. So we try to avoid those conflicts at the bar and Happening by asking folks to dial it back. That's all."

"So it's a safe space thing? Doesn't that sound a little progressive left woke to you?"

"No, man, it's a vibe thing. The people come to our bar and the Happening to leave the day's worries behind. You know, take a short tropical mental vacation. But, unfortunately, politics and religion can drag you back into reality, which can be a serious buzzkill for some. Totally harsh your mellow, man."

"I have to agree with you that reality does sometimes suck. That's why God invented weed. But, speaking of God, do you believe, Don?"

Don thought for a moment. "Sky daddy…for me, that's a philosophical thing, man. I can't say for certain that the existence of sky daddy is known or even knowable. If I say sky daddy exists, that would be theism. If I say sky daddy doesn't exist, that would be atheism. If I say I don't know if sky daddy exists, that would be agnosticism. There are a lot of moving parts to this, man! I'll keep an open mind."

"You are certainly well versed on the topic!"

"I'm a bartender, man! We hear things."

"I guess you do. So, why the Happening Hour? How did that come about?"

"It's another case of happenstance, man. I was just handed the keys to the former church building when a lady showed up in emotional distress. We chatted a bit, and I gave her some friendly bartender advice. It seemed to help, and she asked if she could bring her sister to talk to me. Next thing I know, more people are showing up, and it took on a life of its own."

"It certainly has, and you are very popular these days. So where does the Happening Hour go from here?"

Don scratched his head as he thought. "I don't know, man. The Happening thing started accidentally. There isn't some grand plan. The bar is Jane and my livelihood, and the Happening is a hobby, I guess. We just show up each Sunday and wing it."

"Speaking of the bar, I understand your family started it as a speakeasy during prohibition. Did you know your family had this shady past?"

Don laughed. "I knew about the speakeasy's history and how it became our current bar. I didn't know that my family built the church at the start of prohibition or the lease arrangement with the town. I also didn't know the church had a purpose-built false wall in the basement where they hid the booze that supplied my family's speakeasy. And to top it off, the local fishing boats were used to bring the booze ashore from the rum runners anchored in international waters. There were a lot of people involved, man."

The host laughed. "It almost sounds like the pot industry here in California before it went legit. What people will do to get a little high…or tipsy! So, you didn't answer my earlier question on religion. Are we brothers in the belief that religion is dangerous?"

"I wouldn't call it dangerous, man. I think people can be dangerous when they take a belief of any kind to a bad extreme."

"There are good extremes?"

"Sure, man. Kit Kats are a good example."

"Kit Kat, the candy bar?"

"Yeah, one and the same, man. We have chocolate and maybe a couple of other seasonal flavors here in the U.S. But in Japan, there are over 300 flavors of Kit Kats. They have taken the flavor experience to the extreme in a good way. I'd give the Rum Raisin Kit Kat a try. Rum makes everything better!"

"You do have an interesting take on things, Don. One last question before we have to go. What about Jane? You two have been a couple since high school. I've seen her on The Happening, and she's an attractive woman. But, my friend, a lot of time has passed, and you haven't put a ring on it. We didn't agree on religion. Can we agree on bachelorhood? Are we brothers in the belief that marriage is a bad deal and that you will be single, probably with Jane, forever?"

Don smiled. "Jane and I talked about this in great detail, man. We haven't married because it doesn't add anything to us. We have commitment, love, and trust and have for decades. We share everything. The bar, the church building, and the house are all in our trust. We have power of attorney and medical directives for each other. We even have our burial plots in the cemetery that Jane and I walked through when we first started dating. We will be by each other's side forever, man."

"His and hers burial plots? Wow, when you commit, you commit! My girlfriend is lucky to get me to commit to putting the toilet seat down. Anyway, it has been a pleasure to meet you, and I will consider you my bachelor brother with Jane forever. Thank you, Don, and I look forward to your next Church of Don Happening Hour. And I must stop by your bar to meet Jane on my next comedy show tour through New England."

The host stood, shook Don's hand, and went to greet his guest panel.

Back at the bar, the crowd broke out in applause. Olivia switched the screens to a video of old surf scenes and put on tiki background tunes. She turned to Jane. "When I heard the burial plot thing, I thought it was…a little morbid. Creepy. But then my eyes got a little misty when I thought about being by each other's side forever."

Jane smiled. "It's Don! There is no one else on this planet whose vibe perfectly harmonizes with mine. I will do forever with Don!"

Chapter 40 - The aluminum chair recognizes John
October 3rd 10:52 a.m.

Jane paused before entering the back door of the little church building. She looked up at the trees and slowly took a deep breath of cool morning air. The earthy scent meant autumn had begun. The green leaves were slowly giving way to the vibrant color palette of fall. She closed her eyes and smiled. Happy memories of New England fall seasons past filled her with childhood nostalgia. Playing in the piles of raked leaves. Walking the dirt roads at historic Old Sturbridge Village while snacking on warm Indian Pudding. The colorful foliage backdrop at high school football games. The school trip to Plimoth Patuxet Museum and the Mayflower 2 just before Thanksgiving. It was also the romantically colorful start of the holiday season that she and Don both loved. Jane considered herself fortunate that Don embraced the holidays too. Their inner children were happy.

Over the next few weeks, the leaf peepers will be coming to town. Brite Rock has another temporary increase in tourists traveling through New England to enjoy the fall foliage and the cranberry harvest nearby and on Cape Cod. The Town Common has several large maple trees that turn colors from yellow to orange to brilliant scarlet. They frame the Town Hall for one of those iconic New England autumn scenes. It's a favorite spot for fall foliage photographers and outdoor fall weddings. It's also good for the bar and Shanty businesses, especially when the buses stop in town for a lunch or dinner break.

Don caught up to Jane with a mug of hot apple cider in each hand. "Here you go. This should help warm you up."

Jane wrapped her hands around the large mug. She immediately smelled a hint of Tuaca liquor. Tuaca in a mug of hot apple cider with a cinnamon stick and a dollop of whip cream tastes just like hot apple pie. These are fall and winter flavors to Jane.

She took a sip. "Oh babe, I don't know what I did to deserve this treat but let me know so I can do it again!"

Don smiled. "You didn't do anything. It's chilly this morning, and I thought you would enjoy sipping this while curled up on your special chair."

Jane leaned in and kissed Don. "You know me so well."

The back door creaked open, and Wally stuck his head out. "You both need to be on stage now. We go live in one minute." He held the door open for Jane and Don.

"Hey, Wally, is everything okay? You look used up, man!"

Wally glanced again at his watch as he walked. "I'm just tired. Shūlíng and I were up most of the night pushing out social media. I'm hoping for a good bump in stream traffic today. We also updated the opening graphic, and there is new intro music. That plays for about ninety seconds, but we can fade it out whenever you start talking. And remember, we will take some viewers' social media questions for live answers today. I'll feed you the questions. You need to be on stage now."

"Sure, man. Turn on the thing, and let's see what's happening today."

Don looked around the packed room, acknowledging a few people as he crossed the stage.

Wally counted down. "We are live in 5…4…3…2…" The song *At the Tiki Bar* by *Kenny Sasaki & The Tiki Boys* plays as the *Church of Don Happening Hour* graphic appears on the streaming video.

Don hangs his jacket on one of two wrought iron lantern hooks on the side wall of the stage. An antique lantern that Jane found in the attic of the building hangs on the other hook. The lantern was rustic, almost two feet tall, and about eight inches square. It holds a single tall, tapered candle. He made a mental note to get one.

Don looked over at Jane as she curled up on her leather chair on the other side of the stage, sipping her drink.

The music faded out. "How is everybody doing today? Enjoying that first fall chill in the air? Soon enough, we will be complaining about snow and temperatures that are colder than a witch's…"

Jane didn't look up. "Go ahead. I dare you! Say it!"

Don enjoyed the laughter as he settled into the aluminum chair center stage. "Jane, you can sit next to me center stage if you want."

Jane giggled and shook her head. "No, this is your thing. I want to be at a safe distance in case the crowd turns on you. Some look like they could do some damage, particularly those D.A.R. ladies. But I also want to sit close enough to share any kudos coming your way. This is the perfect distance for that, babe."

Don scanned the room until he spotted Lily. "I have to agree about those D.A.R. ladies, Jane. Lily is a wildcat in a bar fight. Your choice to sit close to the back door is a wise exit strategy."

Lily raised her hand. "The aluminum chair recognizes Lily. You look well this morning, my dear!"

"I am, Don. I had a lovely breakfast, and my prune juice worked wonders this morning. You could say I'm as clean as a whistle, inside and out." Lily stood staring at Don.

"Well, thanks for sharing, Lily. Do you have anything else to comment on this morning?"

Lily thought for a moment. "Oh yes, this was amusing. At lunch at the Shanty yesterday, Doris leaned over to me and said she just let out a silent fart and asked me what she should do. I told her to replace the battery in her hearing aid. She had ripped a doozie! Such vibrancy from a one-inch speaker!"

Don waited for the laughter to settle down.

"Lily, may I ask why you have this fixation with flatulence?"

Lily smiled. "When Jane is our age, you will understand. It will be quite the experience the first time she lets out a little toot with every step as she crosses the room. I call it old-lady marching music. Golden years my ass!"

Don waited again for the laughter to die down. "I'm afraid to ask, but do you have anything else to add to the conversation this morning?"

"Only I don't think the people at the other little church program this morning have laughed as much as we have. It's good medicine to laugh. Come to think of it, I doubt that Smyth fellow has laughed, or farted for that matter, in years. I don't know; maybe he needs to get laid. Anyway, I yield the floor, Don."

Don again waited for the laughter to subside. "Well, that sure gets this Happening off to a good start. Who would like to follow that act?"

Wally raised his hand. "The aluminum chair recognizes A-Wall. What's up, man?"

"We have an e-mail question from Jake in Shreveport, Louisiana. He asks who Smyth is and why is he streaming a religious service from the Church of Don?"

"Aloha, Jake. Thanks for the question, man. Unlike me, Pastor Smyth is in the religion biz. He first got into it by doing his thing here in the Historic Sailers Church of Brite Rock. I guess he digs the vibe of the place, so he built an exact copy next to his new big church. That's why it looks like he's doing his thing from our humble Happening shack. I hope that answers your question, man. Oh, if you ever take a road trip down to New Orleans, check out Beachbum Berry's joint, Latitude 29. Seriously tasty island food and tiki libations. The man is a tropical beverage historian, an inspired cocktail artist, and a superior mixologist! Okay, who wants to contribute to the conversation?"

Wally raised his hand. "The aluminum chair recognizes A-Wall again. Another question from the beyond?"

"No, Don, I just wanted to introduce Shūlíng to everyone. She is helping me produce the show this weekend, and I hope she makes being around a habit. Everyone, this is Shūlíng. You can call her by her full name, Shūlíng, or simply Shū." Wally points the camera at Shūlíng so the stream audience can see her.

Shūlíng looked into the camera and smiled. "Thank you all for your kindness. I feel very welcome here. Now going back to the stage." Shūlíng pressed one of the buttons on the video switcher to select one of six cameras that Wally now uses for streaming the Happening.

Jane started a round of applause. "Welcome, Shū! She and Wally came to the bar the other night, and he introduced her around. She is not only gorgeous; she is brilliant too. Shū and Olivia were talking deep nerd about Liv's bar sound system, artificial intelligence, and other tech stuff. Smart chicks rock!"

Don nodded and applauded. "I concur, man! That's why I have one in my life."

Jane held up her mug and winked at Don.

"Moving along, who would like to be next?" Don scanned the room as hands went up. "The aluminum chair recognizes John Lennon. What's on your mind this fine day?"

John stood and tapped Brad on the shoulder and motioned him to stand up too. "All right then, how is it that daft wanker Smyth and his dodgy little copy of this building is on the internet same as us? It's confusing now, isn't it! He's trying to nick your show and ruin it for all of us. Should me and me mate, Brad, have a word with that smarmy prat about this? It's no bother."

Don smiled, recalling John's past run-ins with Smyth. "Thanks for the generous offer, but you getting arrested for punching Smyth in the nose isn't a good look for your message of peace and love, man."

Brad, still standing next to John, raised his hand. "I'll punch him!"

"No, mate. Donny's right. It's best to avoid a stint at the Governor's pleasure. Besides, you're too handsome for prison. They'll be passing you around like a bottle of port at Christmas dinner."

Brad's eyes opened wide. "I never thought about prison. My girl thinks I am crush-worthy cute. Oh, and I sometimes randomly yell things out that the other prisoners may find offensive! I'm not going to punch Smyth. Bad plan!"

"Yeah, mate. We should take a pint and think on this." Brad nodded in agreement as they both sat down.

Don pointed to the Rules of the Happening paper taped to the wall. "I believe this situation falls under Rule number 12 of the Happenings."

John was bewildered. "Is that the no gratuitous nudity rule? We weren't gonna show Smyth our naughty bits, now were we!"

"No, man. Rule number 12 is no violent acts here or in my bar, and... Look, I get it, man. I believe Smyth is a pompous dick, and others think the guy is golden. I'm good with both views. It's everyone's choice to believe in him or not. So no, I don't want you two punching Smyth in the nose for doing a show from his replica of this building. We are better than that, man!"

Pete raised his hand. "Moving along, the aluminum chair recognizes PP. What's on your mind, man?"

"You say no violent acts in your bar, yet you have told me on several occasions that you will let Jane and Red kick my ass or rip my hand off and feed it to the cat or tap dance on my balls and other violent acts. Aren't you being a hypocrite here?"

Jane sat up straight in her chair. "PP, think about what happened just before each of those threats.

Do you remember sitting at the bar and reaching over the top for a napkin or plugging in your phone charger, which I have repeatedly told you not to do, and your several resulting boob grazes? Or the so-called accidental brushing of your hand against my ass when you would walk by me? Then there is the time when you took a picture of me bending over to pull a bottle of wine out of the cooler and posted it on Yelp with an entertainment review. The list goes on, and that's just me. Add Red's list of your offenses, and your pervie behavior is over the top. All very sexual harassmenty. We don't need Don's help to deal with you. This one Red and I got!"

Pete sat down and stared at the floor. Jane looked at Don. An awkward silence filled the room.

The aluminum chair squeaked as Don leaned forward. "P, do you know why you are allowed in the bar and the Happening?"

Still looking at the floor, he shook his head no.

"It's because Jane and Red asked me to allow it, man. I would have bounced you a long time ago for your behavior, particularly when it comes to touching. Jane and Red both told me that you don't do it to customers and that they will manage it. They said I didn't have the right to be offended for them. It is their choice to let you stay. Getting bounced from our bar would likely mean the Shanty and McCabe's Pub would probably do the same. So, you may want to think about it before you get handsy with the ladies again. They own the biggest part of your social life, man."

Pete slowly stood and looked at Jane. "I'm sorry, Jane. I never wanted to…I never meant… You and Red mean the world to me. I love you and Red and promise I will be a perfect gentleman. Wait, I can still look – right?"

Jane sighed and relaxed in her chair. "Look but don't touch. And no more photos or creepy behavior in general. If you do, the hammer gets dropped, and then you get exiled. Agreed?"

Pete agreed and sat down.

A hand went up in the back corner of the room. "The aluminum chair recognizes James Freeman. How's it going, Best?"

Best stood to talk. "It's going well. I just wanted to offer up support for PP. Since his actions in the bar are limited to Jane and Miss Kelly Rose, and he just said that he loves both of them, he may be in a state of limerence."

Jane was baffled. "Limerence? What's that? It sounds like something I would name my pet unicorn if I had one."

Best looked at PP and then back to Jane. "If I remember my college psychology correctly, it's a state of mind caused by a romantic attraction to another person. You know, obsessive thoughts and fantasies and a desire to have a relationship with you and Miss Kelly Rose where physical love is reciprocated."

Jane had never considered the cause of Pete's behavior before. "PP, are you infatuated with Red and me? Is it what Best just described?"

Pete stood. "No, it's not! I love you and Red as family, and I don't have what Best described. I have a run-of-the-mill sex addiction. Nothing special, more of a fetish, really." PP glared at Best.

Jane slowly stood. "A sex addiction? That's why you touched me?"

Pete shifted his attention to Jane. "Yes…I mean, no. Not really. My thing is for very tall blonde Viking-looking women like my ex-wife Eva and my ex-wife Anna. Women like…oh, Lars Van der Berg's daughter Johanna that works at the post office. That breathtaking statuesque young Dutch beauty is a goddess! Johanna's taller than my ex-wives but worth the climb." Jane clenched her fists and started to walk toward PP.

Don pointed at the paper list of Happening rules tacked to the wall. "Jane, Happening Rule number 12." Jane looked at Don. She stopped and focused on reading his body language. He continued to point at the paper on the wall.

"Rule number 12, Jane." She sighed as she let go of the fight in her and returned to her special chair. She slowly sat, folded her arms, and stared icily at PP. It unnerved him.

"Ah, Don, I think Jane is casting a spell or putting a curse on me or something. Please make her stop. It's creeping me out."

Don knew Pete was superstitious and Jane was taking advantage of his paranoia. "Jane…um, babe…are you putting a curse or spell on PP?"

Jane's expression didn't change. "Yup!"

"Are you almost done, babe?

Jane's expression still didn't change. "Nope!"

Don looked at PP. "I've found that it's best to let her finish. Things can get dicey when the ends aren't neatly tied up. You know, doors to other worlds left ajar, unintended consequences, things like that, man."

Pete looked forlorn. "Oh, absolutely, that isn't something to trifle with!"

Jane energetically smiled. "OK, I'm back. What did I miss? She picked up her mug and took the last sip of the cider.

Jane's antics amused Don. "Well, I will summarize this for you. PP doesn't have limerence as Best suggested but does have strong physical and emotional feelings for exceptionally tall blonde women. PP publicly named Lars Van der Berg's daughter Johanna, meaning he will need to lay low for a while and not go to the post office. Speaking of Lars, have you seen the muscles on him, man? It's an impressive sight as he handles the heavy nets on his fishing boat." Jane laughed and pointed at PP. She stopped when Don gave her the look.

"To continue, PP said some things that incited your ire, and you went into search and destroy mode. I reminded you of Rule number 12, and you sat down. You then communed with your coven and dropped a fresh one on PP. He then committed himself to behave or be gone. You or Red can make that call anytime, so PP is on notice. And limerence does sound like what you would name your unicorn if you had one." Jane laughed and nodded in agreement.

Don scanned the room again. "I see Juan Carlos Batista has his hand up, so the aluminum chair recognizes him. What's hip J.C.?"

"I just wanted to thank you and Jane for holding this Happening thing. I have gotten to know more people in town, and they have gotten to know me. And I have my face and name on a t-shirt that people pay money for because of this and the bar. All my cousins in Calexico have them. So, thank you for including me. I'm honored."

Don waited for the applause to die down. "You are welcome, and thank you for being in our bar and Happening family, man. For those who don't know J.C., he works in a shared arrangement for the Mariners Shanty Restaurant and our bar. He manages the bar food menu. He's the captain of the Crab Rangoon. The prince of the Pu-pu Platter. The king of the Kalua Pork Nachos. That's why the dude with the food is on a staff t-shirt. Now, time for one more."

Don scanned the room. "Officer James Dillard, Brite Rock's finest, is here today. The aluminum chair recognizes him even though he didn't raise his hand. How's it going, man?"

Dillard stood. "Hi Jane, you look spectacular as always. Is Don behaving, or is he being himself?"

Jane laughed. "Well, Jimmy, Don did return to the scene of the crime. Handcuffs were involved, and he surrendered himself to me. He then performed a community service to my satisfaction. So I guess he's a good Don!"

Don nodded. "I am a good Don!" The song *The Enchanted Sea* by the *Islanders* began to play. "Well, that's my traveling music. Thanks for dropping into our Happening. Please feel free to hang around and talk story or stop by the bar later. And thanks to everyone watching from the beyond. Aloha!"

Don and Jane stood, walked toward each other, and hugged. Attendees mingled as the room took on a party atmosphere.

Wally looked at the data on Shūlíng's laptop, smiled, and motioned for Don and Jane to come to him. "I thought you may like to know that we had almost 302,000 attendees on our live stream today, and Smyth's live stream was just over 9,000 for his copycat little church show."

Don stared at Wally in disbelief. "289,000 people watched us today? Why would they do that, man? Don't they have other places to be or better things to do?"

Wally laughed. "I keep telling you, Don, that you are a somebody. People like you and Jane. We will get thousands more views from the recorded version of today's Happening once we add the merch advertisement at the end and post it online in a few minutes."

The perplexed expression returned to Don's face. "How did 289,000 people find us?"

Wally looked at Shūlíng. They both started laughing. "Let's just call it creative advertising."

Chapter 41 - We need to get rid of the competition
October 5th 9:36 a.m.

Smyth glared at Caruso and Reed as they stood uncomfortably in front of his desk. He was seething just below the surface but had to calculate where to focus his ire. Of course, it wouldn't be at either Caruso or Reed. They were critical to his operation. He reminded himself of a quote he came across while looking for preaching material. *Speak when angry, and you will make the best speech you will ever regret!*

Smyth slowly and methodically tapped the ring on his right hand firmly on his desktop as he thought. Each tap was louder than the previous.

The tapping stopped as Smyth leaned back in his chair and looked up at the ceiling. "Tell me the numbers again, Paul."

Caruso cleared his throat. "The bartender's event had almost 300,000 live views. Our Founding Church special had just over 9,000 live views. Our Hour of Reflection had 16,427 live views. I don't have the data for the broadcast views yet."

Smyth's jaw tightened as he continued to look at the ceiling, "And how did he get that many live views, Paul?"

"Well, he got a lot of publicity from that HBO show he was on. People probably looked for his online shit show out of curiosity. Probably just a one-time blip in the data." Smyth nodded slightly. That was a possibility.

Caruso continued. "Now, our social media analytics team found one anomaly that they need to look into. Using the online search term for anything Brite Rock returned the top URL, *Historic Sailers Church of Brite Rock Sunday Event*. Clicking on that took them to the Church of Don Happening URL. Somehow our URL...well, they outranked us in online searches. Our social media team thinks that a lot of our people stayed on the Happening site once they found it."

Smyth leaned forward, staring directly at Caruso and Reed again. "So are you saying that a search for Brite Rock Cathedral by the Sea brought up the bartender's site first? How the fuck can they do that when I own the trademark for Sailers Church of Brite Rock? Ideas, anyone?"

Caruso took a deep breath. "I don't know. I spoke to our lawyer this morning. He called the Brite Rock town lawyer, who confirmed that the term Historic Sailers Church of Brite Rock is used in town documents, maps, Chamber of Commerce tourist literature, and on the plaque on the walkway to the building. We would have to sue several organizations, including the town, to enforce the trademark. Needless to say, that would be expensive and make us look like assholes."

"What about Hour of Reflection? Did they use that name too?"

"Not exactly, George. They used the term Hour of Reflection without caps in several sentences and as their search keywords. It was usually about letting rum breathe for an hour and then reflecting on how it had changed. They called it the rum's hour of reflection. The phrase was used enough to have the search engine rank it. Our analytics people said it was a pretty clever job. They can explain it a lot better than I can."

Smyth sighed deeply. "What is our recourse here? I want this to end, but I don't want a protracted legal battle with the town. We may win in legal court, but we would lose in the court of public opinion in Brite Rock. Or, as you so eloquently put it, make us look like assholes."

"Our lawyer says that we should send a cease and desist letter to the bartender telling him to stop infringing on the trademarked name Sailers Church of Brite Rock and that the potential consequences of not complying with our demand may be litigation. We need to do that to show the enforcement of our trademark. I doubt they will stop the infringement, but it establishes our position for anything we want to do. Or nothing. I don't know. Because of the word historic in front of the Sailers Church name, our lawyer says it's a messy challenge, George."

Smyth pounded the desktop. "We can't do nothing! The hippie bartender is getting between us and viewers that send in donations. This shit has to stop. He's a major fucking irritant!"

Caruso tapped Jim on the arm. "Do you have the numbers from the online take from yesterday?"

"No, I can call down and…."

"Give me a minute here, Jim. Why don't you walk down to accounting and get the numbers? And have them print a trend chart so George can see week-on-week growth." Jim thought that was a good idea and happily left the room.

Smyth glared at Caruso. "We need to get rid of the competition – now! Do a little research and find a guaranteed window for taking out the hippie's building. I need a time at night when he won't be around the old church building or his house, for that matter."

Caruso was surprised. "The house? What are you going to do, George?"

Smyth squinted and firmly pointed at Caruso. "Like I said before, you don't need to know. What you don't know can't hurt you or me if things go sideways. I don't want anyone to get hurt. The house could get some minor collateral damage. Nothing serious or intentional. That's all."

Caruso had never seen Smyth that worked up.

"George, take a breath. You have a plan to fix this. I'll do some digging and find out when the best window of opportunity is for you to…you know." Caruso pointed to his right ear to remind Smyth that Reed was expected to enter the room and could overhear their conversation. Smyth nodded; he understood.

"You're right, Paul. This is fixable. Find me that window, and I want you to have eyes on them for that time period. Do you understand – they never leave your sight."

"Yeah, I got it, George. I'm on it."

Reed was talking as he entered the room. "So, the numbers for online viewer donations are down about forty-two percent. It looks like the majority of our viewers that clicked on their link by mistake stayed with them."

Smyth listened half-heartedly, waiting for Reed to finish talking. "Okay, thanks, Jim. We'll have to work on getting the online business fixed. If you two will excuse me, I have a few calls to make."

Caruso told Smyth he and Reed would catch up with him later and exited the office. In the hallway, Caruso asked Reed what it was like in Don's Tiki Lounge.

"You know, Paul, I think it may be a fun place. It's decorated like an old bar that you would find in the South Pacific. People wore Hawaiian shirts; they played tropical music and offered interesting drinks. I wanted to try one, but I was with George, and we were on business, so it was not a good idea."

"No, George would not have been happy with you drinking during a meeting. Is the bar successful?"

"I'm guessing it is. It's been in Don's family for three or four generations. A poster in the bar's front window promotes a big birthday celebration for the bar in a week or so. It says it's one of their biggest events of the year. I'd go back there, but I'm afraid the crazy person that attacked George would recognize me."

Caruso feigned concern. "Of course, you wouldn't want to run into that crazy person again. Probably best to steer clear of the place."

"I couldn't agree more, Paul. So, why are you asking about his bar?"

"You know, Jim, I'm trying to understand the person that's giving George a run for his money. Finding that middle ground so we can negotiate for the church building is easier when you understand both parties' personalities."

Reed nodded. "Ah, that's true. Well, I hope you can find a way to put an end to this animosity."

Caruso smiled broadly. "I'm sure we will, Jim. I'm sure we will."

Caruso drove by the bar on his way home to read the poster. He took a photo with his phone and went home to make a few calls. Caruso needed to find a ticket and order a colorful tropical print aloha shirt online. He had to stand out in the bar on that night. Being seen there is his alibi.

After buying the shirt and ticket to the luau, Caruso drove to Smyth's house. He didn't dare have this conversation on the phone.

Smyth answered the door. "Are you alone, George?"

Smyth looked past Caruso. He squinted as he scanned the dark surroundings. He didn't see anyone. "Yes, come in."

Caruso entered and closed the door.

"Okay, so on October 14th, there is a huge party at the bar. It's a big deal, so the bartender and his girlfriend will both be there all evening. So that's your window of opportunity."

Smith opened the calendar on his phone. "The 14th is in 9 days. Good! So, starting at 9:00 p.m. on the 14th, you must have eyes on both of them. I will be done and back home by 9:45 p.m. Can you guarantee that you will have eyes on them for that time, Paul?"

"Yes, George, I will be there with eyes on them. The party they are throwing at the bar has been sold out for weeks, but $50 got me a ticket. I bought it from some loser in town who broke up with his girlfriend, thank god! So, I'll be watching them, and if something goes wrong at the bar, I will text you."

"No text, Paul – call me! I don't want anything written down about this. Phone calls or in-person conversations only."

"Okay, will do, George.

"Thanks, Paul. And please know that I appreciate your help on this. I wouldn't do it if it weren't important to our plan."

Chapter 42 - It's going to be a busy night
October 14th 3:20 p.m.

The Don's Tiki Cocktails & Lounge annual luau was a significant undertaking for the bar and Shanty. The larger-than-usual staff was busy decorating and preparing for the 5:00 p.m. start time. A.J. hung up the phone and yelled across the bar to Jane. "The florist said she will be here at 3:45 to drop off your order."

"Thanks, A.J." Jane walked to the stage, where Don adjusted the luau birthday party sign. "Hey babe, when will you and Darlene address the ohana? Time is getting tight." Jane held up her wrist and pointed at her watch.

"I guess now is good. Let's do this in the Shanty so the cooks can keep working if they aren't at a stopping point."

Don called the bar staff into the Shanty, where Darlene and her team joined them.

"First of all, Darlene, thanks for continuing the tradition and closing the Shanty early to cater our luau again. And I want to thank every one of you for helping to put this luau on tonight. This annual bar birthday tradition has been going on since the bar opened as a backroom speakeasy in October of 1920, 10 months after Prohibition started.

Darlene knows this story well. But, for those that don't, in 1920, Darlene's grandmother, Emma, was the cook at my grandparent's summer home in Brite Rock. My family encouraged Emma to rent space in this building and open a restaurant. The rent was one dollar per year. The restaurant opened in the spring of 1921. The speakeasy and restaurant kept each other afloat through the Great Depression of 1929 until it and Prohibition ended in 1933.

In 1934 the speakeasy was converted into a full public bar. In 1948, my grandfather and father changed the bar to Don's Tiki Cocktails & Lounge. I was born and named Don after my dad. But that's only part of the family story. To tell the whole story, you have to speak of the ohana. In Hawaiian, Ohana means your family of close relatives, cousins, in-laws, neighbors, and friends. It's an extended family bound together. In this room is our ohana. In this room is love." Don paused, a little misty-eyed. Darlene gave him a long hug.

Jane smiled. "You'll have to give these two a moment. They grew up together in the bar and restaurant and have this weird non-sibling relationship. I'll carry on for Don and Darlene while they compose themselves. So, let's talk about who will do what tonight.

Don, me, Red, A.J., Shakemaster Sam, Geezer, and Sarah from McCabe's Irish Pub will be slinging drinks on the bar side. Sarah will fill beer and wine orders. Lindsay from the Black Cat Diner will be bussing tables. Since we will be slammed all night, we are going with restaurant-grade compostable cups, cutlery, and plates to eliminate some dishwashing, just like they do at most Hawaiian luaus.

Also, in the luau tradition, we will offer a limited selection of tropical libations this evening. Cocktails include Mai Tai, Blue Hawaii, Pina Colada, Rum Old Fashioned, Pain Killer, Jane's Jungle Juice, Day at Brite's Beach, and Lava Flow. The non-alcohol cocktails will be the No High Mai Tai, Virgin Lava Flow, and the No Pain Killer. Each is five dollars, and they get one complimentary drink ticket with their paid admission. And yes, we are sold out on admission tickets.

Now, six rum companies have donated several cases of rum to the bar. In addition, three companies will have their product ambassadors pouring and serving three-dollar shots of the good stuff. All the money from the shots goes into the Ohana tip jar for the evening. A few special bottles have also been gifted to the bar to partake of at the afterparty. Of course, the full luau menu will be available too. We deserve it!

Live entertainment this evening will be Mike & The Swinging Coconut Farmers opening for the Curly Wave Chasers. And then my favorite tropical all-girl party band, Kalani & The Ōkole Shakers. She is the cutest thing, and what a voice. I may also shake my Ōkole a little tonight, but you already knew that.

And finally, for security and age verification, Officer Jim Dillard will be at the door tonight with Kamekona, or Kam for short. Kam is Hawaiian and on the Boston College football team. Don and I met Kam on the flight from Kauai to Boston this past spring. He said he would work the door at the luau in exchange for island cooking. He won't be disappointed. We open the doors at 5:00 p.m. and do last call at 11:30 p.m. And now I turn it over to Miss Darlene. Tell us about the tasty this evening, sweetie!"

Darlene wiped her brow. "I'm looking forward to that afterparty drink already!

We will use three food buffet stations around the bar and walking hors d' oeuvres service tonight. This way, we can control the flow of the kitchen and grill better so we don't put ourselves ass deep in the weeds.

On the kitchen side for this event are me, my line cook Tommy, and Tommy's cousin Mason who line cooks in New York City. Their sous chef is Connie, and her cooks are Kerry and Tim. J.C. is on the wood grill, and the kalua pork imu pit out behind the bar. The food runners are Kevin from the Black Cat Diner and little Lisa from Rudy's Clam Shack. The hors d' oeuvres servers are Stephanie, Jenna, and Becky. David is the dishwasher, and his brother Joe is on bussing, trash, and recycling. My boo, Andy, will be on the pass-through door to keep it clear for servers and runners and keep people from entering the Shanty.

The menu is kālua pork, ahi poke, beef teriyaki, huli-huli chicken, char siu pork, Don's guava barbecued ribs, coconut shrimp skewers, lumpia (Filipino spring rolls), Hawaiian style macaroni salad, and Hawaiian fried rice, coconut cake, pineapple upside-down rum cake and haupia, a coconut dessert with the texture of stiff pudding. We start serving at 6:00 p.m. and end at 10:30 p.m. That gives us time to prep for our after-party that will begin in the Shanty at midnight.

The bar and the Shanty open at four in the afternoon tomorrow, so everyone can get their party on tonight, sleep late tomorrow, and still have time for cleanup before it's business as usual. That's it!"

Don looked around the room. "Thanks, Darlene! I am happy to announce that the Ohana tip jar is expected to be big tonight and will be evenly divided between the staff, excluding us owners. The bar's liquor purveyor, three of our favorite rum companies, and two beer companies have made cash contributions to the tip jar, so you are starting the evening at $3,900 in tips even before the doors open. Now, let's get ready to get our tiki on and welcome our luau guests. Servers, give yourself time to get dressed in your finest aloha wear. It's going to be a busy night!"

Chapter 43 - Don't worry, Paul, I've got this
October 14th 3:45 p.m.

Smyth looked at his watch again. Caruso could see that he was anxious, and that bothered him. Nervous people often make careless mistakes. Smyth started tapping his ring on the desktop and was deep in thought when Jim Reed walked in. "It's quiet in here. What are you boys up to?"

Smyth glanced at Caruso and then back to Reed. "Nothing. It's been a long week, and I think I'm about to call it a day. Dinner and a movie at home tonight sound great to me. What about you, Jim?"

"I'm leaving in a few minutes for Boston. My wife's sister is ill, so she gave us her tickets to a show at the Cutler Majestic Theatre tonight. Dinner at the Union Oyster House after the show and a room at the Four Seasons. You have to get out of Blight Rock now and then and enjoy a little culture."

Smyth laughed. "Blight Rock does describe the lack of cultural offerings in this town. It sounds like you have a wonderful getaway planned. I need to do more of that. Boston is such a great city."

Smyth looked directly at Caruso. "So, what are your plans for the evening, Paul? Anything special, or will you be a boring homebody like me?"

Caruso flashed that big smile of his. "It's funny, ever since Jim mentioned that luau party at the bar on Jetty Road, I have been craving Hawaiian food and drink. So I may try to get in. If that doesn't work out, I can always find a pint or two of Guinness at McCabe's Pub. The fish and chips are good there too! Wherever I end up, I will make an evening of it."

Caruso looked at his watch. "You better get a move on, Jim! The traffic on Route 3 North into Boston is horrible during rush hour."

"You are right about that, Paul. However, if you do end up at the luau, watch out for the Beatle John Lennon. She punched George hard, bloodied his nose."

"Thanks for the tip, Jim! I'll keep an eye out for the Beatle. Travel safe!"

The door clicked shut behind Reed. Caruso laughed. "You know that story about John Lennon punching you in the nose never gets old, right?"

Smyth still doesn't see the humor in it. "I only wish it were the actual John Lennon that punched me in the nose. That would mean he was still with us, and I had done something spectacular to provoke the man of peace and love to violence. But, instead, a nut case that thinks they are him attacks me in a bar. I tell you, Paul, this is a fucked up world."

"I agree, George. So, let's look at where we stand. Jim has unwittingly provided himself with an alibi. My alibi will be my presence at the bar when, you know, that thing happens. What about you?"

Smith smiled, confident that he had come up with a solid plan. "I will order Chinese food delivered to my house at 8:30 p.m. It will be just enough food for one person. Next, I will find the newest hot Netflix movie to rent and talk it up to the delivery person. I'll give them a big tip. Service people always remember big tippers. Then I will rent and pay for the Netflix movie, starting around 8:45 p.m.

Then, I will drive to the hippie's church in a dark-colored SUV I borrowed from Ernie Chapman in Providence this afternoon. I parked at the train station in the west lot. There aren't any security cameras in that lot. I made and printed a set of counterfeit license plates using Photoshop that I will tape over the SUV's license plates. I will then drive over and park on Abigail Road. It's a short walk to the church building from there.

The backdoor alarm hasn't worked in years. So that's my way in. I should be back home just about 9:30 p.m. at the latest if someone calls to tell me about what happened. My alibi is being home alone that evening. The food order, the delivery guy remembering me being home, and the record of the rental movie at the time of the thing support that. Have I forgotten anything, Paul?"

Caruso thought for a moment. "I think we are all covered. Just be careful. If anything looks the least bit wrong or someone gets a look at you near the target, walk away. We can regroup and try again later."

"Don't worry, Paul; I've got this. You do your part, and we will be golden."

Chapter 44 - It's showtime baby
October 14th 4:37 p.m.

The kiawe wood smoke from the imu pit and grill pulled at Don as he walked out the doorway to the bar's back parking lot. Kiawe, a slightly sweeter Hawaiian mesquite, reminded him of the campfires a few locals would make at sunset at Shipwreck Beach on Kauai. The expense of shipping the kiawe firewood, banana leaves, and ti leaves from Hawaii for the annual luau is fine with Don and Jane. That smoke flavor was a must-have for an authentic luau.

The traditional luau main dish, kālua pig, was slow-roasted pig wrapped in banana leaves and ti leaves in a Hawaiian-style imu underground oven behind the bar for several hours. Delicate kiawe wood smoke and banana and ti leaves give kālua pig a distinctive flavor. J.C., Tommy, and Mason removed the kālua pig from the imu and took it to the kitchen to be shredded at 4:30 p.m.

J.C. returned to masterfully grilling the huli-huli chicken, the barbecued guava ribs, and the red char siu pork. The pork had the traditional red color courtesy of vegetable-based food coloring added to the marinade. Red is an auspicious color in Chinese culture and is included in the luau menu in hopes of bringing continued success to the bar and Shanty.

"Don, get away from the grill. You'll smell like a brush fire from the smoke."

He looked up to see Jane standing in the back doorway to the bar. She was dressed in black linen slacks and a v-neck Hawaiian floral print top. The top was custom-made for her by the fabric shop on Kauai. A fresh plumeria and purple orchid lei was draped around her neck. A single plumeria flower was carefully placed in her hair behind her left ear. That lets those looking for love know she was unavailable. Don couldn't take his eyes off her.

Jane folded her arms. "Do I have to come down there and drag you away from the grill? Get your smokey ass upstairs and change out of that nasty t-shirt and shorts. We open in ten minutes."

Don quickly walked past Jane and bolted up the stairs to their old apartment above the bar to change. Nine minutes later, he appeared at the bar showered, dressed in white linen slacks, a new white aloha shirt with colorful tropical accents, and dress leather sandals.

October 14th 5:00 p.m.

Shūlíng turned on the camera and started live streaming. Wally introduced himself to the viewers as the streaming host for the evening's luau. Shūlíng panned the camera off of A-Wall and focused on Jane as she adjusted the collar on Don's shirt. Jane took the kukui nut lei from its container, placed it around Don's neck, and kissed him.

She smiled. "It's showtime, baby!"

Jane walked behind the bar, grabbed the cord to the wall-mounted cast iron rooster bell, and rang it three times. She announced, "all is well, and let the luau begin!"

Don opened the front door and greeted the long line of people outside the bar. He walked the line talking to people as Officer Dillard and Kam checked IDs and tickets. Most of the usual bar patrons were there (Jerry, Olivia, Ed and Cindy, Roger, PP, Best, the D.A.R. ladies, Brad, John Lennon, Karen and her sister Kathy, Spider, Been Dead Billy, Pudsy, Douche Bag Danny, Benny the bear, Cyclops, and his girlfriend Bent Betty) along with people from the area and some from seeing the Happening online. Don recognized the loud blonde in her signature polka dot dress and her boyfriend, who drove in from Connecticut.

Most wore aloha wear and were very much in the island party spirit. One woman near the back of the line wore a tropical print evening dress and an impressive Niʻihau shell lei.

"Thank you for coming. You are rocking that dress, and that shell lei is beautiful. The craftsmanship is impeccable!"

The woman reached out and took Don's hand. "Thank you! My name is Alonna. My grandmother made this lei for my mother many years ago. My mother moved to Kauai when she married, but my Tutu lived all her days in Ni'ihau.

The lei was handed down to me when my mother passed, a family tradition. And I made my dress. I got the material from the same shop in Kapa'a where Jane got the top she is wearing tonight. Your shirt, too, I think."

Don was surprised. "How do you know that?"

"I heard it on the coconut wireless. My son told his girlfriend about you, and she told the fabric shop owner, and they told me. Small island!"

"How does your son know me?"

Alonna proudly points. "Kamekona is my son. I am visiting him this week. He told me about meeting you and Jane on his flight to Boston and how kind you were to him. Several weeks ago, he bought me a ticket to the luau, so I drove down from Boston with him this afternoon. Traffic here is much worse than Kauai."

Don laughed. "Yes, it is! Now, you shouldn't stand in line way back here. You are ohana! Come with me."

Don presented his arm, and she locked hers in his. They walked to the front of the line. Kam smiled when he saw Don escorting his mom.

"Mahalo for helping my mom. She doesn't know anyone here besides me."

Don smiled. "The building is full of ohana that she hasn't met yet. Let's get you settled inside, Alonna, so that I can get to work. Let me see if I can find you a table."

Alonna hesitated. "Would it be all right if I sat at the bar? I bartended for a while in Poʻipū and would like to watch you folks in action."

"Of course. This seat will give you a primo view of the bar. The couple seated to your right is Olivia and Jerry. Let me introduce you to a few others."

Don held up two fingers and waved them, signaling Red to ring the bell twice to get people's attention.

"Aloha, everyone, and welcome. Tonight's luau honors this fine establishment's longevity and the Hawaiian and Polynesian cultures that influence us. Before we get started, I want to introduce Alonna. She is from Kauai and is visiting her son Kam, the gentle giant Boston College football player, at the door. Please introduce yourself to both of them this evening in the luau spirit.

Alonna, that brown-haired buxom beauty behind the bar to your right, is Jane, my girlie. Standing before you is ginger-haired barkeep extraordinaire Kelly Rose, but you must call her Red. The barkeep to Red's right is Shakemaster Sam. The gray fox at the end of the bar is Arthur Johnson, better known as A.J. The lovely lass next to A.J. is our unofficially adopted daughter, Sarah. She is probably the best cold water surfer here and rules at Narragansett and Ruggles. So, Red, take good care of Alonna; she is Ohana.

As you can see, the food service has begun and will continue until 10:30 p.m. There are a few grazing stations are around the bar, and waitstaff will move around with tray service. There is plenty of food, so don't freak out if something momentarily runs out, man. Fresh refills from the kitchen and grill will not disappoint.

Luau drinks listed on the bar signs are five dollars each. There are four rum producers here that will be pouring three-dollar shots. All proceeds from drink and shot sales go into the tip jar. That pink ticket you received at the door is your complimentary free drink. It's a cash bar tonight, so see Miss Sarah if you need to break a bill or want to buy drink tickets on a credit card. The minimum credit card purchase is two tickets.

Now, live music is medicine for the mind. It reduces stress and makes us happier. We have three bands tonight to help enhance your mood. Mike & The Swinging Coconut Farmers will kick things off starting at 7:00, followed by the Curly Wave Chasers. And then Kalani & The Ōkole Shakers will take us to midnight. The last round will be called at 11:30. Bar rules apply. Luau responsibly." The song *Let's Lounge* by *Richard Cheese* began to play on the bar sound system.

October 14th 6:10 p.m.

Don stood near the Shanty passthrough door. From this vantage point, he could see the flow of the thirsty and hungry crowd. The bar was handling a completely packed house that all needed drinks. He could tell by the sound of Darlene's voice that the kitchen was in good shape, even though the food stations were quickly picked clean as if set upon by locusts. Stephanie, Jenna, and Becky walked their hors d' oeuvres service trays near the depleted food stations to provide a buffer zone for Kevin and little Lisa to refill them. It was an impressive diversionary tactic to keep the food flowing seamlessly.

Shūlíng live streamed as she followed A-Wall around the bar. They approached Don.

"Don, this luau rocks! The people are partying hard. But we have just completed a behind-the-scenes look, and there are nothing but smiles from the bartenders, cooks, servers…everyone! This is hard work, but everyone is happy. What do you attribute that to?"

"It's not work, man."

Wally looked confused. "But the staff is busting ass to make and serve food and drink at a breakneck pace. So how is that not work?"

"It's not work if you love what you are doing. We have been preparing for this for weeks and love the challenge of pleasing our guests. That's the nature of our business, man. When we do it well, it's all smiles."

Wally continued interviewing Don as Paul Caruso maneuvered his way behind him so he would be seen on camera. Caruso then went across the crowded room to the bar to order a drink from Jane. He made small talk to annoy her so she would remember him. He needed to be seen and keep his eyes on her and Don.

At the front door, Dillard greeted someone that he knew very well. "Anthony James Foonman! Are you working tonight, Mister Foonman, or is this a drinking night for you? Better not be both since you are in uniform!"

Foonman laughed. "No worries, Officer Dildo, I'm here for a takeout food order for the station. Darlene called and said they had some island treats for us to pick up."

"Wow, Foon, you fire department guys have an easy life. You sit on your asses waiting for something to happen while we police cruise the city protecting the citizenry."

"And a fine job you do, Jimmy! Those black and white patrol cars look nice too! Kind of like superhero cars. Do people say the penguins of justice are here to save us when you roll up?

"No, Foon, it's nothing but respect from everyone in town except you boys. All you boys do is stand around with your hoses in your hand. Have you ever considered looking for honest employment?"

"No time for that, Jimmy. Being on the BRFD is a calling. Many apply, but those who don't make the fire department become cops, I guess. Hey, my takeout should be ready. Give us a call if someone falls off their bar stool and needs a ride to the hospital. We just finished thoroughly cleaning the ambulance, and it's springtime fresh, so no pukers. That's what police cars are for!"

"I'll be sure to ask for you by name when I call, Foon."

"You do that, Jimmy! Take care tonight. It's a full moon. There is something in the air beside the bar's barbeque grill smoke!"

Chapter 45 - Smyth practiced his plan
October 14th 6:27 p.m.

The full moon lit the unseasonably warm October night. Smyth opened the power panel and turned the lights off for the parking lot on the right side of his Brite Rock Cathedral by the Sea. The founding church was thrown into darkness. Having an exact copy of Don's Sailers Church building provided the perfect training location for Smyth to practice his plan.

He exited the side door of the Cathedral and stopped to adjust the shoulder strap on the heavy duffle bag. The four-pound steel hammer, one-inch wide cold steel chisel, and heavy-duty wrecking bar weighed down the bag.

Smyth carefully scanned the empty parking lot and the surrounding area for any activity. Then, satisfied that he was alone, he casually walked to the back door of the founding church.

Time Check... 6:32 p.m.

He slipped the key into the lock, opened the back door, and entered the service and storage room. The duffle bag made a metallic thud when Smyth set it down. He closed the door, slipped on the LED headlamp, turned it on, and adjusted the strap.

Smyth slowly opened the door into the nave and studied the pews. He walked in and stepped up onto the chancel. An office chair was placed where Don's aluminum chair typically sat. He smiled as he walked past it and over to the wall where the old lantern was hanging. He opened the lantern door, took one of the three lighters out of his pocket, and lit the long tapered candle. He left the lantern door open.

Time Check... 6:34 p.m.

Smyth walked to the back door, picked up the duffel bag, and turned to his left. The basement door creaked as he opened it. Walking down the stairs carrying the tools and trying to illuminate the steps with his headlamp was challenging.

Time Check... 6:37 p.m.

Except for the light coming through the basement window and from his headlamp, the basement was dark. He paused to run the scenario through his head and soak in the surroundings.

Time Check... 6:41 p.m.

Satisfied that he knew all aspects of the plan, Smyth went upstairs, extinguished the candle, and returned to the Cathedral by the Sea.

Time Check... 6:44 p.m.

It took just 12 minutes to complete his plan. He smiled. He was confident. He's got this!

Smyth paused, standing in the shadow by the Cathedral's back door. Then, scanning his surroundings again, he returned to the back door of his Sailers Church replica to practice his plan again. And then one more time after that.

Time Check... 7:09 p.m.

It was time to get ready to execute his plan.

Chapter 46 - I bet Jane says it first
October 14th 8:53 p.m.

Applause filled the room. "Thank you! I'm Mike, and these are the Swinging Coconut Farmers. It's been our pleasure to lay down some tiki and surf tunes for you this evening. Up next, the Curly Wave Chasers will be jammin' some island reggae to keep this luau thumpin'. Finally, my favorite wahines, Kalani & The Ōkole Shakers, are closing the stage tonight. And don't forget the big tip jar at the end of the bar for your cooks, bartenders, and waitstaff. They're working hard so you can luau hard. Mahalo!"

Don delivered drinks to Jerry and Olivia, turned, and pressed the juke control on the iPad. The song *Panito* by the *Fathoms* starts to play in the background. Olivia smiled; she could hear the music clearly and at the perfect volume in what was the noisiest she had ever heard in the bar. Her audio system was performing flawlessly, as designed.

Sarah worked her way around a busy Red to get to Don. "I need a keg change on the Sam Adams SAIL. I don't know your keg system."

Don smiled. "Okay, I'm on it. I'll signal you in a moment when it's done."

He headed for the keg cooler in the back room. "Jane, do you need anything from the back?"

She looked around. "No, I'm good for now. Hustle back, baby. There are beer customers lined up."

Caruso watched as Don left the bar for the backroom.

Don opened the keg cooler door and efficiently pulled out the empty SAIL beer keg. He slid one of the cold spare kegs into place, tapped it, and checked the CO_2 tank gauges for the beer distribution system.

He returned to the front of the bar and flashed the shaka gesture to Sarah, signaling that she was back in business. Don then returned to the back, placed the empty keg under the stairs, and put another full keg into the cooler to chill.

The smell of the grill drew Don to the back door again. Curiosity finally got the better of him, and he stepped outside. The portable flood lights around the grill should have attracted moths and other such bugs, but the smoke kept them away. Don inspected the cooking food.

"The grill looks a little light, man. Are people slowing down on eating?"

J.C. laughed. "No way, I am barely keeping up with them. These people are eaters! I just sent the food runners back to the kitchen to bring me more chicken, guava ribs, and char siu pork."

Just as J.C. finished saying that, Kevin arrived with more chicken and ribs to cook. J.C. gave Kevin the cooked ribs, chicken, and pork off the grill to take to the kitchen to be prepared for the food stations. As Kevin entered the bar's back door, he nearly ran into Jane. She was looking for Don.

Jane finds him next to the smoky grill again. "Hey, babe – I know the 9-year-old in you finds the grill fascinating, but I need the adult you to get your happy ass behind the bar and let J.C. do his job. I need you now!"

Don fist bumped J.C. "I've gotta run, man. I look forward to some of your killer barbecue at the after-party!" Don jogged toward the back door. Jane heard footsteps behind her and stepped aside as little Lisa headed to the grill with a large pan of char siu pork in red marinade. Lisa looked up as she passed by Jane and thanked her for stepping aside.

Don entered the doorway as little Lisa exited. Neither saw the other until they hit. Jane caught little Lisa as she fell backward. Don grabbed the pan of marinated pork, preventing it from hitting the ground. The food was saved. Lisa was fine. Jane gasped!

"Oh, my god. Where are you hurt? Oh, baby, no...." Jane panicked.

"Fuck me, man! No, I'm fine, Jane. It's the red marinade. It spilled all over my crotch. It looks like someone cut my dick off, man!"

Jane took a deep, cleansing breath. "You scared the shit out of me!"

J.C. ran over and took the food pan from Don. "Nice catch, but those white linen pants are ruined."

Little Lisa's eyes were wide. "I'm so sorry. I was looking at Jane. It's my fault!"

"No, Lisa. I wasn't watching where I was going. It's just an accident, man. But I do need to get out of these slacks. I don't have anything presentable here. I need to go home and change. Jane, please get my house key and cell phone out of the office and bring them to me." Jane went inside to get them.

Don again assured an emotional little Lisa that it was just an accident. He laughed. "I know you will tell people you porked me in front of Jane."

Little Lisa giggled. "I bet Jane says it first!"

Don agreed as he looked around the parking lot behind the bar. "J.C., I walked here tonight from home. Can I borrow your bike, man?"

"Sure, Don. Grab a plastic bag and wrap the seat. I don't want that red sticky shit getting on it. That food coloring stains the skin too. You are going to have a red dick for a while." J.C. laughed at his own comment.

Jane handed Don their house key and his cell phone. "Hurry back; we need you mixing drinks if we are going to keep our heads above water. And I just saw Captain Morgan and his two hot wenches, or whatever they are, walk in the front door."

Don nodded, took a deep breath, and peddled off into the night.

Chapter 47 - Smyth angrily tugged at the zipper
October 14th 9:06 p.m.

Smyth parked the borrowed SUV on Abigail Road, a short walk from Sailers Church. He thought no one would associate the SUV with him since he drove a top-of-the-line white Mercedes. He also knew that the security camera on the house wouldn't see the SUV or his approach on foot on that side of the church building.

Smyth pulled the black hoodie tight around his head and adjusted his baseball cap to shield his face from view. He walked around the side of the church building to the back door. He hadn't taken the light from the full moon into consideration. It bothered him.

Smyth scanned the area again to be sure that he was alone. Then, he nervously took the phone out of his hoodie pocket.

Time Check... 9:09 p.m.

He slipped the phone back into his pocket and set the duffel bag down. He tried to open the bag to get the wrecking bar out. The zipper was stuck. He tried again. It wouldn't budge.

"What the fuck?" Smyth angrily started to tug at the zipper. Finally, he stopped and took a deep breath. Relaxed, he adjusted the bag's position. It opened easily. Smyth tried to reassure himself. "Slow down – think! You've got this!"

Smyth reached into the open bag and took out the wrecking bar. He wedged the straight-end blade into the space between the door and its frame, just above the deadbolt. Smyth slowly pulled back on the bar. The wood around the door made a cracking sound but didn't budge. Smyth tried again with the same result. "Oh, come on!"

Smyth forcefully pushed the blade in as far as it would go and pulled back on the bar with all his strength. The sound of the breaking wood was surprisingly loud. The door effortlessly swung open.

Smyth nervously looked around as he placed the wrecking bar back in the bag. He was feeling confident about his plan again.

Time Check... 9:12 p.m.

He tucked the phone back into the pocket of his hoodie and entered the service and storage room at the back of the church building just as he had practiced. The bag made the familiar metallic thud when he set it on the floor. An unexpected breeze blew the door closed, startling Smyth. His heart raced.

After a few more deep relaxation breaths, he entered the nave. Light from the full moon shining through the stained glass windows produced an eerie scene of dark shadows and otherworldly light patterns. Smyth half expected to see a ghostly apparition sitting in one of the pews. He quickly took off his baseball cap and put on his LED headlamp. Even as an adult, he was not comfortable in the dark.

Smyth stepped up onto the chancel and walked behind the aluminum chair, knocking it aside as a sign of disrespect to Don. He opened the glass door and lit the candle. A pang of guilt started to well up in him. Smyth crushed it, walked to the back room, and picked up the duffle bag.

Time Check... 9:15 p.m.

Smyth opened the basement door. He had become accustomed to tilting his head down so the LED headlamp could light the stairs. Smyth balanced the weight of the duffle bag as he carefully walked down to the basement. He wasn't aware that the last step from the stairs to the basement floor was higher than the others. The weight of the duffle bag pulled him forward as he stumbled.

Smyth quickly became incensed. The last step height was different than in his newly constructed replica. If the builder got that wrong, what else is different? Smyth started to doubt his plan and paused.

"Fuck it! It's now or never!" Smyth took a deep breath and walked over to the old furnace. He flipped the power switch off.

He then turned his attention to the old iron gas line that came in through the stone foundation. Smyth had never actually done this part of his plan before. First, he studied the stones around the pipe to find the best leverage position for the large chisel. He carefully aligned the chisel blade against the top of the iron pipe and the stone above it.

The four-pound hammer felt cumbersome as he picked it up from the duffle bag. Then, with the hammer raised high, he swung and firmly came down on the chisel head. The loud sound of the hammer striking the chisel and the sparks flying as the chisel hit the stone next to the pipe sent a wave of instant terror through Smyth. The brittle gas line cracked open, and gas leaked into the basement. He was thankful that the sparks hadn't reached the escaping gas.

Time Check... 9:21 p.m.

Don looked around as he leaned the bike against the side of his house. He couldn't identify the source of the odd sound he had just heard.

Chapter 48 - Let me go; I have to save Don
October 14th 9:24 p.m.

Caruso couldn't decide if the buxom buccaneer that arrived with the Captain Morgan character was actually into him or if it was just part of her act. He looked at his watch and reluctantly excused himself from their conversation. Caruso hadn't seen Don in a while and needed to be sure he was still in the back room. Caruso went to the bar and asked Jane if he could speak to Don. She told him he had just gone home for a moment and would be back soon. The color drained from Caruso's face as the bar phone rang. Jane answered it.

'It's hard to hear you, babe. Speak up!"

Standing by the back door of Sailers Church, Don whispered as loudly as he dared to. "I heard a noise and saw a flashlight in the basement window of the church building. There's someone in there, man. Ask Jim Dillard to…"

The backdoor of Sailers Church flung open. Don instinctively turned away from the rapidly approaching wrecking bar. But he wasn't fast enough. Searing pain from the glancing blow to his head brought him to his knees. The phone call abruptly ended. Smyth stepped back into the church as Don lay motionless in the shadows outside the backdoor.

October 14th 9:26 p.m.

Jane desperately listened for Don's voice as she repeatedly called his name. She knew that something was dreadfully wrong. The phone fell from Jane's hand. She grabbed the rope to the bell and rang it frantically to silence the bar. She yelled to Dillard.

"Jimmy – Don's at our house, and he said someone broke into the church building and is still there. I was talking to him on his cell phone, and it went dead. I feel he's hurt. Please hurry!"

Jim ran out the front door of the bar. As he ran, he called 911 on his cell phone and put it on speaker. "Brite Rock Dispatch, this is off-duty

Officer James Dillard. Possible 10-64 [crime or criminal act in progress] at the old Sailers Church on Main Street. Requesting 10-33 [need immediate assistance]. Be advised the owner is there and may have engaged with one or more suspects. My ETA is 2 minutes approaching from the east on foot on Main Street...standby Dispatch."

Dillard heard a noise and turned to see Jane running about 100 feet behind him. Directly behind her was Kam, Captain Morgan, and nearly half the bar patrons. Even though the situation was deadly serious, Dillard wondered for a moment what people would think if they saw the aloha-shirt army led by a pirate running down Main Street.

"BR Dispatch, I am being followed by a large group of civilians. I will lead them to the Bay Colony and Main Street intersect at the front of Sailers Church and hold them there."

BR Dispatch: "10-4 [message received, affirmative]. 10-26 [estimated time of arrival] of Two-One [Unit 21] is 5 minutes. Wait for backup before entering the building. Please leave this line open."

Dillard, still catching his breath, replied. "10-4."

Dillard paused in front of Jane's house for the approaching group. Jane was the first to reach him. Instead of stopping, Jane ran past Dillard and started up the dark driveway toward the back of the Sailers Church. Dillard called out to Kam to stop her. As if it was a football play that he had practiced hundreds of times, Kam quickly chased Jane down, swept her up with his right arm, and promptly carried her to Dillard, who was shepherding the crowd down the street to the corner of Bay Colony Road and Main Street.

"BR Dispatch, please be advised civilians are present and listening."

BR Dispatch: "10-4. 10-26 on Two-One is less than 3 minutes. 10-26 on Two-Zero [Unit 20] is 5 minutes."

Jane continued to struggle as Kam held fast. Finally, Dillard got in her face. "Jane, stop! You can't go in there right now. You could be putting Don and yourself in danger if you do. Let the police handle this!"

They could hear the sirens getting closer. Jane stopped resisting, so Kam slowly let go of her. He knew he could quickly chase her down and tackle her if she ran again. Jane nervously paced.

October 14th 9:33 p.m.

The left side of Don's head throbbed and was sticky from blood. He was disoriented and in pain. Believing whoever attacked him had run off, Don got to his feet and cautiously entered the service and storage room. He hoped the church building hadn't been vandalized.

As Don slowly walked through the service and storage room toward the nave, he was startled by the unexpected sound of the door blowing closed behind him. His heart pounded from a rush of adrenaline that momentarily dulled his pain and sharpened his mind. He took in a deep breath and continued.

It took a moment for his eyes to adjust as he walked into the dark nave. The light coming through the windows created an eerie scene as the partially lit tops of the pews appeared to float in the black shadows. Don felt high, but not in a good way.

Another flash of pain was followed by another moment of clarity. A new sensation registered as Don looked around the nave. He was starting to feel nauseous and thought he might have a concussion. He stood, staring blankly at the lit candle, but had no recollection of lighting it. He was confused but knew that he was injured and needed help.

As he turned to exit the back door, he heard a cell phone ringing from somewhere in the black shadows of the pews. He had heard that song before. It was in the opening of Smyth's YouTube video of his replica church dedication show. It's the Brite Rock Revivers song *Here Because of Him*.

October 14th 9:37 p.m.

Caruso, overweight and far from being athletic, ran one block from the bar before he had to sit down on the bench at Rudy's Clam Shack to catch his breath. He called George's cell phone to tell him about the crowd running towards Sailers Church. "Come on, George, pick up!"

Smyth slowly stood, rising out of the shadows in the middle of the pews on the left side. He answered the call on speakerphone out of habit.

"George, the dipshit bartender, and a group of people are heading your way. They know someone broke into the church building. Get out of there. Now!"

Before George could answer, Don spoke up. "Did he just call me a dipshit bartender, man?"

Smyth hung up on Caruso and slipped the phone into his pocket. He reached down and lifted the heavy hammer shoulder height. Smyth took an unsteady step forward before throwing the hammer in Don's general direction. Both men watched the heavy tool fall to the floor far short of its intended target. Neither moved for a moment and then both lunged at the object neither could see in the shadows. They frantically searched in the darkness, but the hammer was nowhere to be found.

Feeling the ill effects of the gas, both men slowly stumbled to their feet. Smyth's LED headlamp had fallen off and was lying on the floor. It had turned on, and the light beam illuminated Don's legs. Smyth stared in disbelief.

"What the fuck...what happened to your....?" Smyth pointed at Don's crotch.

Don's head ached, and he felt like throwing up. His breathing had become labored, and his confusion was getting worse. "No, man, my dick's fine. I got porked by little Lisa. Jane watched the whole thing...and...she...um...and then...hey, are you following any of this, man?"

Smyth was dizzy and had difficulty concentrating. "I have no idea what you are talking about."

Smyth made a fist and awkwardly swung at Don with all his might, missing him and striking the end of one of the pews. The sound of the loud impact startled Don. Pain raced through Smyth's shattered hand and up his arm. Clutching his hand, he doubled over in pain. Don saw this as his opportunity to take down Smyth. He clumsily rushed toward him. Instead of the skilled moves Don thought he could pull off, his foot landed on the headlamp, crushing it and sending him tumbling on top of Smyth.

Both men were disoriented as they pulled themselves up out of the shadows. Smyth gathered his strength and took another swing at Don. This time he connected enough to knock Don back down on the floor. Smyth moaned as he held his badly swollen hand and doubled over in pain again. The nausea was worse. He knew he needed fresh air. He turned and started toward the front door. He had taken two steps when his foot caught the strap of the duffle bag in the dark aisle. Smyth wasn't fully aware that he was falling until his chest and face slammed into the floor.

Despite the pain and severe headache, he slowly untangled his foot from the duffle bag strap and rummaged in the dark, searching for the chisel. Then, with it in hand, Smyth stood to find a wobbly Don facing him.

Don squinted as he looked at Smyth. It took Don a moment to recognize him. "What happened to your face, man?"

"I fell down!"

Don squinted again as he studied Smyth's bloody face. "How many times?"

Smyth raised the heavy chisel and slowly brought it down toward Don's chest as if trying to stake a vampire in the heart. Don effortlessly took the chisel out of Smyth's injured hand.

Don paused and sniffed the air. "It smells like hard-boiled eggs in here. Did you eat an egg salad sandwich, man?"

Smyth was indignant. "No, you idiot, I cut the gas line into the building!"

"Why would you do that, man?"

Smyth aggressively pointed his finger at Don. "Because you don't fucking deserve this building."

Smyth shoved a bewildered Don back a step and staggered toward the front door. Don coughed, mustered all the focus his blurred vision could provide, and prepared to throw the heavy chisel at Smyth.

October 14th 9:42 p.m.

The first of two responding police cars arrived in front of Sailers Church.

"BR Dispatch, Two-One is on the scene at Main and Bay Colony."

BR Dispatch: "10-4 Two-One."

Officers McClelland and Brown exited the cruiser as Dillard approached. McClelland took his flashlight from his belt and shined it at the front of Sailers Church. "What do we have here, Jim?"

Before Dillard could respond, Jane stepped in front of him.

"Don interrupted a break-in, and somebody must have jumped him. So why are you still standing out here, Mac? Get in there and get him out!" Jane put her hands on her hips to emphasize her point.

At that moment, the wayward chisel from Don's poor throw crashed through the stained glass window above the front door of Sailers Church.

McClelland pointed at the police car. "Everyone get behind the cruiser and stay down. Jim, cover the front. Brownie and I will go in through the back."

Brown grabbed the shotgun from the cruiser and handed it to Dillard. He and McClelland ran around to the back of the church and slowly opened the door. The pungent odor of gas forced them back immediately.

October 14th 9:51 p.m.

Smyth moaned as he tried to open the front door of Sailers Church. His badly broken right hand was too deformed and painful to work the lock. He was about to try with his left hand when Don pulled him back from the door. Both men stumbled and regained their footing the best they could. Don made a fist and awkwardly swung at Smyth, missing him completely. Smyth shoved Don with all his remaining might, sending him crashing against the back of the last row of pews. Don, unconscious, crumpled into a heap on the floor.

October 14th 9:54 p.m.

McClelland and Brown ran back to the front of the church and started to move the crowd. "Everyone, you must evacuate the area; there's a gas leak. You have to leave now!"

Jane heard the words but couldn't comprehend the situation. In her mind, this was someone breaking into the church building and assaulting Don, not a gas leak. It wasn't making sense to her.

Jane angrily pointed at the church. "You go in there right now and get Don out! Now, Mac!"

"Jane, we need to secure the area before we go in. Get behind the cruiser and stay there, or I'll lock you in the backseat." Jane stomped her foot and defiantly folded her arms.

McClelland started to open the back door of the cruiser.

"All right, I'll get behind the car! Now go get Don!"

McClelland turned and spotted Shūlíng live streaming Wally with Sailers Church in the background.

"Brownie, get those two off the church walkway while I call in the gas leak."

Officer Brown grabbed Shūlíng and Wally by their arms and escorted them behind a cruiser. "Stay here!"

Shūlíng stared at the front door of the church and pointed. "But I saw the door move. It opened a little."

Brown pulled his flashlight from his belt and aimed it at the church's front door. Smyth had managed to open it a few inches and was peeking out at the crowd. He raised his hand to shield his eyes from the bright flashlight. Jane squinted as she tried to see who it was. She could barely control her urge to run to the church.

"Two-One to BR Dispatch."

BR Dispatch: "Go Two-One."

"BR Dispatch, we need immediate assistance from Brite Rock Gas & Electric. There is a major gas leak at Sailers Church. Notify Brite Rock F.D. of our situation too. We will start to evacuate people in the vicinity of...."

"Fuck it!" Jane started to run toward the front of the church.

McClelland spotted Jane as she sprinted up the walkway toward the front of Sailers Church. "Brownie – stop her!"

Brown started to go after Jane. He had taken only two steps when the gas ignited.

Jane was halfway to the Sailers Church front doors when they splintered in a cloud of debris and fire. The sudden impact of the thunderous blast hit Jane, knocking the wind out of her as she slammed into the ground back first.

Terrified, she desperately struggled to breathe. She tried to inhale. She tried again. On the third try, Jane's lungs moaned as air rushed in. Her stomach ached. Her face and body stung from the numerous cuts and nicks from flying debris. She had difficulty keeping her right eye open. Her ears were ringing, and her senses were overloaded. What felt like minutes were seconds.

Jane slowly propped herself up and looked in awe at the devastation. Debris, much of it burning, rained down around her. Most of the building's roof, side walls, and back were gone. Only the front wall and a small section of the front of the roof were still standing. The cupola that held the bell was on fire and leaning precariously inward. Jane looked through where the front doors had been a moment ago to see a wall of orange flame. A column of fire fed by the gas pipe stood straight, reaching 20 feet into the night sky.

Jane got to her feet and suddenly found herself running awkwardly toward the remains of the building. It was an uncontrolled physical reaction to the scene before her. She fell to her knees next to the person lying face down on the ground, hoping it was Don, yet rationally knowing it wasn't.

She quizzically looked at the wisps of smoke as they rose from the man's shredded and smoldering hoodie. His shoes were missing. What seemed like a foot-long splinter of wood was embedded in his left butt cheek. A small flame, about the size produced by a birthday candle, danced at the tip of the splinter. Jane let it burn.

Rage suddenly filled her. The injured man moaned as Jane grabbed his shoulder and forcibly pulled him onto his side so she could see his face. Although battered and bloody, she recognized Smyth. Jane made a fist and punched him in the face.

She leaned over, inches from his ear, yelling. "Where is Don? Where is Don? Tell me!" Jane again made a fist and raised it into the air. She was on the thinnest edge of self-control. "This is your last chance, asshole!"

Smyth feebly raised his left arm and pointed at the remains of the burning church. Jane mercilessly pushed Smyth back over and pressed down on him to get to her feet. He groaned loudly. She started to run toward the church but immediately felt an arm wrap around her waist from behind. She fought to free herself, but Dillard held her tight.

"Jane, you can't go in there! It's not safe!" Dillard tightened his grip as a determined Jane tried to free herself.

"Let me go; I have to save Don! Get the fuck off me!" Jane kicked and scratched. Dillard held fast.

"It's not survivable, Jane. No one could live through that."

"Fuck you! Let me go. I will…" Jane reached back and scratched his face.

Dillard tightened his grip. "I just lost one friend, and I'll be damned to let you make it two! Stop, god damn it! Jane - stop!"

The fight was slowly going out of her. "But I still feel Don. He can't be gone. He can't…."

Jane stood motionless as her brain registered the words *not survivable*. She turned to look at Dillard. Tears ran down his cheeks, mixing with blood from her scratch marks. His lip quivered as he drew shallow breaths.

Jane felt her world slipping away. She couldn't accept that she had just lost the love of her life or fend off the growing sense of extreme emptiness. Jane cried out in anguish and slowly collapsed to the ground. Dillard sank to his knees beside her and went silent as she sobbed uncontrollably. His left hand rested on her shoulder to comfort her. And to comfort himself.

Dillard took a deep breath and raised his cell phone. "BR Dispatch, please advise BRFD that we have one unaccounted for in the building, one on the front lawn in serious condition, one with injuries that…I don't know. The blast roughed her up. There may be others with injuries that I am not aware of. Send EMS [Emergency Medical Services] to the front of the church immediately. BRFD should request mutual aid. More ambulances."

BR Dispatch: "10-4 Officer Dillard. Be advised that BRFD is arriving on the scene, and mutual aid has been requested and is en route. The Command Center is in the parking lot at Main Street and Muhsachuweesut Camp Road. Chief Tim Polk is Ops Commander, and Greg Walker is the EMS Supervisor. I will notify both of your situation and location."

"10-4 Dispatch." Dillard stayed by Jane.

Officer McClelland was now attending to Smyth while waiting for EMS to arrive. He yelled to Dillard.

"Jimmy, are you okay?"

"Yeah, Mac. I'm good!"

"Is Jane hurt bad?"

"I don't think so. She put up one hell of a struggle, but you know how adrenaline can be."

Darlene ran up to Jane and Dillard and knelt next to them. She gently hugged Jane. Both were inconsolable.

McClelland listened to Smyth's erratic breathing. "Jimmy, can you go find EMS…10-18 [urgent]. This guy sounds a bit juicy."

"I'm on it, Mac!" Dillard ran to the arriving ambulance to get priority assistance for Smyth before he bled out.

"Wow, this is quite the mess, isn't it?" Lily was standing over Jane and Darlene, looking at the remains of the burning building. She looked down at Darlene with a curious face.

"Why are you two so upset? It's just a building. It can be rebuilt. And I'm sure the fireman will save the house. Oh, I really do need to stop calling them firemen now that Emily Morse has joined the firefighter ranks. She's delightful!"

Darlene was stunned that Lily was being so insensitive. She took a deep breath. "Lily, Don was in the explosion. He's gone, so please show some compassion."

Lily's gaze returned to the front doorway of the burning church and then back to Darlene.

"Don's gone where dear?"

Darlene could hardly contain her anger. "Lily – Don is dead!"

Lily folded her arms and glared at Darlene. "Don't take that tone with me, young lady! And if you say Don is dead, then who the hell is that?" Lily pointed at the church.

As the smoke momentarily cleared from the church doorway, Darlene saw a battered and disoriented Don. He stood, vacantly staring up at his mangled aluminum chair hanging from a tree branch amid random debris, some burning.

"My god!" Darlene stood and quickly ran to Don. Jane looked on as Dillard returned to help Darlene move Don away from the building. The burning cupola crashed onto the floor, sending sparks and flaming debris out of the doorway. It was where Don had been standing a moment before.

It was hard for Jane to accept what her one good eye showed her. Deep grief blurred her rational thoughts. Jane tentatively got to her feet and slowly walked toward Don.

She whispered to herself with each step. "Please be real…please be real…please be real."

Darlene stepped aside as Jane took Don in her arms. He stood motionless as Jane held him. His eyes slowly looked around as he tried to comprehend the surreal scene. Jane lightly kissed him. Don did not respond.

"Babe, where are you hurt? Talk to me, please. Don! Words!"

Tears welled up in Jane's eyes. "Darlene, something is wrong with Don. He doesn't answer me when I talk to him. I just kissed him, and he didn't…" Jane paused, exhaled, and smiled softly. She gently held Don close again. Darlene looked down to see Don holding Jane's butt with both hands. He had responded.

Don again looked up at his mangled aluminum chair hanging in the tree. "We need to call the fire department. Does anyone know the phone number for nine one one?"

Dillard glanced at Darlene. "It's okay, Don. The fire department is here. Why don't you and Jane sit on the ground while I talk to the firefighters? Darlene will keep you company." Dillard went to get medical help.

EMT/Paramedics Tony Foonman and Kevin Washington finished evaluating and stabilizing Smyth. Foonman attached a Red Tag to Smyth's foot, identifying him for Immediate Treatment and Transport.

Washington and EMT/Paramedic Moreno loaded Smyth into the Brite Rock town ambulance and departed for the South Shore Trauma Intensive Care Hospital, a short six minutes away.

Another ambulance arrived as Greg Walker and Foonman performed triage evaluations on Don, Jane, and the other eleven injured people. Four would be treated at the scene and released. Five had minor injuries and were Green Tagged as walking wounded and held for transport. Another ambulance arrived.

Walker adjusted the trauma dressing he applied to Don's head injury and tied a Yellow Tag on his wrist. He was stable but wobbly. Walker noted several injuries on the tag, including potential undiagnosed internal injuries from the blast. Jane was angry about Smyth being prioritized over Don, even if he had suffered worse injuries.

"It was Smyth's fault, Greg! He did all this!"

"I know, Jane, but Smyth is in pretty rough shape. Now, hold still, and let me look at you." Jane appeared to have numerous minor wounds, blunt trauma contusions on her back and shoulder, an eye injury, and a possible broken hand. Walker attached a Yellow Tag to Jane's good wrist and put her in the same ambulance with Don as it departed for the hospital. Another ambulance arrived for the others.

Darlene followed Don and Jane's ambulance to the hospital. She needed to be with them. They are her family.

October 15th 1:58 am - South Shore Trauma Intensive Care Hospital

Jane sat in the ER waiting room, exhausted and emotionally drained. She stared at the cast on her right hand and slowly shook her head. Her face, arms, and body had numerous adhesive bandages covering her cuts and scrapes. Her right eye had two moderate corneal abrasions that were treated with antibiotic ointment and covered with a black eye patch. She was unhappy to learn that she would need to wear the eye patch for ten days. Large bruises on her back and right shoulder ached as she tried to find a comfortable position on the uncomfortable bench seat.

"I talked an ER nurse out of a blanket. This will help warm you up." Jane was shivering as Darlene wrapped the blanket around her shoulders. The thin fabric of Jane's short-sleeve tropical shirt was no match for the hospital air conditioning.

Darlene gently adjusted the blanket to cover Jane's back. "I don't know why they keep hospitals so cold. It's like a restaurant walk-in refrigerator in here. Anyway, I called Andy to check in while waiting for the blanket. I told him to tell everyone that you two will be fine and not to come to the hospital and that if you or Don need anything, you will reach out to them."

Jane nodded. "Thanks; I don't want to be around people right now. I just need you and Don. Did Andy say anything about the bar and the luau?"

"Yes, Andy said they heard the explosion. It rattled bottles and glasses. Jimmy called Red right after you and Don left for the hospital, filling her in on the details. Red told the bar and Shanty crews to keep the luau going for those that stayed. Most of the luau attendees that had run to the church returned to the bar. From what Andy said, Geezer climbed up on a table, with assistance from the voluptuous Captain Morgan sidekick he was hitting on, and told the crowd it was their responsibility to keep the luau going for you, Don, and the bar. I hear it was quite an impassioned speech. Andy said it was one hell of a party until last call."

Jane smiled. "Fucking Geezer! I love that old goat!"

"Red also told Andy that she, Shakemaster, Geezer, J.C., Sarah, and A.J. closed tonight, and they will cover for you two for the rest of the week. The bar and Shanty crews are running up a well-deserved after-hours bar and food tab tonight."

Jane rested her head on Darlene's shoulder. "They are all such good people. And thank you for helping us. The day was going so well, and then this?" Jane sighed.

Darlene gently kissed Jane on the forehead. "Of course! I love you two. I'm so glad you only ended up with a few scrapes, bruises, and a hurt paw. And I think you can pull off the pirate eye patch look with the right ensemble. You already have the pirate attitude."

Jane smiled. "I do, except I only day drink when on vacation, and this pirate doesn't hide her booty!"

Darlene laughed. "That's you, a socially responsible pirate witch."

Jane reached to adjust her blanket with her injured hand and winced with pain.

"Oh, sweetie, is there anything on you that doesn't hurt?"

Jane gently shook her head. "No. I'm a hurting puppy for sure, but the doc said I'll be fine. I keep thinking back on punching Smyth in the face. He was defenseless! I am so disappointed in myself. That was like a road rage reaction, Darlene. They can lock me up for assaulting a badly injured man!"

Darlene adjusted Jane's blanket again. "Jane, it was in the moment, and you said you held back on the second punch. I'm not sure I would have had the strength to hold back if it were me in that situation. Smyth hurt Don. Fuck him! I'm pounding that son of a bitch into the ground!"

Jane sighed as she looked at her cast. "I guess it's appropriate that my hand injury is called the boxer's fracture. A broken fifth meta something bone. It's a reminder of my dickish behavior.

Oh, and then I scratched Jimmy's face trying to get him to let me go so I could run into a burning building. What was I thinking? Jimmy's my friend! And he's a cop! I assaulted a cop! I can be arrested for that too!"

Darlene smiled. "If you ask nicely, Jimmy will probably just taser you a little and call it even."

Jane nodded. "I will consider myself lucky if that's my penance. Being a pirate witch is tough!"

"Excuse me." Darlene and Jane looked up to see Doctor Jensen standing in front of them. Jane winced as she slowly sat up straight and prepared to concentrate on every word he was about to say. Doc Jensen scanned the medical charts as he started to speak.

"I'm sure it's been a long day for both of you, so let's get right to the good news. Some of this you already know, so bear with me. Generally speaking, Don is doing well and resting. We gave him a mild sedative to make his x-ray and MRI tests less uncomfortable. Unfortunately, he does have a Grade 2 Concussion in the right temporal lobe, likely from a fall. He did experience a loss of consciousness. Typical for this grade of concussion are headaches, temporary memory problems, confusion, dizziness, nausea, and irritability."

Doc Jensen paused to see how Jane was receiving the information. She listened intently as the doctor continued.

"The penetrating trauma on the side of his head required five internal stitches and seven external staples. It's in the hairline, so it won't be noticeable when healed. He will need to have the staples taken out in ten days. We didn't find any broken bones or other significant internal injuries."

Jane's expression did not change.

"Don passed his lung function tests, and we didn't find any significant damage from inhalation of heat or smoke. He is, however, receiving oxygen therapy to help get the gas and toxins out of his system and his blood oxygen saturation level up. He has minor, second-degree burns on his left ear and left arm. His tympanic membranes and the middle ear appear normal, but he may experience ringing in his ears from the explosion. That will fade over the next several days.

In addition, he has numerous minor skin wounds, bruises, and a swollen jaw. All that said, he is lucky. Nevertheless, we will hold him for forty-eight hours for continued observation and testing."

Jane took a deep, cleansing breath and stared intently at Jensen's eyes. "What about the bad news? What are you looking for over the next 48 hours?"

"Nothing serious, Jane. It's standard procedure to hold someone with a Grade 2 Concussion for observation and rest. Now, Don has shown signs of vertigo. While the concussion may be the cause, it is more likely the result of an impact, such as hitting his head in a fall. Such impacts can cause debris in the inner ear canal to break free and float around, signaling Don's brain that he is moving when he isn't. If Don has this, we can place the head and body in various sequential positions to move the debris out of the affected ear canal. That will alleviate the vertigo symptoms. He's also going to be very sore for several days. Everything on him is going to ache, so I have prescribed pain medication for him. He cannot drink alcohol while taking it."

Jane looked up at Doc Jensen. "Is that everything?"

Doc Jensen looked at Don's chart again. "Yes, that's the comprehensive summary. Ah, no, there is one thing we couldn't figure out. Do you know why Don's genitals are bright pinkish red? We need to confirm his explanation."

Jane answered without thinking. "Oh, yeah, he got porked by little Lisa. It's fine. I saw the whole thing."

Doc Jensen was processing Jane's explanation when Darlene added that it was a red vegetable-based food dye from her kitchen and how it got on Don's genitals. Doc Jensen laughed.

"Well, that matches Don's explanation. The color will fade over time."

Jane didn't see anything humorous in that. She felt relief that Don's prognosis was good but was still visibly angry. "What about Smyth?"

Doc Jensen sighed. "You know I can't talk about him, Jane. Patient confidentiality and all, plus he is under arrest and in our care, so there is that too."

"What about the piece of wood that was stuck in Smyth's ass? Did you remove it?"

Doc Jensen looked at Darlene and then back to Jane. "Well, I understand that his surgeon has removed the large splinter of wood and debrided the wound."

Jane squinted, and her jaw took on a determined set. "Tell that surgeon to put it back in his ass!"

Doc Jensen couldn't believe his ears. "I'm sorry; what did you say?"

"I said tell that surgeon to stick that piece of wood…" Darlene quickly stood and took Doc Jensen's hand. "Thank you, doctor. Jane is obviously overtired and emotional. We'll be leaving now. She'll be staying at my house tonight."

Doc Jensen smiled sympathetically. "I understand. Jane, it's been a stressful day for you, and you will be sore from your injuries. May I prescribe something to help you sleep tonight?"

Jane shook her head. "No, my honey is alive and will get better. I want a hot shower and to put on one of Don's favorite aloha shirts. I want a glass of his favorite rum before crawling into bed for a good cry. I'll be back here tomorrow morning to be with Don."

Chapter 49 - Lady Luck cut me some slack, man
October 17th 8:17 a.m. (2 days later at the Hospital)

Larent, the orderly from Jamaica that helped Don during his hospital stay, held the wheelchair steady as Don gently settled into it. "You small you self up now. Make it easy to fit in the chair, mon."

Don tried in vain to find a comfortable position in the wheelchair. "I still don't get the hospital rule that says you have to wheel me to the exit, and then I can stand and walk away. Do they charge extra for wheelchair rides, man?"

Larent grinned. "If they do, they don't share with Larent!" Don smiled and winced.

Larent paused in thought. "I think some hospital lawyer came up with the rule. It's silly enough to be lawyered. I will find out the reason, so when my wife and I open our clinic back home, we will know if it's good for the patient." Don agreed with Larent's take on the wheelchair rule.

"You stay in the chair. I'll give you the VIP door-to-door service." Larent wheeled Don through the hospital exit to Darlene's borrowed minivan parked outside the door. A mentally and physically exhausted Jane leaned against the van's open side door, smiling softly.

"Here he is, Miss Jane! Good enough to take away!"

Don slowly stood and gently hugged and kissed Jane. Then, he turned and expertly completed the complicated Caribbean handshake with Larent. "Thanks for the ride and everything, man. Also, thank your wife, Amancia, for me too. She's a good nurse! And please, stop by the bar, and we'll make you and Amancia an authentic Jamaican Rum Cream. Of course, we have Wray & Nephew rum to make it with."

Larent laughed. "You got Uncle Wray? We will definitely come to the bar. Now, me and Miss Jane will help you into the van."

Jane closed the van door and turned to Larent. She gently hugged him. "Your visits and talks with Don about Jamaica and the islands have brightened his stay here. Please give us a few days to recover, and do stop by the bar for that rum cream or whatever else you and Amancia would like. It's on us."

"We do that, Miss Jane. Now, you drive safe and rest you self up too!"

Don flashed a shaka sign to Larent as Jane drove away from the hospital. "Larent is something else, man! Working part-time as an orderly while being a full-time medical student is impressive! It's cool that he and Amancia want to open a clinic back on the island. Do you think we should donate a few dollars from the bar's community cookie jar to help them? They're good people."

Jane agreed and continued muttering under her breath, irritated by the visual challenge of driving while wearing the eye patch. The annoying sound of several rattling metal serving trays and empty wine bottles didn't help her disposition. Darlene had catered the annual Red & Blue fundraising event for the Brite Rock Fire and Police Departments at the hotel conference room a few weeks ago and hadn't cleaned out her minivan. Don and Jane had donated a few cases of wine for the event. Jane now thinks providing boxed wine would have been a quieter donation.

"Babe, does the rattling of the trays and empty bottles back there bother you?"

Don thought for a moment. "Not really. I think I may still be comfortably numb from the meds, man."

Jane sighed. "Wonderful. Am I going to have to take a step – drag Don with my one good hand, take a step – drag Don, or are you up to walking around our house?"

"I'm good for a walk. We need to know where things stand. By the way, I couldn't help but notice that you seem a bit agitated this morning. Talk to me."

Jane slowly turned left off of Brite's Jetty Road onto Main Street. Working the steering wheel with a cast on her hand was difficult. "Sorry if I'm cranky, babe. I'm just used up. My body aches, one hand is nearly useless, and my eye is uncomfortable. I haven't slept well for the past two nights with you in the hospital. I kept reaching out with my foot to touch your foot. You know I like to touch feet when we sleep, so I know you are there. Maybe I have abandonment issues. I don't know. I'll sleep better tonight with you in our bed."

Jane pulled up to their house and parked at the curb. The State Fire Marshall's car and two police cars were in the driveway. In addition, several cars and pickup trucks were parked along the street. Don grumbled about the stupid child door lock holding him hostage. Jane pressed the driver's armrest button to open the motorized sliding door. Don took a deep breath as he gingerly exited the backseat. Despite his discomfort, he voiced his appreciation for Jane's help and Darlene's minivan's extra legroom and sliding door.

Jane handed Don his prized walking stick to help steady himself as the occasional momentary remnants of vertigo passed by. The walking stick belonged to his great-great-grandfather. He would use his common stick on walks through his large shoe tool factory. It was a simple oak shaft with a turned knob at the top. It was unlike his ornate and expensive day or evening walking sticks that were indispensable fashion accessories for men of means in the 1800s. But, like the old aluminum beach chair, Don felt the old walking stick had stories to tell. It had been places and was well experienced. It had a good vibe.

They stood for a moment in the driveway taking in the scene. Debris was cleared from the street and sidewalk but had only been pushed aside in the driveway. Don looked up at his badly mangled aluminum chair that was still hanging from a tree branch among other debris. Jane studied the damage to the house's side and the plywood covering the blown-out windows and side door. She sighed heavily. They gently hugged each other as they continued to absorb their loss.

Jerry was talking with Brite Rock Police Captain Bob Hamilton and Officer Dillard. Another man in a tan jacket took notes and stood close enough to hear their conversation.

Don and Jane turned their full attention to what was Sailers Church. They were in awe of the devastation. Only a part of the front wall remained standing. The acrid smell of the burnt, wet building was somewhat nauseating to Don. He wondered if it was from the concussion, a reaction to the pain medication on an empty stomach, or vertigo. He told Jane that he was feeling queasy so she could note it in the phone app as his doctor had provided.

They slowly walked around the debris as they made their way to the back edge of the burned-out church building. The State Fire Marshall stood ankle-deep in water in the basement, examining the incoming gas line. He looked up at Don and Jane. "Can I help you?"

"We're the owners, man. I'm Don, and this is Jane. I was in the building when it…you know."

The Fire Marshall pointed to the stone and concrete wall in the middle of the basement. "I have to tell you, you are one lucky man. That wall deflected most of the blast up and toward the back of the building. If that wall weren't there, you and I wouldn't be having this conversation. It appears the blast threw those old oak pews toward the interior front of the building, where they stacked up on each other over you. So you were essentially sheltered from the worst of the initial explosion and fire."

Don winced as he shifted his weight. Jane put her arm around him for support.

"I guess Lady Luck cut me some slack, man. I'm a little messed up around the edges, but you should see the other guy."

The Fire Marshall nodded. "I hear he was pretty banged up in the blast — broken bones, burns, skewered by a sizeable piece of wood, and other injuries. I almost hate to make his life more miserable, but I'm about done with my physical investigation. It looks like he purposely severed the incoming gas pipe to the furnace. The tool mark on the pipe matches the chisel that he used. That filled the building with gas and caused the explosion. Unfortunately, we haven't found the ignition source yet."

Don replied instantly. "He lit the candle in the big room, man. I saw it was lit when I entered the room. It was the only light except for what was coming through the windows."

The Fire Marshall wrote *lit candle was the source of the ignition* in his notebook. "An open flame, that will do it! Thanks for the information. I'll update the ATF on that. They left just before you got here, and they weren't happy about the cause of this explosion."

Don took a deep breath and sighed. "Well, at least our house is still standing."

"You got lucky there too! The windows and siding on this side will need to be replaced, but the smoke and water damage aren't bad. The boys did a good job protecting your house. Aside from trashed window treatments and wet carpets, the interior looks pretty good. The blast blew a lot of the shingles off the roof edge, so plan on reroofing the place too. The house's power, water, and gas have been turned off. The utility companies said it would take a few days to complete their inspection and testing and get services back on. So you should grab some clothes and things and find alternate housing."

Jane nodded. "That's exactly why we are here. We have the apartment above the bar. We're good!"

As he approached Don and Jane, Jerry stumbled over a piece of metal debris. "Shit – I just ruined my Ferragamo loafers!"

A quick smile flashed across Jane's face. "Sorry about your shoes."

"Thanks, Jane. I was hoping they would last more than a year but... wait, didn't you say the same thing about my shoes several months ago? They were fine, and you said sorry. So why did...how?"

Don looked at Jane and then back to Jerry. "Welcome to my world, man!"

Jerry had a bewildered look on his face. "I don't think I want to know. Anyway, it's good to see you two up and about! How are you both feeling today?"

Don looked at the remains of the destroyed church building and the damaged house. "Physically not too bad, man. But when I look at this mess, it rips my heart out. You know, I really didn't want that church building when this whole thing started. But then it slowly grew on me, man. It became the center of an odd little universe, not just for me but for a bunch of people looking for a place to fit in. Now it's gone. The house is a different story. I was thrilled at getting the house. I wanted that for Jane. She deserves much more than an apartment above a bar."

Jane leaned in and gently kissed Don. "There's nothing wrong with the apartment as long as you are there with me."

Don hung his head. "Thanks, babe, but the side of the house is trashed and needs some serious cash to fix it. Cash that we don't have. And the sad part is it's my fault for not having insurance on the property. Things got so busy so fast that I lost track of that. So now we have to get a loan to fix the place."

Jerry stood smiling at Don and Jane.

"Are you OK, man? You are smiling at, well, our kind of shitty circumstance. It's a little hurtful, man."

"About that insurance, Don. The way the Town's sublease agreement for Sailers Church was drafted, the sublessee, in this case, Smyth, pays for the nonrefundable annual insurance coverage in advance. The town, as the lessee from the estate, would receive any insurance payment to make the property whole should there be a loss. But, upon turning the property over to you, the town is no longer a lessee, so the town assigned the prepaid insurance policy to the trust. That's you!"

An exhausted Don and Jane silently stared at Jerry. It was clear that neither of them comprehended what he was saying.

"Okay, see that nice man over there in the tan jacket? He's from the insurance company. I called them on your behalf. He said your losses are fully covered. He will call you tomorrow once he files his report."

Jane gently hugged Jerry and kissed him on the cheek. "Thank you for helping Don and me. It is deeply appreciated, Jerry." Jane started to tear up in her one good eye but quickly composed herself.

Don scratched his head. "I'm blown away, man! This is all so weird!"

Jerry laughed. "Oh, it may get even weirder. Can I meet you and Jane at the bar at noon time today?"

Don looked at Jane and then back at Jerry. "Sure, man. We don't open until 1:00. Is everything okay?"

"I think it is. So, I have been contacted by another party that wishes to pitch you an offer. They are pulling the terms together now and asked to meet today at noon. They want to come to you."

"Can you tell us who this other party is and what they want, man?"

"Not yet. I'm not sure who all the players are or what their pitch is about. I suspect it's damage control. They are probably trying to get in front of potential liability exposure. You know, more of that legal stuff."

Don nodded. "Okay, well, we better grab some clothes and a few kitchen items and head back to the apartment. I want to shower to get the hospital smell off of me."

Jerry snapped his fingers. "That reminds me. When Brad heard that they were cutting power to your house during the fire, he, John Lennon, and PP came right over, boxed up everything in your refrigerator, and stored it in the Shanty's cooler and freezer."

Don grinned. "We have some pretty cool people in our orbit. But, you know Jane, PP will expect you to be nice to him for a while."

She smiled. "One attaboy doesn't erase a long list of his illicit touching complaints. But for this, he deserves a…robust handshake."

Jerry looked at his watch. "You two should get a move on. Don needs to shower, and you both need to eat something before the meeting. See you at noon."

Don and Jane went to the front door and entered the house.

Chapter 50 - Rum makes everything better
October 17th 10:36 a.m.

Jane's bruised back and broken hand ached as she carried the last box upstairs to the apartment. She wouldn't allow Don to help her. Instead, she told him to go take a shower and rest. She was being fiercely protective of him.

Don clumsily stepped into the shower and slid the glass door closed. Pain rushed up his burned left arm the moment warm water touched it. He instantly dropped the soap and held his arm above his head. As he awkwardly bent to pick up the soap, waves of moderate pain and vertigo unsteadied him.

"Jane, can you help me? I dropped the soap, and my body isn't working well enough to pick it up. You may need to wash my back too."

"Sure, babe, I'll be right there." Jane set the box down on the bed. She stripped, put the waterproof cast cover on her arm, and stepped into the shower behind Don. She immediately put her hand over her mouth to muffle any sound she may make. She was nearly overcome by the sight of the enormous purplish-black bruises and scrapes covering Don's back and legs.

"I couldn't reach the bandage on my back. The doc said to gently wash the wound and apply the stuff in the blue and white tube after I've dried off. He gave me bandages to cover it again. The other tube of stuff and the gauze roll is for my burned arm."

Jane studied the bandage. "At least they shaved the hair on your back shoulder before they put on the bandage and tape. It looks like the water has loosened it. Here goes…"

Jane gently peeled off the bandage exposing a five-inch gash on his back shoulder. She didn't know about this injury or missed hearing about it in the medical debriefing by Doc Jensen. Her breath quivered as she counted 14 staples and fought back the urge to cry.

"The nurse did that to me last night when I wouldn't let her have her way with Moby at sponge bath time. How bad does it look?"

Jane quickly composed herself. "I have seen you do worse on a broken bar glass. And sponge bathing you is my job, so don't get any ideas, bucko!" Jane smiled. She knew both were hurting, yet they tried to comfort each other the best they could with silly humor.

"Babe, put your good arm by your side and cup your hand. It will be our soap dish." Jane picked up the soap and gently washed Don's backside with her soapy hand. He turned to face her so she could wash his front. He closed his eyes as her lathered hand washed his face. She was careful not to touch his burned ear.

Jane continued lathering her hand and working down his bruised and scraped body. She couldn't help but giggle a little when she gently washed his bright pinkish-red penis.

"Well, hello, Moby. It looks like you've missed me!"

Don sighed. "Not now, Jane."

Jane giggled. "You know, babe, I am open to trying new things in the romance department to keep things fresh, but the red penis isn't a good look. Does Moby come in any other colors?"

Don smiled. "You have no idea how popular my penis was in the hospital. The sponge bath nurse said it was the talk of the ER. Moby is a local celebrity!"

"It doesn't surprise me that you had a celebrity red penis at the hospital, babe. It's so you! Now let's get you rinsed off, dried, and dressed. I want food before this meeting with Jerry. I haven't had an appetite for a few days. But now I'm jonesing for a burger and extra crispy fries from the Shanty. You need to eat too!"

October 17th 12:04 p.m.

Jane pushed two tables together for the meeting. Don settled into one of the chairs as Jane unlocked the bar's front door and let in Jerry, Jim Reed from the Brite Rock Cathedral by the Sea, and two men in expensive-looking dark suits that were with Reed.

Jerry had his game face on. Don found it amusing that he spoke in a different cadence and tone than when hanging around the bar with Liv.

"Don and Jane, allow me to introduce Randal Hallet and Trey Jackson from the church up the road in Strathford. They are here representing Pastor McCarthy. I believe you already know Jim Reed. Please, everyone, take a seat."

Reed's eyes widened when Don raised his walking stick and laid it on the table as if it were some form of medieval weapon. "We are familiar with Mr. Reed, man. How's your boss? If he still wants to buy our church building, I'll sell it to him now. Some assembly required!"

Jerry immediately saw that things were getting tense with both Don and Jane. "Let me set the stage for today's conversation. Randal and Trey have been looking for land to build a larger church. They heard about what happened to Pastor Smyth. Opportunity knocked, and here they are."

Don was confused. "I'm not interested in selling our place, man. Not if the insurance can fix up the house."

"They aren't interested in buying your property, Don. The night of the explosion, one of Jim Reed's staff called him to say Smyth was in the hospital. Jim then called Paul Caruso to ask what happened to Smyth. Caruso advised him to skip town like he was doing. Jim wasn't involved in the plot and knew nothing about it, so Jim called the police and told them about Caruso. The State Police arrested Caruso at Logan Airport yesterday morning as he tried to board a flight to Bahrain. That country doesn't have an extradition treaty with the

United States. Thanks to Jim's timely call to the police, Smyth's co-conspirator Paul Caruso is behind bars."

Reed cleared his throat. "I'm third in the line of succession at the Brite Rock Cathedral by the Sea behind Smyth and Caruso. I called an emergency board of directors meeting early yesterday morning. The board authorized me to offer to merge the Cathedral by the Sea's assets with the Strathford church and put Smyth in the rearview mirror as fast as possible. Pastor McCarthy would be the new pastor at the Cathedral by the Sea."

Trey Jackson spoke up. "Yes, the only caveat to Jim and the Cathedral board from the Strathford church is to clean up Smyth's public relations nightmare. We can't have that besmirch our good name nor be exposed to the liabilities from his actions."

Reed agreed. "Of course not, and that's why our board has decided to spend money to erase Smyth's legacy and make things as right as humanly possible.

Don, Jane, I am so sorry for what George Smyth and Paul Caruso did to you. I don't know what drove them to cross so many lines, but their actions are beyond horrific and in no way representative of any church I know. Like you, the Brite Rock Cathedral by the Sea is a victim of their incredibly poor judgment and disgusting behavior.

George Smyth's fixation with the original Sailers Church of Brite Rock has always been an unhealthy fascination. He longed to possess that building, so he built the exact replica when he couldn't purchase it. I have come to believe that building was a trophy to him, something he used to create a story bigger than the man himself. In our eyes, what he built is Smyth's folly. For that reason, we have decided that the replica building constructed by Smyth is a moral affront to our church and our beliefs, and it must go. But seeing that your original Sailers Church building was taken from you by Smyth, we are offering to sell you our replica church building for the sum of one dollar. We will pay to move it, including all permits and related installation costs. We hope this reparation helps get your Happening community program going again. You have a…a unique rapport with people."

Jane looked at Don. "He has a point, babe. You always seem to have the most interesting people orbiting you."

Reed paused, unsure if Jane was making fun of Don or simply pointing out the obvious. Reed continued. "Next, we will sign over the trademark on the Sailers Church of Brite Rock to you for one dollar. Pastor Smyth…I mean, George Smyth coveted the public Sailers Church name and never should have laid claim to it. Selling you the trademark will right that injustice.

Now, regarding your unfortunate injuries, our insurance company will pay for all of your medical bills related to the incident for both of you. It has been a traumatic ordeal, and we want to ensure you are both properly taken care of.

And lastly, I am authorized to offer you and Jane a cash settlement of $500,000 for loss, pain, and suffering as long as you and Jane agree not to sue Brite Rock Cathedral by the Sea for anything Smyth or Caruso have done. And, of course, you don't disclose the terms of this generous settlement. Do you accept our offer?"

Don started to answer. "Well, I…."

Jerry interrupted. "I think you need to rework the cash settlement, Jim. Between your insurance, their insurance, and your generous offer of the replica church building, Don and Jane will be made whole regarding property loss. But look at Don. Look at Jane. For the physical and emotional injuries they have suffered, $500k is woefully insufficient!"

Jane sat up and slowly pointed to her eye patch with her broken hand. "You made me look like a fucking pirate!"

Reed cleared his throat. "Well… yes… um… $1 million… that's our final offer."

Don's eyes got wide, and he looked at Jerry. Jane was absent-mindedly squeezing Don's injured arm. He didn't notice the pain.

Jerry reached over and tapped Don's walking stick on the table with his hand as he stared directly into Reed's eyes. "Your church nearly killed this man and…"

"It was not the Brite Rock Cathedral; it was Smyth and Caruso!"

"That depends on how the story gets told, Mister Reed! Now, as I was saying, your church nearly killed this man. This woman was violently thrown to the ground and injured by the blast. The visible injuries inflicted on both people have been extensively documented and photographed. The medical records are highly detailed. There are dozens of very credible witnesses. The physical evidence is clear and incontestable. Now, let's start talking real settlement numbers."

Reed was stressed. "All right, all right! $2 million! That's the best I can do. One penny more, and the board said it has to go to court, and all the other parts of the offer are off the table. That would kill the Strathford merger and shutter the Brite Rock Cathedral by the Sea. No one benefits from that."

Jerry leaned in. "You are wrong about that, Mr. Reed. We will go after the property and cash holdings of your Brite Rock Cathedral. That's valued much more than the $5 million that Don and Jane deserve as a settlement. Agree to $5 million, and everyone walks away feeling good about the deal."

"No deal!" Reed stood and prepared to leave.

Jerry's face was expressionless. "Then we will see you in court for a very public trial."

Randal Hallet took hold of Reed's right arm and gently lowered him back into his seat. Then, Hallet leaned over and whispered to Reed what appeared to be lengthy instructions.

Reed swallowed hard and sighed. "Okay, all of the terms previously stated and a settlement of $5 million. That will be the total settlement with the agreement that Don and Jane waive the right to sue Brite Rock Cathedral by the Sea, or me, regarding this…incident. And when Don and Jane are called to testify in the trial of Smyth and Caruso, it will be specifically about those two individuals. Don and Jane will hold Brite Rock Cathedral by the Sea harmless. That's everything on the table."

Jerry thought for a moment and then addressed Don and Jane. "You have a decision to make. The offer on the table pays for all your current and future medical bills related to this unfortunate event. You get your Sailers Church building replaced, and it's a free turnkey installation. They do it all at their expense. Your insurance policy will pay for all repairs to the house. I believe the cash offer for pain and suffering and your agreement not to disclose the settlement terms are reasonable, but it's up to you. You may get more if you go to court, but it will be a long, expensive process, and it's possible the cash amount could be increased or reduced or not awarded at all. What do you two say, accept the offer or court?"

Jane whispered something into Don's ear. He smiled.

Don looked at Jerry and nodded his head. "We have a deal, man!"

Jerry reached out and shook Reed's hand. It was clear that Reed was greatly relieved. Randal Hallet and Trey Jackson smiled and thanked everyone at the table. Finally, they got the results that they wanted.

Jerry stood and walked Reed, Hallet, and Jackson to the door. "I'm glad we came to a mutual agreement. I'll meet you at the Cathedral by the Sea at 3:00 p.m. to discuss the details." They shook hands one more time. All left happy.

Don and Jane sat at the table, trying to sort out what had happened. Jerry came back and sat down. "Okay, Jane, what did you whisper in Don's ear about the decision on Reed's offer?"

Jane couldn't contain her smile. "Oh, the whisper had nothing to do with accepting the deal. We gave each other a little pat on the butt at $1 million to let each other know that we were all in on the offer. When you threw down the public trial, and he offered $2 million, we were thrilled. Then things got dicey when you went for $5 million, and Reed stood. But then he settled down and agreed to $5 million. You play rough, Jerry!"

"That's called negotiating, Jane. So, getting back to the whisper, what was said?"

Don smiled. "Jane came up with a nickname for you. It fits, man! It's cool."

"I earned a nickname? What is it?"

"Sorry, man, you have to wait until Friday happy hour. Make sure Liv is with you. So, changing the topic back to the deal, did you just act as our lawyer, man?"

Jerry laughed. He was enjoying this. "Well, kind of yes and no. As Town Counsel, I can't represent you. I strongly suggest that Attorney John Scofield handle the paperwork. I can call John and have him come to the Cathedral by the Sea to document the offer if that's fine with you. He will be your Attorney for this."

Jane was still processing it all. "Okay, it's been an insane couple of days, and I'm mentally exhausted, so I want to be sure I have this straight. We are getting a new church building to continue with the Happenings, and it will be delivered and installed for one dollar. They will pay all our medical bills. We will get a check from our insurance company to fix our house. The trademark for the Sailers Church name will be ours, and we will get $5 million in cash. All of that is really happening?"

Jerry nodded for each item that she listed. "Yep, that's the deal. The only strings attached are that you can't disclose the terms of the deal, and you waive the right to sue the Cathedral by the Sea."

Jane leaned over and gently hugged Jerry. "I can keep that secret."

"But Jerry, what about negotiating the cash, man? That's a shit load of cash that you just got us. We need to pay you or something."

Jane agreed with Don. "We need to share the wealth with you. That was over the top generous to step in and help."

Jerry shook his head no. "I didn't do anything. I merely had a conversation with Mr. Reed to be sure there weren't any potential legal entanglements for the town in this deal, and there aren't. The $500k was their opening offer. I assumed that they had more set aside to make this go away. I just had to motivate him to put another $4.5 million on top of his original offer."

"Jane is right, man. Please let us fatten your wallet or something."

Jerry sighed. "Okay, if it will make you feel better, how about I do not pay for my drinks at the bar for one year? Oh, and that includes free drinks for Liv too."

Don thought for a moment. "As long as you and Liv agree to come on the next rum crawl trip with us for some of those free drinks. It's the Caribbean, and for you two, it's all expenses paid by us! Sipping rum in Barbados, Puerto Rico, Guyana, and Jamaica. That's the least we can do, and we feel it settles our debt for legal services rendered and for Liv providing the awesome sound system in the bar."

Jerry knew the game had changed when he saw Jane's mischievous grin. "You know, Jerry, Liv would not be happy if you turned down that free Caribbean trip on her behalf. Don't you want to make our bronze goddess happy?"

Jerry paused. Jane made an excellent point. "Will Liv and I sipping rum with you two in the Caribbean truly mean all debts are paid?"

Don smiled. "Yes, it will, man! Rum makes everything better!"

The End ~ Aloha

Visit the Church of Don website at www.churchofdon.com.

References

Books

Beachbum Berry's Sippin' Safari: 10th Anniversary Expanded Edition
By Jeff Berry ~ Cocktail Kingdom.

Smuggler's Cove: Exotic Cocktails, Rum, and the Cult of Tiki.
By Martin Cates with Rebecca Cates ~ Ten Speed Press.

The New Rum: A Modern Guide to the Spirit of the Americas
By Bryce T. Bauer ~ Countryman Press.

Tiki Road Trip: A Guide to Tiki Culture in North America
By James Teitelbaum ~ Santa Monica Press.

Trader Vic's Bartender's Guide Revised (1947, 1972)
By Vic Bergeron ~ Doubleday & Company

Periodicals

Exotica Moderne (Magazine)
House of Tabu, LLC

Imbibe Liquid Culture (Magazine)
Imbibe Magazine

Author Bio

Don Thomas was born and raised in southeastern Massachusetts near Cape Cod and Boston. As a young boy, he was fascinated by the stories of family wealth and a large summer home in a quaint seaside town during the late 1800s through the early 1900s.

Those stories of the heady days of prosperity through the Roaring 20s always ended with the 1929 stock market crash. It was the beginning of the great depression. Reminiscing and family stories about the glory days were over.

So were those family stories true? Were they once financially well off? Did a family member make frequent boat trips to Canada to bring back adult refreshments during prohibition? And what of the passing comment that the family put up the land to build a small church to serve the community? What could have possibly happened after 1929?

While sipping a Mai Tai on Kauai many years later and thinking back on family lore, the concept of a "what if" story came together. The seaside town of Brite Rock and the delightfully odd cast of characters in the "Church of Don" were born.

"Church of Don" is the first fictional book by Don Thomas. He graduated from Emerson College in Boston and Anna Maria College in Paxton, MA, and resides in California and Massachusetts. There is a home tiki bar in the California house. After all, rum does make everything better!

Made in the USA
Las Vegas, NV
23 August 2023

76475811R00157